Also, by David Beeley

THE WATH MILL ALLOTMENTS SERIES

SECRETS, LIES, AND RHUBARB PIES

SECRETS, LIES AND TWO LEG BYES

SECRETS, LIES AND SEAGULL CRIES

THE STOCKWELL COLLEGE SERIES

LET SLEEPING SECRETS LIE

Jenny Clutterbuck

Reluctant Traveller in Time

David Beeley

This book is dedicated to Eveline Beeley, long-suffering
wife and supporter of 52 years.

Table of Contents

Chapter One: This is, Without a Doubt, the Last Time... Maybe

Jenny Clutterbuck hated few things, if any, but time travel was definitely on top of her noticeably short list. Broccoli was most certainly another.

This was her ninth intervention in the past, and each one seemed to be the worst. Was it worth it, she thought, pale-faced and very queasy, sitting on a park bench in Thornbury in July 2024.

Usually, dog walkers and joggers would have quickly noticed a smiling, confident sixty-year-old with perceptive brown eyes, which people often described as kind and thoughtful. Her short, fair hair, parted on the right and swept behind both ears, was like her clothing, simple but in a smartly elegant way. Jenny dressed herself, the epitome of confidence. But not today, at that precise moment and for very good reason.

Today, she leaned forward, her stomach more than borderline queasy and her head spinning most unpleasantly. A seasick-like hangover without the red wine or the sea.

Jenny worried that each intervention travelling into the past seemed to take an increasingly long time to recover, the horrendous period when her eyes would focus on an object only for it to dance horizontally unbidden.

With her face bathed in a sheen of sweat, she fought the urge to vomit and forced herself to sit upright. The first rule of time travel: Be discreet and blend into the background. Do nothing to make yourself conspicuous.

With determination, she tried to overcome her nausea and dizziness while pondering the fast-developing world of the discovery of travel back in time. Jenny took a deep breath and kept her eyes open, focusing on a nearby flowerbed to settle her mind. This would pass as it always did, but recovery seemed slow. Too slow, this had to be her last journey; age was increasingly against her, and gradually taking its toll.

The reluctant time traveller thought of standing but decided against it, the dizziness was too much of a threat to her and being upright would have to wait for a few moments more.

Of course, no one would believe that the lady on the bench was sixty; she looked around mid-fifties and had taken good care of herself. The passing dog walker with a graceful red setter glanced across and wished Jenny a cheery good morning. She would certainly have been shocked and certainly disbelieving to be told that the lady, a stranger to her on her regular walk, had been born in 1996 and should have been 28, but had travelled back through the time portal in 2056 when she was sixty, a widow with two children and three grandchildren, Jenny managed a small smile in return, and the dog walker continued with her routine.

The highly secret time portal base was set amidst an industrial estate in Swindon. It was bland with the appearance of a warehouse, non-descript and deliberately unremarkable. There, in May 2032, Jenny had been recruited as one of the first experimental time travellers. Her physics lecturer at York University, Professor Thomas Goodwin-Rowe, had discreetly approached her to sound her out about her suitability for the task of time travelling and her willingness to enter the potentially deadly research study. He had always admired her sharp, curious intellect and cheerful disposition; they had kept in touch after she left university and decided to go into teaching.

Thomas had been part of the groundbreaking team that had developed the concept of time travel and turned it into a reality ahead of their Saudi, Russian, and Korean rivals. His specific role was in recruitment, and his position as a university lecturer was ideal, especially in the science faculty.

Jenny trusted her old lecturer, but, of course, had been, as most were, dubious and certainly sceptical. Once given proof at the Time Research Interventions Portal (Environmental), or TRIPE, as those involved loved to say, she had signed the Official Secrets Act and undergone strict security training. The financial rewards were considerable and certainly helped, although as a small school headteacher married to an architect, Steve, they were comfortable in life. Looking back, she realised that it was heightened curiosity and a sense of pioneering adventure that had led her to agree to the astounding role offer.

Thomas Goodwin-Rowe had patiently spent two days explaining the science behind time travel, answering all of Jenny's flood of questions. He did not minimise the potential dangers, although earlier interventions had given them enough data and experience to reduce risk as much as possible.

There were definite restrictions. Only travel back, never forwards, at the current stage of research, although work was in progress in this area. Time travel interventions involving family or friends were strictly forbidden. The Portal cost billions, discreetly hidden in budgets with vague code names and unfathomable acronyms, and was not for personal use. It was soon apparent that going back thirty years was the approximate limit, and the human frame was not to be subject to more than ten interventions. Jenny had quickly seen the immense potential for power in the hands of disreputable states, as Thomas had outlined. Winners write history, but the Portal potentially controls history. A mind-staggering thought, difficult to absorb.

Sitting upstairs in an animal welfare charity shop in the outskirts of Brighton, Jenny had completed her assessment for suitability to begin intervention training. The shop was discreet and very secretly owned by the government. Customers browsing the shelves and racks for bargains would never even begin to suspect that this was a cover for its use by TRIPE, well away from the Portal in Swindon. A perfect place for assessments and interviews. It had all the attributes of a small, nondescript, and very bland flat with no links whatsoever to Swindon or Whitehall.

More women than men, especially older ones, were chosen as it was thought that they could blend in better into their environment. The invisible grey ones, as Thomas would say, although Jenny, at 36, was still worthy of the proverbial second glance.

Jenny had not been disappointed not to go back in time to see momentous events in world history. Not for her, a place at the seemingly serene and calm birth of Jesus in a little town called Bethlehem. We three kings and a girl from Scarborough in the late twentieth century. Carols would have to be rewritten, and Jenny suspected that the reality of the birth of Jesus, homeless and in an occupied country, would spoil the Christmas card image. Thomas soon squashed this idea as he informed her that time travel away from the Portal was limited to about four hundred miles. He had gone on to explain that going back to assassinate Adolf Hitler, for instance, was tempting but futile. It was against their intervention rules, and besides, it was a popular rising rather than the leadership of one man with hypnotic speaking capabilities that led to devastating war.

Interventions were meant to have positive outcomes, designed for the greater good, and were enough to outweigh the considerable risks. Of course, some would argue that the slightest intervention could have enormous implications later, but this was science being rewritten, if only secretly, as knowledge rapidly developed. Nevertheless, travellers in time were trained to minimise all contacts in the past. 'You can't play God,' people argued from a necessarily ignorant and understandable viewpoint, but it was in Jenny's nature to help, even if only in a small way. Decades of teaching and headship had embedded this fine quality into her very soul.

Over the years, Jenny Clutterbuck had gradually become increasingly reluctant to travel back in time. She had married Steve, a young architect in Haltemprice in East Yorkshire, on August 5th, 2018, and had lost him when he was swept out to a stormy and grim North Sea by strong waves from the rocks near Scarborough, thirty years later, whilst fishing, his passion second only to Jenny's. His body had never been found, and Jenny missed him deeply, every moment of every day.

Somehow, her interventions had seemed meaningless ever since she knew full well that she could not travel back to that horrendous point in her life to draw him back from the waves and keep him safe for always.

Jenny was one of the most successful travellers or interventionalists, and she had been increasingly in need of persuasion to continue. She had to admit, if only to herself, that most of her interventions had been successful to a greater or lesser degree, and she had been able to stave off disaster, even if only in a small way.

Jenny decided to sit back, to be less conspicuous and was pleasantly surprised that her eyes focused properly without dancing images, and the nausea was gradually abating. Several deep breaths of fresh South Gloucestershire air filled her lungs, although she noted that the air didn't seem quite as clean and fresh as in her mid-21st-century time.

Standing was probably a step too adventurous, and she seriously feared a return of the appalling dizziness, so it was postponed for a few minutes more. Best to consolidate and sit to observe her surroundings.

There was a pleasant warmth to the July morning sun, and this gave a sense of well-being. Dog walkers would address her with a convivial morning greeting, and some tried to engage her in conversation but soon moved on when it was quickly clear that the stranger did not wish to be drawn into small talk about the weather. Joggers were easier; they would ignore her, intently concentrating on their personal efforts and time schedules.

Jenny liked dogs and owned two back home, a stubborn beagle named Dottie and a younger, keen tail-tail-tail-wagging spaniel named Cassie. Both rescue dogs are from a Dogs Trust centre in Woodlands Farm, Leeds. Both were adored and adoring. It was a sobering thought that neither dog would be born for another quarter of a century. Her children, Georgie and Rebecca, would be four and two, respectively and with her other younger self and her beloved Steve. She wondered what they were doing at that moment in time. Jenny's head knew that she could never meet them or even see them, no matter how much she wanted this potential breach of protocol. The enormity of that single thought was almost overwhelming, and a small tear rolled unbidden down her cheek.

No, this would be her last intervention, and no amount of artful persuasion would change her mind. On her return to her own time, she would take Dottie and Cassie to her local park in East Yorkshire, free to exchange morning greetings and chat with fellow dog walkers well known to her.

Jenny was determined to visit her children, Georgie, now thirty-six, and her beautiful Rebecca and their delightful children, her parcel of grandchildren or munchkins as she called them. It was time to retire and let others take up the baton, time to enjoy retirement both from headship, which had happened in 2051 and from time travel, albeit without her beloved Steve. So close, yet so far and alive. Jenny felt a surge of grief and deepest sorrow.

She sighed and stood, relieved to find herself mostly without any aftereffects. Her trusty over-the-shoulder blue sashiko bag was adjusted slightly. It was her constant companion, bought on a wonderful trip to Japan with Steve and full of information which may help her in her quest, whatever it turned out to be. There was usually a sealed envelope and materials necessary for her to blend into the past.

A facsimile of a newspaper dated several days in the future was unfolded. The headline screamed Local Bus Crash: Three killed and eight critically injured. Quickly scanning the front page, she realised that it was light on detail. Police had not released the names of the victims until families were fully informed.

Sitting back down on the bench, she realised that she would need a base to sleep on and look over the sealed envelope in private. Inside the bag were details of a motel about a mile away up a winding hill overlooking a local cricket ground. How to get there? Further investigation brought forth an old person's bus pass with her picture and details. Jenny half smiled to herself; she certainly didn't see herself as old.

Looking around, she noted the two adjacent car parks and a small queue at the bus stop. She decided quickly to swallow her pride and be one of the grey-haired invisible ones, not that her hair was truly grey, just fair.

Taking the bus pass, she walked quickly across the small park area with its wonderful flowerbeds and shrubs and crossed the road to join the queue,

At that moment, a blue double-decker with side panels advertising what to Jenny was an old film but just recently released. The destinations panel clearly said T1 Bristol via Bradley Stoke. Within the next few days, this vehicle would be on its side with smashed windows and three dead and eight fighting for their lives.

Jenny Clutterbuck, reluctant time traveller, presumed that one of the passengers was important to the future and had to be saved. But which one, and could she possibly save all the passengers? Her last intervention would potentially be the hardest yet.

Chapter Two: Drab, Dreary and Boring with a Splash of Razzle-Dazzle

Frank Matthew Nelson's life, the one he allowed to be revealed to all and sundry, was one of routine and timetables. Today, as in all workdays, he took a cup of tea and marmalade-covered toast on a small plate to his wife, Lillian, waking her gently with a kiss. He was up and dressed as usual in his tracksuit bottoms, cheap battered trainers and bright red and white hooped Gloucester rugby shirt, ready to leave their modest Eastville terraced home for the short car journey to Bristol bus station.

Lillian Nelson loved her husband dearly, despite his boring routines or perhaps because of them. Every morning was the same for Lillian, not that she didn't appreciate Frank's kindness, but she was woken early by either the dawn sunshine or his cheerful clattering as he prepared his breakfast and sandwiches for lunch. She knew full well that it would be cheese with a thick slice of onion, with an apple and a small chocolate bar. Frank's diabetes restricted his diet, but he didn't mind. Lillian loved him even more for that; he wasn't a martyr to his condition. His gregarious cheerfulness would not allow him to stagnate into self-pity; it was not in his nature.

Each morning was the same: an identical cup of tea and toast, only the morning light changed. Today was a bright July dawn with the promise of a good summer's day. As Frank came up the stairs, she closed her eyes as she did each morning and pretended to be asleep, knowing that he took delight in waking her with a kiss as he had for the last nineteen years of married life. He loved the routine of first warming the blue teapot with steaming, boiling water and, a few moments later, adding freshly boiled water to the teabag and covering the teapot with an old, well-loved knitted tea cosy.

Later, when the forty-two-year-old Frank had left the house to go to his job as a bus driver, Lillian would sit up in bed and enjoy the luxury of the brief time to herself. A time to read before she would get up and prepare for her job as an assistant in the local corner shop. Before she picked up her book, usually a detective mystery novel bought in a charity shop, she would wish her beloved husband a safe day driving. As usual, it was the T1 Thornbury to Bristol run. A popular easy run with newer roads and a bus lane past the heavy traffic on the M32 down to Bristol.

To his fellow drivers, Frank was the epitome of a lock forward in a rugby pack without the cauliflower ears, mainly because he had never played rugby since leaving school in Stroud. He had blue eyes, clear and smiling, with brown close-cropped hair which easily allowed for outrageous wigs, although his colleagues were not to know that and hopefully never would. His cheerful banter made him popular with his fellow drivers, and he lifted the spirits of the room even on drab mornings, or worse, the icy ones, the dangerous ones.

But today was bright, and conditions for steering the large double-deckers around familiar routes were perfect. As usual, Frank hid his worries and unusual ambitions behind his facade of humour. His condition, diabetes, did not worry him too much; it was type 2 and manageable with tablets and a careful diet. His only daughter, Jess, was seventeen, and Frank was immensely proud of her. For him, she was the perfect child, well suited to the loving banter between him and Lillian. It was a close-knit, devoted family, and Jess was socially at ease with everyone she met. Her feet were well grounded, but she wished to go to university; Bath or Bristol were her immediate choices, not that she wanted to live at home to save money. Jess and Frank recognised that part of the unit, as she called it, was to take part fully in the social as well as the academic side.

Frank left the driver's room and went across to board the almost new double-decker. As he settled himself into the cab, he allowed his worries to surface briefly but powerfully. Jess's going to university was expensive, and he was a bus driver, and Lillian worked long hours in a corner shop, not a good baseline for the upcoming huge expenditure. Together, they had tried to save, but the cost-of-living crisis had hit them hard.

Frank's mother, Dorothy, would certainly have helped if she could, but all her assets were tied up in her modest house in Stroud. She was sixty-three and a fit and healthy farmer's wife; it was very unlikely that she would pass away before Jess needed the money to go to university. As her only child, Frank had been a disappointment to her. Not that she didn't love him, but he had refused to continue the long line of generations of farmers in the beautiful valleys around Stroud. He had read Cider with Rosie and felt the need to leave and explore the world and find adventure. He felt different, and whilst he had the build of a farmer, his heart was not in the farming life.

He had joined the army and eventually became an army driver, having proved himself more than competent at handling the large, powerful trucks. After years of steering huge tractors around Gloucestershire fields, he was certainly not overawed, as some were, by the size of the trucks. Frank was careful, and on country roads, he would, from being seventeen, stick rigidly to speed limits. He recognised that being in his tractor cab high above the road gave protection, which the driver of a Ford Focus suddenly appearing round a narrow bend did not enjoy. Drivers did not relish meeting his tractor coming the opposite way, but they were at least safe.

In the army, Frank was reliable and well regarded as a truck driver, and during his time serving the Queen, he did tours in Norway, Cyprus and Germany. This was the nearest that he came to his desire for adventure and colour. Drab army camouflage was the order of the day.

On leaving the army, Frank looked at his options. He had sat down after a large welcome home meal, his mother's gift: roast lamb, mashed potatoes, roast potatoes done in goose fat and peas, followed by a large helping of rhubarb pie and custard. Frank had eaten well in the army, but never on this scale of Mother's farmhouse cooking. No wonder he was stockily built, but thanks to the active army life, he did not run to borderline fat.

On the old, well-worn table, scene of generations of Christmas family feasts, he had taken a large pad of paper, bought for the very purpose and written options at the top. Decisions taken now would affect the rest of his life; careful thought was needed.

- Rejoin the army. He enjoyed the routines and orderly life, and the regimental camaraderie

- Go back to farming and the lonely life. Long hours are determined by weather conditions

- Driving – set up his own company, haulage or coaches. Frank crossed this out at once as too expensive, as he had little capital

- Coach driving would use his considerable skills both as a driver and his gregarious social skills

- Lorry drivers work long hours for someone else's profit

- Bus driver, routine and set hours, plus he would meet many people, perhaps a nice girl to settle down with and the delightful prospect of children

- Ambulance driver Frank considered this seriously; it appealed to his strong sense of being useful, but it lacked routine and held little prospect of meeting a girl, unless smashed up in a car accident

Frank had paused and taken a sip of home-made cider, realising that his limited academic achievements and meagre available capital were reducing his options to what he was truly best at, driving large vehicles. Not for him the life of a Formula One driver; he was too careful and steady for that. The army had never approved of its vehicles being driven at 130 miles per hour around in circles. Frank considered this a waste of fuel and time. He had gone back to his list, aware that his mind was wandering away from the point of this important exercise. Thinking broader, taking in all possibilities, now was the time to widen his opportunities list. He picked up his cheap biro and continued as his mother came in, wiping her hands after washing up. She considered this her job, a role too skilled to allow the men of the house to take part except perhaps at Christmas. She was a traditionalist and glad to have her son home safe from the wars, as she liked to put it to friends, although Frank had thankfully never experienced battlefield trauma apart from simulated exercises.

'Writing your memoirs, are you, son?' Molly Nelson had asked, sitting down in her favourite fireside chair for her usual after-dinner nap. Frank had smiled whilst at the same time deciding that his mother did not have the breadth of experience to offer advice. His father Tom was, on the other hand, always keen to offer advice, but this was trickier. It was certainly unsaid, but Tom was disappointed that Frank seemed determined to leave the farm and not follow in his footsteps. He did little to offer advice, which would take his son away again. Tom was getting older and needed the help of the young man, to say nothing of the chance to gradually wind down. Retirement for farmers was not a real option.

'I thought that I would become a famous author like Laurie Lee,' he had smiled in answer to her query. He knew that the literary reference to 'Cider with Rosie' would pass over his mother's head, but it was meant in a kindly way and not as an attempt to belittle the old lady's lack of further education.

Looking down at his list, he knew that being an author was beyond his scope, and yet he could never write down his real desire; the unwritten number four was consigned forever to the secret compartment of his mind. Frank's parents would never ever understand, perhaps even Frank did not understand why he wished for the unthinkable, the unspeakable desire.

Since being a boy, Frank had been fascinated by the glamour of that specialist area of show business, the drag queens. Men dressed as women with their flamboyance and ready caustic wit, on stage, putting down hecklers with skill and humour. In recent years, it has become more widely accepted and seen as a legitimate and established area of entertainment. Fank would watch these acts on television, appreciating the hours that went into the hair styling and the outrageous top make-up. He would have loved to have tried, if only once, to emulate these 'ladies', but it was not to be. The British army was not renowned for fostering regimental drag queens, and a farming life gave little experience of wigs and make-up. Frank had no contacts or links to the magical glitter of show business. He sighed, knowing full well that he could never add number four to his list, his parents would never understand and probably be hurt by his seemingly outlandish thoughts. Driving was the only avenue of escape from farming.

Looking back all those years, he realised that for him, driving was his only real choice. When his father had died, he had been very tempted to go home and be a farmer to fulfil his father's wishes, but that would have bred resentment, and so it was that the farm was sold to buy a comfortable house for his mother in Stroud, Stroud and Proud as she liked to say. The line of generations of farmers named Nelson was broken.

Frank sighed as he settled himself into the cab of his double-decker and put aside his memories as he began the process of starting his day. He loved this vehicle, his vehicle, almost brand new and costing nearly £400,000; it was his responsibility to bring the twelve-ton bus home safe each night. Twelve tons, even without up to eighty-five passengers, and Frank took their safety very seriously.

Frank put aside idle memories and concentrated on reversing his bus out of the bus station parking bay. He made the difficult manoeuvre look easy, and shifting the gears, he moved the giant bus smoothly forward to start what was to be one of his last before a momentous and terrible day.

Chapter Three: Times Change, and We, with Time

Jenny tried hard not to look closely at the others waiting in the queue; discretion was her watchword, but this was difficult. These might not be regular passengers, but if they were, they might be among the critically injured or even dead. Just a short time left in life. Her mind slipped as it always did to her wonderful lost husband, claimed by the mighty North Sea, but at that moment alive and with her and their children in Yorkshire. She felt an overwhelming desire to throw caution to the four winds and catch a train to Hull and at the least see him again. Impossible but very, very tempting.

As the bus approached and came to a stop, Jenny followed the lead of the other passengers and put her OAP bus pass on the card reader. She glanced at the driver and smiled, and Frank returned the silent greeting before adding good morning.

Jenny quickly decided that she liked the bus driver, but then had to choose whether to go upstairs or stay down where most older people stayed. Given her recent dizziness and nausea, she opted for a safer seat downstairs. It was only a short journey up the long, winding hill, but her stomach did not relish the twists and turns.

A rear window seat allowed her to observe the other passengers. Most had bus passes or phones to pay for the journey, but she was amazed to see one older lady opening her purse and paying by coins, a transaction almost unheard of in 2056, her time. Cash had become redundant, especially coins. Numismatists or coin collectors had flourished as the minting of new coins had ceased, creating a thriving market for the increasingly rarer coins.

Jenny was followed by an attractive young girl of about sixteen who had allowed Jenny to go ahead of her, a sign of welcome if unexpected respect. Unlike Jenny, she went easily upstairs and sat near the back to observe her fellow passengers.

Madison Olivia Marsden opened her rucksack and was very annoyed with herself. The earlier bus would have taken her to her new school in Bradley Stoke in good time, but she had missed it. Not her fault, she said to herself. The alarm, which she had not set, had surprisingly not gone off, but she didn't care one way or another. Her parents had said that a change of school would do her good, but she found herself indifferent. Madison, or Maddie as she preferred, was tall for her age and aloof with her blondish, unruly hair and thoughtful, steady brown eyes. Today, upstairs on the back seat of the T1, she was doubly annoyed as she had forgotten her smartphone.

For Maddie, the last year had been the year from hell, the worst of her young life.

The loss of her granny had left a huge emotional gap in her life, but then she had met her grandfather, estranged from the family for decades, when she had delivered a brilliant eulogy at the funeral. The newly met couple had been thrown together for three weeks when her family went on holiday, and Maddie had firmly refused to go. They had quickly formed a strong bond of friendship, respect, and love. Both had regretted not meeting earlier, and now it was too late.

The old man had finally succumbed to cancer, and Maddie mourned deeply once again. Her life seemed to be shadowed by tears and grief. She had travelled to Bromley in Kent and been met by her grandfather's partner Emma, a long-lost love from his college days. At the now familiar house, she had cried together with Emma and Joanie, her close Polish friend. Joanie, or to give her proper name, Malgorzata Wisniewski, had been her grandfather Daniel's housekeeper and close companion for many years before she had married, a fellow Pole, in the summer.

Maddie sat on the bus and had taken out her pen and notebook by habit. Laying down her pen, she sighed deeply. Two beloved grandparents lost forever, and she recalled the optimism and hope during those heady summer days. She had returned home after three weeks with a superb laptop and a wonderful puppy called Rosie, gifts from her newfound family and friends. But more importantly, she had a sense of growing understanding and wisdom. Her grandfather and Joanie had shown her that she was special and that being different was not somehow second-class. Maddie had realised that she preferred girls and had formed a loving relationship with a girl at school named Poppy. They had shared so many common interests and viewpoints. Maddie felt sure that Poppy's parents had taken her off to a private school in Wiltshire to get her away from what they considered a bad influence. Gay tendencies were certainly not on the agenda for their Poppy.

Maddie considered the impact of loss and newfound love. In the last year, she had lost both grandparents, two special and only friends, at school and a dog, Daniel's ancient cocker spaniel. On the plus side, she had gained, through her quest to find her grandfather's long-lost college friends, several new friends, especially Jan and Joanie, her Polish friends or family, as they preferred. Joanie's newborn twins had been a delight, and she had travelled to Bromley to meet them, but therein lay the problem. Her friends were older, apart from the twins, of course. And living some distance away.

It was difficult to balance the scales of her relentlessly unkind fate. Maddie smiled to herself as she recalled the delight at meeting a tiny baby who carried her name and her brother, who had her grandfather's middle name.

One of the great pleasures of life was holding those two tiny scraps of humanity; they would grow up with a proud Polish heritage, and Maddie looked forward to being their unofficial aunt. If only they lived closer. Her fast-growing puppy, Rosie, a Bocker, a cross between a beagle and a cocker spaniel, was the delight of her life, someone to share secret thoughts with as well as long walks together.

Maddie pondered the strange elements of time. If she could go back in time, an obvious impossibility, she knew she would go back to when her beloved grandmother, Martha, was alive. Although at that time she had not even met her grandfather, Daniel. A compromise was called for; Joanie and Jan's magical wedding would be her preferred destination. But then her Granny, Martha, would have passed, and the twins safely nestled in Joanie's womb.

Difficult decisions, but totally irrelevant, and she determined to be positive, as her grandfather had taught her. Live for the here and now, not in an untouchable past or uncertain future. Daniel had said that the Japanese had it right, their appreciation of the beauty around them and their search for perfection in all they did was legendary.

Daniel Caleb Finney had written several books, which he often decried as waffle and fluff, outstandingly mediocre, as he would say. However, Maddie had read them and been entranced by the world they portrayed. His stories were intriguing, warm, and funny, with gems of wisdom about small human interactions. He had encouraged Maddie in her writing, which he praised. Her eulogy at her granny's funeral had been a wonderful piece, and he realised that Maddie had real potential as a serious writer. But his wise guidance was sadly gone, and Maddie was left feeling empty and alone in a world which didn't understand her.

The pen and notebook on her lap were ready to note any quirks amongst her fellow passengers, or wherever she happened to be at the time. Their mannerisms, speech, movement, and dress were noted in a succinct way to be stored for future use as a writer's storeroom. Maddie was determined to carry on with her writing, which she enjoyed immensely as it took her into her created worlds and away from reality.

Maddie was aware of the sign at the front of the bus, Bus Stopping. The ill-fated double-decker had pulled into a bus stop outside the local cricket ground with its sign announcing the next fixture, which would attract a small crowd and several dogs. She noticed one passenger alighting; it was the elderly lady whom she had allowed to go before her at the Thornbury Rock Street stop. It seemed obvious that the disembarked passenger did not know where she was going as she looked uncertainly around. Maddie tried to guess her age and put her in her mid-fifties, a decision which Jenny Clutterbuck would have been pleased with, as she was sixty. Maddie noted the simple elegance of her clothing and her blue sashiko bag, a pattern Maddie was familiar with after conversations about her grandparents' visit to Japan. That was in the gloriously heady days of love before their bitter divorce, long before Maddie was born.

There was something about the lady which Maddie liked but could not easily define, she seemed independent and confident and at the same time vulnerable. As the bus pulled out once again into the traffic, Maddie looked back, sure that she had not seen this lady before, but strangely, she hoped to meet her one day. Perhaps it was that she reminded Maddie of her deceased grandmother, or was it the air of self-reliance? Maddie wished that she could give that impression herself, although without knowing it, she probably already did.

Maddie put her pen and notebook into her rucksack and allowed herself the luxury of pondering on Jenny's background story. Would she make a character in a story?

Maddie would have been staggered to find that Jenny was from the year 2056 and was merely thirteen years older than herself in 2024. Looking back out of the rear window, Maddie saw the lady walk towards The Ship, a coaching inn built in 1589 with ancient wood beams and flagstones, with a more modern sixties Premier Inn motel alongside. Due solely to the time of day, Jenny deduced that her destination would be the motel, a long, low two-story building made for function rather than grace or architectural elegance. The girl pondered the reason for her visit to the motel, alone and with no luggage, just a sashiko bag. There might be a short story there, if only she knew the mind-blowing reality of Jenny Clutterbuck's journey back in time, she would have the story to rival any in human history.

The subject of the would-be author's creative thoughts turned to see the double-decker preparing to turn south onto the A38, the Ridgeway, the ancient road from Gloucester to the Roman port at Sea Mills. Jenny sighed, suddenly keen to look carefully at her intervention pack from TRIP(E) at Swindon. From experience, she knew that her preparations would be thorough, but there was always the unexpected. She had rarely been given an intervention of such proportions. It was usually an individual who needed a slight change of direction to avoid a poor decision or even impending death., The person in question would go on to be of great service to society and well worth the risk of potentially devastating changes to the continuity of time. It was a delicate process, and errors were inexcusable.

Jenny walked towards The Ship and saw that across the courtyard cum car park was a reception office for the Premier Inn. This was always the fun part; she was always accustomed to a hologram AI-generated receptionist, but this would be old school, a human being. There was always a chance that the technicians at the Portal in Swindon would make a mistake, but they were usually thorough and reliable.

As always, Jenny waited for the door to open automatically before reading the stick-on sign instructing her to push. Jenny smiled to herself and noted the young but slightly plump receptionist who cheerily greeted her. Her name badge said Jill, Jenny briefly pondered on the fact that Jill in the year 2056 would probably be on a computer-generated individualised course of food intake in conjunction with an exercise regime. Jill in the future would be different, but Jenny liked her cheerful and plain jolliness. It was easy to see her as a buxom waitress in the sixteenth century in the old coaching inn opposite. Now came the moment of truth.

'Good morning, my name is Jenny Clutterbuck; I believe that you have a reservation for me. '

Jill smiled, wondering at the lack of luggage. She assumed that a case would be in the guest's car, although she hadn't noticed one enter the car park. Not to worry. A quick referral to the list of arrivals revealed a reservation for a Mrs J. Clutterbuck made in the name of a company called Portal Ltd. Not one that Jill knew, but a reservation was always welcome. The motel was only a third full.

Jenny noted with some amusement the newspaper on the office desk; she had obviously disturbed the receptionist's morning coffee and perusal of the news. Newspapers had died a death in the 2030s, unable to compete with the internet and television. A hologram receptionist would be indistinguishable from the real thing but would have electronic updates almost instantly and no need for a morning latte and custard cream, or two.

'Upstairs or downstairs?' Jill asked, bringing Jenny back to the present.

'Upstairs sounds OK, I think.'

'Back or front?' Jill went on to explain that the back rooms, especially the upstairs ones, had a superb view over the Thornbury cricket ground, spoilt only by the busy A38 and a Hyundai car franchise.

Jill sensed that the new arrival seemed keen to move on; nevertheless, she went into her well-rehearsed routine. W.G. Grace and his brother played cricket here, one of the most famous Victorian cricketers. Big chap with a large bushy beard. Some of our guests ask for upstairs rooms at the back to watch Thornbury play, quite a good standard for local cricket, I believe.'

'Yes, I had heard of him, my family were from Yorkshire, so we were deeply into cricket.' Jenny said before, silently cautioning herself. Beware of offering too much information about yourself. Discretion always. Listen, observe and be invisible. Don't be noticeable.

'Yorkshire, you say, a lovely part of the world. I have a cousin in Huddersfield.'

Time to quickly change tack, avoid being drawn in.

'Yes, we enjoy it. Where will breakfast be?' Jenny asked, trying to avoid further conversation.

'Just across the courtyard in The Ship, they do a very good full English there, I can personally recommend it.' Jenny looked with a smile at the plump receptionist and thought that she could well believe it.

'There's your key, room 17 upstairs, enjoy your stay. If you need anything, don't hesitate to ask.'

Room 17 is her base for her final intervention. Jenny took the key and wondered if this would be a failed mission or a glorious success.

Time would tell as it always did.

Chapter Four: A Dreamer of Dreams

Mel Chandoo hated jury service, and at 30 years old, the psychoanalyst reckoned that she was liable to be called again to Bristol Crown Court for potentially another 45 years. A daunting and despairing thought. For the last nine days, she had boarded the T1 from Rock Street in Thornbury to attend a particularly nasty case at the Crown Court in Bristol, close to the harbourside. She was not against Jury service in principle, and for the first two days, she had found it most interesting. Not being able to discuss the case was particularly frustrating. It was more than she had decided early on, the guilt of the obnoxious child abuser; it was part of her job to assess people, but she found the foreman of the jury to be almost as bad as the defendant.

Iris Melanie Chandoo had gradually eased herself from her parents' West Indian heritage. She regarded herself as 100% British and had ditched her first name, Iris, as being too Trinidadian and too flowery. Instead, she preferred her middle name shortened to Mel. It seemed to suit her dark, curly hair and large glasses. Looking in the mirror that morning, she liked her light brown skin tone, and at five feet nine with a slim frame, she reckoned that she was worthy of a second glance.

Friends would call her calm and intelligent, shrewd with an orderly mind. The perfect fit for jury service, not that this was an assessment shared by the foreman of the jury, Terry Gilligan. He lost few opportunities to niggle at Mel's background. It was usually done in a quiet but persistent way, enough to make Mel seethe with polite anger. The man's racism was obvious, and he disliked the idea of what he saw as a black foreigner sitting in judgment on a white man. A spot ironic as Mel was born in Kings Heath in Birmingham, and the defendant is from Bulgaria.

Mel smiled at the bus driver as she followed the young girl, obviously late for school, upstairs. Sitting near the stairs, she was glad of the smoking ban which had once made the upstairs on buses no-go areas for non-smokers or those who valued their health.

Mel's journey had settled into a routine, boring and very predictable. She had decided that, as she could not avoid jury service, she would embrace it to assist the wheels of fairness and justice. Having explained her new role to her employers at the NHS, she realised that her absence would put more pressure on an already stretched service. Her boss was, however, understanding, and Mel had worked out she could claim the £64.95 per day for loss of earnings if she needed to. There was also a food and drink allowance of £5.71 a day, which would more than cover her lunch and refreshments. Travel to and from the court had been trickier. Petrol costs were covered, but parking in Bristol would be scarce and expensive, particularly difficult with the early morning rush hour traffic. No, Mel decided on the T1 bus, which used the bus lanes to speed her to the very convenient final stop close to the Bristol Crown Court. A nearby coffee shop was a bonus. She decided that it would be more economical and less stressful than driving.

The forty-minute journey allowed her to think about the forthcoming case, which was horrendous in detail but clear-cut. Terry Gilligan, the pontificating racist fifty-year-old bane of her life, would soon be a brief footnote in her life story. The judge had predicted a twelve-day trial, and this was the ninth. Mel would be glad to get back to the backlog of work with the NHS, work she thoroughly enjoyed as it combined her skills as a psychoanalyst with the pleasure of helping people. It felt good and clean in a way that Mister Gilligan with his snide remarks and unsatisfactory underachieving life could never be.

Mel sat on the bus looking forward to her pre-court latte coffee and a tea cake before joining the rest of the jury. She closed her eyes as the familiar journey with its different perspective of height no longer needed her attention.

However, her dreams certainly did.

At around thirteen, Mel had found that her dreams had an unnerving way of becoming true, although rarely directly. She had long ceased to try to explain this to parents or friends as her special talent seemed ridiculous in the cold, clear light of dawn. She did not dream every night, or if she did, they drifted quickly away from her before she was fully awake, the in-between time of consciousness, as she called it.

Mel's analytical and most logical mind had at first refused to accept that she could in any way dream of the future, but it had happened so often that she had grown to accept her talent if that was what it was. Mel had decided that her observational skills had merely projected and predicted what might happen. Her dreams were not of major world events and never involved people she had not met. She could, thankfully, not dream of ordering.

The first dream she could recall happened at around the onset of puberty, and she was unsettled to have had a vivid dream of the death of her auntie's terrier. Sid was ancient, snappy and bad-tempered, willing to attack cars, cats or anyone he took a dislike to. Mel was on that list, and she, in turn, was terrified of him and his snarling ways. She had had a strange dream in which Sid had died but, in the morning, Mel decided that he was old, and his time was due, not a stunning prediction but later in the day she had been told that Sid had run into the road chasing a Honda Jazz and been instantly killed by a motorcycle coming the other way. Mel had found this news to be very sad and unsettling, following as it did on her dream.

Over the years, Mel had come to accept that she could not control her dreams; therefore, large lottery wins were impossible, and she could not change events. She was learning to accept her gift, if it could ever be called that, but at times she wished she could enjoy more dreamless nights. She had learned not to share her special dreams, as she called them, she didn't want to be labelled weird or a freak.

People were afraid of those who were different. In the seventeenth century, she may well have been called a witch. Best to keep her dreams private.

Last night, she had spent a few brief and very discreet hours at the house of Joel McCarthy, a local travel agent who arranged holidays and tours to wonderfully exotic destinations. This was in sharp contrast to his own dull and predictable life with an equally dull but domineering wife. Mel had met Joel when she had arranged a short holiday to Corfu through Joel's agency. She found him physically attractive and safe, but married. He had asked her out to a restaurant in **Bristol**, carefully orchestrated away from the watchful eye of his wife. Mel was aware of his marital status and enjoyed Joel as a friend with benefits, a naughty secret life, although she knew that she could never marry Joel, even if he left his wife, as he often promised. No, the arrangement suited them both as a pleasurable interlude if Gill, his wife, was away.

Yesterday, Gill had been away on an overnight stay with her ailing mother, although she often used this story as a cover for her clandestine meetings with the owner of a large garage. These convoluting arrangements suited everyone as long as all remained discreet. Variety is the spice of life, as the saying goes, yet Mel was a realist and expected Joel to satisfy her needs. She would have much preferred her husband and family, but time was moving on.

Last night was pleasant, and Mel had enjoyed the wine and cheese, her weakness, and a glass of rum, a silent nod to her West Indian ancestry. She loved the rich golden colour and warmth of the rum, but rarely had more than one small glass, preferring to sip and savour rather than guzzling the glorious taste. Strangely, Mel never dreamed of Joel, and certainly her predictive dreams were never a subject for discussion. He was not an imaginative man and would never be capable of understanding or even trying to interpret her dreams, which seemed to be a window into the future. She rarely spent the night at her convenient friend with benefits; it was more routine for him to come to her small flat and leave as discreetly as possible. Both were familiar figures in Thornbury, so meals at local restaurants were off the benefits list. Mel would usually prepare a meal and drinks, and he would later leave wearing a cap pulled low over his face like a classic Victorian villain.

That night, Mel had retired to bed with a feeling of dissatisfaction with her 'romantic' episodes. She knew that it was no more than a pleasant interlude for them both, but it could only end in tears despite their pragmatic approach. No, she wanted something more, something more settled; she wanted a man of her own to share her whole life. She was on the wrong side of thirty and wanted children. This feeling increasingly dominated her thoughts, but strangely never entered her dreams. Mel had often found herself entering the crafts shop on Castle Street and perusing the many finely crafted items, but her focus was on the tiny, knitted cardigans on a rack. At one moment, she considered buying one and pretending they were for a nephew or niece, but held back and bought a decorated Christmas tree star to cover her feelings of guilt.

After kissing Joel briefly on the cheek last night, intimacies done with, he left, and she decided to leave the washing up and go straight back to bed. Once asleep, her dream was startling and harshly vivid. The main player in her court case, the Bulgarian driver of juggernauts, Bogdan Petrov, serial abuser of children, allegedly, was dead on a cold slab in a mortuary. Mel had never been in a mortuary but had watched enough television dramas to recognise where her dream had led her. The body, and body it was, had a label tied to its big toe with his name marked. She looked down at his large face, brutal even in death, and felt no pity whatsoever. He drove lorries from the continent to the UK and was often drunk, drugged or half asleep. Slight collisions were ignored as his mighty lorry roared on, impervious to the horns hooting in anger. He used his trips to England to stalk, kidnap and abuse children, usually young girls, and he enjoyed their pain. Mel certainly felt no pity for his death, even though he was still technically innocent until proven guilty. But she felt a growing anger at the vileness of this sexual predator. Although still in her disturbing sleep, she vowed that he would never leave the court a free man, whatever the efforts of the jury foreman to oppose her.

Mel awoke with a start, and a glance at the bedside clock showed it to be 3.33 am, and she was covered in a cold sweat. A terrible dream, and she went to make herself a cup of cocoa to try to settle herself back to sleep.

Mel was not to know it, but she and most of the jury would be successful in their judgement of guilty, happy to see Bogdan convicted, but all felt intimidated by his stare of pure hatred as he scanned the jury members for the last time. The judge would thank them all for their service in a very difficult and at times harrowing case. Sentencing was to follow later, and Mel would leave the court feeling that she was vindicated, but the man's sentence would be many years in prison and not execution. Mel never found out that he was to commit suicide six months later, unable to endure the anger of his fellow prisoners in Parkhurst prison. No one likes an abuser of children, and he was made to suffer in ways the court could not.

But this was for the future, and it was a future that Mel never discovered. Perhaps her most dramatic of dreams had come true, and she had missed the small piece in the newspaper announcing his suicide. No one would mourn his cowardly way out of a miserable life built on giving pain to vulnerable, terrified victims. Her dream was starkly correct, but she was never to know this.

As Mel Chandoo sat quietly on the T1 bus, which announced the next stop with a taped regularity, she wondered if the driver would ever grow weary of hearing that same message repeatedly. She had only been listening for a few days but disliked the largely unnecessary commentary on their journey. She pondered on planners' ability to give new developments names which reflected a rural past which could never be reached again. At the Willow Brook shopping centre, which served the large overspill of Bradley Stoke, she closed her eyes and tried to ignore the boring, clear, crisp voice announcing their next stop. She was unaware that she had been seen by a would-be author at the back of the bus. Maddie went towards the stairs, ready to go alone to her new school. She took the opportunity to glance at Mel as she left the bus, ready to add details to a potential new character. Mel did not look up but realised that the girl was late for school, but did not seem flustered or rushed, more a calm indifference.

Chapter Five: Check Lists, Missed Buses and a Parallel Marriage

Jenny Clutterbuck had not intended to fall asleep, but sleep she did in a motel room which seemed very familiar to her, but different enough to be part of a museum piece. The bed was utilitarian and did not offer a variety of postures and heat settings. The bathroom was clean but spartan, and the toilet was light years away from the Japanese model which she and Steve had loved on their trip to Japan. The seat was cold, and there was no computer setting to select the pulse of warm water to cleanse the body after use. Light classical music to mask noise was certainly absent. Such features unique to the perfectionist manufacturers in Japan would become commonplace and expected in the mid-2050s.

It was slightly irritating not to control the lights, heating and television by voice control. Nevertheless, Jenny lay on the functional non-interactive bed and took a nap. Half an hour later, she awoke feeling refreshed but slightly annoyed at herself for allowing such a luxury whilst on intervention duty. At home in 2056, she would often take a short nap after walking the dogs, but this was 2024, and there was work to be done.

She decided to ignore the quaint, tiny bedside kettle and two mugs, an ever-present reminder that she was alone and a widow, yet ironically, at this time, she was married and in Yorkshire with her beloved Steve and two small children. The thought again passed her mind to travel to Bristol and catch a fast train to Hull, at least fast by the standards of the time. The delicious thought was swept briskly aside, and she reminded herself to be more disciplined; time travel was not to be taken lightly.

Sitting on the bed, Jenny opened the sealed padded envelope and spread the contents on the worn, cream bedspread. She was familiar with the succinct instructions. There were details of the exact time of the awful crash of the T1 double-decker on its way from the market town of Thornbury to Bristol. Thursday, July 10th, 2024, at 9.45 am at a roundabout near Parkway station. Just a few days. There was a timetable with the specific ill-fated bus highlighted. It left Thornbury Health Centre at 9.16, scheduled to arrive in Bristol at 10.03, but it never arrived as it lay stricken and smoking on its side, like a fallen dinosaur breathing its last. It was surrounded by ambulances and police cars all with flashing lights, and two fire engines which had disgorged their teams of firefighters working quickly to rescue the injured and trapped.

Jenny read slowly the list of names, which were meaningless to her, apart from one which shocked her to the core. Unusually, there was no targeted individual, the one considered important enough to have an intervention to save them for the benefit of the future.

Jenny sighed and closed her eyes. This was the worst-case scenario, a multiple. Two or more lives had to be saved, and the report was nonspecific. It was all related to that double-decker, and she had the task of saving multifarious lives.

She scanned the list of names:

- Iris Chandoo, aged 30, Psychoanalyst
- Madison Marsden, 16, Schoolgirl
- Frank Nelson, 42, Bus driver
- William Hayes, 35, Teacher
- Joy Chen, 22, Teaching assistant and translator
- Amanda Buckley, 61, Music teacher
- John Buckley, 71, Retired architect
- Rosangel Chlebek, 30 Doctor

The final name on the list frightened her; Jenny Clutterbuck's name was there at the bottom.

She allowed logic to take control. She could not be one of the three killed. A return to 2056 would then be impossible, so she must be one of the injured, a daunting and certainly scary thought. But what if she was indeed one of the dead? The implications in terms of time warps were unimaginable. This was proving to be a very difficult case, a multiple with little information to work with. It was obvious that she had to save the whole double-decker; it wasn't just a matter of keeping one special individual from boarding the ill-fated vehicle.

At the bottom of the page was a sentence in bold black letters.

Intervention return: Friday July 11th, 2024, 16.00 hours

A note added, one of the passengers is a potential time traveller. At least she did return, but injured and how badly? The idea that one on the list was to be recruited as a fellow time traveller was intriguing. Her replacement? Despite Jenny's determination to never time travel again, she felt a twinge of jealousy.

The rest of the package held useful items such as money, credit cards in her name and a further reminder to check her watch often. Jenny knew well that her watch, seemingly innocent, was a powerful item vital to her mission. At precisely four o'clock, Friday, July 11th, at 16.00, it would transport her back to the main portal in Swindon for debrief. A quiet place was always needed, but if she was injured, what then? Without the watch, she would be left stranded like Robinson Crusoe, unable to return home. There was a flicker that, at least, she could go and see her family and indeed herself, but that was all. She would be trapped and injured, although she was not sure how badly. It was very tempting to just deliberately miss the bus and return home safe. This was certainly Jenny's most extreme intervention and potentially the most dangerous.

This was unquestionably going to be her last intervention. Raw fear began to creep upon Jenny.

At that moment on the A38, the T1 bus stopped. Frank glanced in his left-hand mirror. The bus had set off from the designated stop opposite St Helen's church with its neat, well-tended cemetery and small west tower. To an American visitor, it would be seen as old; from an English perspective, it was a newcomer amongst the country's rich variety of places of worship. It was built in 1885, thus late Victorian, but boasted a Norman font removed from an earlier St Helen's. The church served the village of Alveston, where John and Amanda Buckley lived in a fine, large semi-detached house across the busy A38 road from the church.

When they moved into what they saw as their forever home with its views to the rear of fields and the church to the front, they were happy and refashioned the 1939 house to their liking. They were Christmas Eve service Christians, going annually and to the occasional wedding and lately funerals, but the sight of the church was comforting, and the house was convenient for travel to Bristol with easy access to the major motorway crossroads of the M4 and M5.

Amanda Buckley sat in her high-ceilinged bedroom, carefully adjusting her makeup. It was her bedroom as she had long since ceased to share her nights with her terminally ill and, as she considered, boring husband, John. He was technically ten years older than Amanda, but seemingly thirty years older with his cancer and alarmingly increasing dementia. When they met at a Vivaldi concert in Cheltenham, John had seemed to her to be the epitome of charm and desirability. He was the older, more experienced man and an up-and-coming architect with real prospects, but since retirement, he had settled like silt in a particularly slow river.

When she had first taken John home and introduced him to her mother, she was doing that thing she did, that thing with a dishcloth and bleach in the sink. Amanda remembered that her mother had raised her eyebrows at her young daughter and the older man.

Her good friend, Elaine, had called her a leech for attaching herself to a well-off architect. Elaine was no longer a friend, and they had lost touch years ago.

Amanda stood and adjusted her figure-hugging jeans and loose, low-cut light blue blouse, carefully chosen for coordination. No, she thought, I am only 59 and 24 months, much too young to settle quietly, waiting to make the short journey across the road to a final resting place. She had places to go and people to meet. She felt trapped, as she was a reluctant, nervous driver, and John was unable to drive due to failing eyesight; they were on the wrong side of the road and increasingly reliant on public transport. John was an experienced driver, and he was alarmed by

Amanda's stuttering driving. The thing she did to the brakes on their old Honda had become the stuff of legend. Crossing the A38 was hazardous, and the destination was a church with a school behind and a considerable walk to the small row of shops which served the village. Not ideal by any stretch of the imagination.

Today was a special day for Amanda, she and John, her husband, turned semi-patient, were catching the T1, their lifeline, into Bristol where they had an appointment. Amanda had seen an advert in the local paper asking for homes for Ukrainian refugees. She had persuaded John that having a family to stay long term would be good for them and part of their duty as committed Christians. The £500 a month would certainly augment her income as a private violin teacher and give her access to a wider range of fashionable dresses and youthful outfits. She was determined to battle the inevitable ravages of time. He had seen the sense of the arrangement, plenty of room and perhaps their Citroen A4 could be used for mutual benefit if the Ukrainians could drive. In his innocence, he had missed the fact that his younger, frustrated wife was yearning for an injection of male testosterone into her boring life. For her, a virile, handsome, blonde, blue-eyed Ukrainian would be a wonderful addition to the household, an object of advanced-level flirting, married or not.

She smiled to herself; the exciting prospect was enticing and delicious in her secret thoughts. A familiar voice cut into her waking dreams.

'Amanda, are you nearly ready yet? The bus will be here soon, and we shouldn't be late.' John shouted from downstairs by the front door. He was organised with a walking stick in hand and front door key ready to lock up, if only he could get Amanda to come away from her bedroom mirror.

'Yes, I'm coming, I'm coming,' she answered irritably.

He was reminded of a fog horn's bleary call, but such thoughts were deeply hidden. His secret compartment, never to be revealed in case Amanda would do the unthinkable and leave him, alone and stranded. He had never even mastered the electric tin opener. He resolved to discreetly buy an old-fashioned one in Bristol as a precautionary measure.

Everything that John did or said seemed to grate on Amanda these days. His habits, once so endearing, seemed designed to get on her nerves. Once her passport to exotic foreign travel, he was now an anchor to her ambitions. His jaunty, carefree walk had become a trudging, slow shuffle, which she hated. The click of his walking stick, slow and persistent, drained her patience, and yet she had always thought herself to be a wonderfully patient individual, as she had had to display heroic stoicism and composed professionalism in her role as violin teacher in the face of screeching strings being abused in those days before retirement. The tortured grating sounds had been replaced by the constant clicking of a carved walking stick. Life was so unfair, she thought as she carefully chose a silk scarf to match her blouse and hide her ageing, wrinkled neck.

'Amanda, please, you know how long it takes me to get to the bus stop, it's almost time and I can't run, as you well know.'

Glancing one last time at the mirror and judging herself to be able to pass as a thirty-five-year-old with an appropriate slim figure, Amanda flounced downstairs, like a film star on the red carpet at the Cannes film festival.

They left the house and reached the end of the drive when Frank Nelson's T1 double-decker went past. Amanda was not going to let this daunt her; she ran, waving her arms and demanding that her private carriage wait for her. It was humiliating enough to have to travel by public transport without the indignity of having to run after it.

Frank Nelson carefully checked his mirrors and stopped gently, not that he was supposed to. He had caught a glimpse of the old lady waving frantically, and he opened his doors. With a small sigh, he realised that the woman was accompanied by a stumbling, stick-reliant older man. This counts as my good deed for the day, he thought, if he could keep up to his timetable and his boss didn't find out.

Amanda stepped onto the bus and began to search in her handbag for her hated bus pass.

'You were early, late, I can understand, but early?' Amanda said without gratitude and a degree of childish petulance.

Frank Nelson raised his eyebrows and refrained from a biting answer. He had to deal with so much, most of which he could tolerate, but today he allowed himself the luxury of a short reply.

'Very sorry, madam, the vehicle set off without me, and I had to run to catch it up. It likes to be on time.'

Meanwhile, John had arrived with a bus pass ready in hand. Touching the plastic over the card reader, he thanked the driver profusely, noting that Amanda had bounced upstairs, murmuring about bloody, sarcastic drivers. He was left to find a seat downstairs, going upstairs was certainly out of the question, and Amanda refused to sit with what she thought of as the oldies.

Frank waited until the old man was safely seated before checking his mirror and easing the giant vehicle into the constant stream of commuter traffic. Strange, he thought, he had assumed that the two passengers were together. He was right in his original assessment, but decided that this was what he thought of as a parallel marriage, a couple going in the same direction for convenience's sake, but tracks never to converge, each with their own life and needs.

He was right.

Amanda sat at the front seat, her rightful place, surveying her vista with an imperious look. She knew that John was incapable of mounting the stairs, especially on a moving vehicle, but he didn't need her company these days, or so she thought. Her mind turned from her increasingly disappointing husband to her hopes for a successful conclusion to their meeting for potential carers for a Ukrainian refugee family, or rather, her husband to be flirted with. She sadly supposed that a single man would be off the menu.

John Buckley, meanwhile, was catching his breath, pleased to have a window seat and, like his wife, was contemplating having a Ukrainian family to stay for a number of months. He hoped for children, small children. He pictured himself with a child snuggling on each side of the settee as they watched television, and he helped with their developing English. He had always wanted a family of his own, but pregnancy would, she said, have ruined his wife's figure, and children would be a tiresome burden. As an only child, John had always felt that their marriage was incomplete, but he was endlessly compliant. His needs were a poor second to the awful thought of losing his younger wife. Nevertheless, he loved the idea of a large Christmas tree with excited children tearing the wrapping paper from myriad presents. Yes, a young family would bring a breath of fresh air to their stale marriage and echoing empty house. Perhaps if the children were older, he could take them to the County ground and introduce them to his love for cricket. It would be Gloucestershire and not his beloved Worcestershire, but no matter. They probably wouldn't know the difference.

Glancing out of the window at the approaching motorway interchange, John thought that the arrangement would give Amanda another female to chat with.

Wrong, and innocent as always.

Chapter Six: A Solitary Life and Twenty-Five Years to go to Retirement

The letter was short and precise, with an official letter heading, Hurst Green Primary School. Bradley Stoke. William George Hayes opened the envelope slowly, expecting the usual rejection letter. He read the words, almost unable to take in the invitation for an interview for the vacant deputy headship. Heart pounding, William went into the kitchen and automatically put on the kettle to make a settling cup of tea.

His flat was modern but small, and certainly big enough for a 35-year-old man living alone. The view from his third-floor window would once have been of the Filton airfield, but now it was a hive of construction as houses and flats sprang up where freight planes once landed, and famously in 1969, the first flight of Concorde took place. William would have loved to have seen that, but it had happened twenty years before he was born in Sheffield.

Now, 35-year-old William was tall, slim and healthy. His eyes were a deep navy blue, and his brown hair was swept back from his forehead like a wave on Scarborough beach. Now flecked with grey, his thick hair gave him a look of gravitas, accentuated by his black rimmed glasses, not that he thought much about his looks. He had never overcome his shyness and dreaded walking into a room full of strangers. Small talk was foreign to him.

William, or Silent Bill as he was known at his teaching job at Middlebrook Primary school, took his plain blue mug of tea and sat down on his two-seater grey settee. He read the letter again, savouring each word, only his second deputy headship interview in fourteen years of teaching. The first had been a disaster as everything that could go wrong went spectacularly wrong on that horrendous day. He had been ill-prepared, unable to respond in a positive manner to questions about his vision for the school. He had stuttered as he desperately tried to think of adequate answers and had then had to request a break in mid-interview to visit the toilet as his bladder had let him down. He had got confused on his return to the temporary interview room and managed to get locked out as he tried to take a shortcut through an outside door and back to the main entrance. No, a day to forget.

Since then, he has sent out many applications to the point where he can fill in the forms and add his CV while he is asleep. This would be different, he decided. His only regret was that he had no one to share his letter with. Unmarried and with both parents, Alan, a caretaker, and Shirley, a dental receptionist, both sadly deceased, he had only one brother, Eric, in Stockport, and he had little interest in William's stuttering career. They were on Christmas card exchange terms, and the increase in the cost of stamps put this fragile relationship in danger. His father, a former miner, died of lung cancer, still bitter about the miners' strike of 1984. He was immensely proud of his son breaking with tradition and going to Nottingham University, although he regarded the Nottinghamshire miner's refusal to join the strike as scabs and beneath contempt. William, or young Billy as his father called him, would have loved to have phoned home to tell them about the interview; his mother would, he knew, have cried with happiness for him. But both were sadly gone, and William missed them each day.

It had been a hard decision to move to the Bristol area away from his parents and his native Yorkshire. He had secured a teaching job, one he had stayed at for fourteen years, and proved he was at best a reliable teacher, fish and chips without the salt or vinegar or even mushy peas. In his time at the school, he had seen three different headteachers. Each regarded him as dull; there was no excitement in his teaching, no flair, and when classes were allocated, there was a collective quiet groan as children realised that William was to be their teacher for a year. Parents accepted that he was slightly old-fashioned in his teaching, but he carefully covered the necessary curriculum. Never absent, never controversial, rarely away on career-building courses. Reliability was his watchword.

In the staffroom, he was quiet. Polite when spoken to, but not part of the banter. Behind his back, he was called Silent Bill, although not in an unfriendly way; he was always willing to help. Several years before, he had applied for the deputy headship at his own school but had not even been granted a chance to put forward his case.

On the day of that interview, he had been asked by the chair of the Governors, a dour Welshman, to bring in a table for the interviewing panel. It was thoughtless and, for William, deeply humiliating. Not good enough to warrant an interview, but worthy of being a table carrier. He should have refused and walked away, head held high, but he had carried the table into the staff room and left. As he sipped his fast-cooling tea, William thought, as he had done a thousand times, that he should have acted differently.

'If you've not to say, say nowt,' as his beloved Yorkshire grandmother would say, but he felt that he had something to say to that mindless Welshman, but he did not. The job went to a young, dynamic teacher at the school, junior to William, but by sheer coincidence, she was sleeping with the headteacher, king of waffle and the latest buzz words.

This time would be different. He was increasingly determined to act and speak; he would be super prepared, his days of being mediocre and safely average were over. His future would be different because of this letter on his lap; he would shine and secure a place in the leadership group in a new school. William wanted to make his old parents proud, even after their passing.

With a sigh, William's thoughts were brought crashing to the ground as he thought of his university love, his first real love, Emily Greenwood. He knew that she would have supported him and helped in so many ways. Those first few weeks at Nottingham University had been confusing and difficult, a Yorkshire miner's son, the first of his family to go on to higher education, but William had felt out of place and out of his depth. Academically, he was comfortable with his geography course, but he began to lean towards a career in education. At a lecture on glaciation, he had heard a laughing, lovely female voice rich with what he felt was a familiar Yorkshire accent. He thought of home and saw that the speaker was a dark-haired, pretty girl wearing a short denim skirt and a sweatshirt with a university logo, two sizes too big.

William was smitten, and he later did the bravest deed of his life: he invited Emily out for a drink. She asked if it was just the two of them, and when he said it was just him, she amazingly agreed. A tumbling, clumsy love affair began that day, a love which even overcame the fact that Emily was from Preston in Lancashire and not the revered broad acres of Yorkshire. William's wrong interpretation of her accent became a standard joke between them, and he was happier than he had ever been before.

They had gone to a university film club night showing a classic film, Seven Samurai, and both were entranced by Japan. Over a drink in the university bar, they had discussed the wonderful thought of visiting Japan together, since then William had tried to learn some basic Japanese and soaked up all the information about the mysterious, unique country. They had even started a small collection of netsuke, those beautifully carved clothing fasteners used in traditional Japanese clothing. Netsuke were used on a sash around a kimono and could be made of boxwood, ivory, walnuts or even peach stones. They decided that they could not afford the old authentic versions, but managed several more modern ones, carved to perfection and very tactile in the palm of the hand.

Emily was William's first and indeed only experience of exploring a female body. He was certainly not an accomplished lover, but nevertheless, she loved this tall, serious and handsome young man. He, in his turn, enjoyed Emily's cute chin and her willingness to be patient with him as he became, for a while, more outgoing.

Neither of them could say when or even why the arguments started, but Emily increasingly saw William or Will as she called him, as moody and petulant. He wanted to be with her alone and shunned friends. In one of their good times, he had revealed that his mother had told him that he would be a wonderful husband and father. Amid a fiery argument, about sausages of all things, she had shouted at him.

'Your mother lied to you, and that is the truth.'

William was deeply hurt, and the arguments kept coming, growing stronger until the end of the Christmas term, when he had helped her with her bags on the journey to the station. Emily had somewhat inevitably been seeing another student at university, and he had seen them together holding hands. Helping with her bags had seemed the gentlemanly thing to do, but he was hurt and anxious at the prospect of losing her. Confronting her was not a good idea. Emily felt constrained and wished to end the relationship. Angry words were exchanged, and Emily cried, anxious to get on the train to her home.

William, he had loved being Will, had gone over that scene a thousand times, and his version was his preferred heroic one. Emily had boarded the train with tears streaming down her face, to the embarrassment of some passengers and the curiosity of others. It was a bleak, unsatisfactory ending, and she silently urged the train to leave. William didn't have a ticket but manfully vaulted the gate and, ignoring the protesting guard, ran down the train looking in each carriage, desperate to find Emily, to apologise and start again, a fresh new beginning. Luckily, she was in a window seat, head down and sobbing. He knocked frantically on the window, and she had left the carriage to join him on the platform in a joyous hug. Tear-wet kisses had followed, and moments later, the train had slowly left the station, but the two lovers did not care. Even the guard at the platform paused and turned away, smiling.

However, this version never happened.

William had stood behind the barrier with a churning stomach as the Manchester train departed, and he was left alone. Strangely, when he replayed this scene in his mind so many times, he had become increasingly aware that in his version, Emily's bags had been left on the train to start the journey without their owner. William's mind was too orderly, and this anomaly disturbed him if he could only go back in time to that bitter, cold sleeting day when his love was crushed forever.

Of course, they had returned to university for the spring term, but things had changed, and William had suffered agonies as he saw Emily walking hand in hand with her new love. It hurt him deeply, and he became more introverted and alone. Suicide crossed his mind, and he went so far as to purchase a bottle of wine and mixed it with ground-down aspirins, hoping to enter a drunken, never-ending sleep. Somehow, the aspirin didn't mix as well as he hoped, and the drink seemed unappetising.

Years later, William sat alone and wondered where Emily Greenwood was now. He had tried to discover her whereabouts on social media, but no doubt she was married with a new surname or perhaps had a hyphenated name. He had been unable to find her and realised that this was a long-lost cause, but he would have liked to have phoned her to tell her of his interview.

William was certainly not hungry, but realised that he needed to eat, perhaps a pizza delivered to the door, but that seemed too much for his excited churning stomach. He decided on a sandwich, believing that there were some ham slices left over in the fridge, and a fresh hot pot of tea would be easier than pizza.

Usually, he would go for a walk after tea past the new houses, many still under various stages of construction and down to the A38, where he would return by a slightly different route. But today was not a usual day. He would not look at his carefully catalogued collection of Cup Final programmes, memorising the missing early years which were proving difficult and expensive to obtain. The collection was unlikely to be completed. His accumulation of netsuke in their display cabinet gave him great pleasure to clean and admire, and it had become a habit to take one and look carefully at the marvellous workmanship. The earlier ones in his array reminded him sharply of Emily, and he would sigh deeply with longing and regret.

But not tonight. This was a time for the future, not the past. He finished his sandwich and sipped his tea before opening his favourite, a Kit Kat, the prince of chocolate biscuits.

Time to plan, and he put the interview date in his diary, usually empty but for school-related events. Taking an A4 notebook, he began to make a list of things to do. A positive reply to the invitation to interview and then inform his headteacher. He decided to be known as Will at his new school, should he be lucky enough to be named as the new deputy head, a wonderful, exciting prospect.

Suddenly, William's stomach gave a lurch as he realised that the relevant date coincided with his five-year-old Ford Fiesta being booked into the Ford garage in Thornbury for major gearbox work, that could not be delayed, and as he could walk the short distance to his present school, this did not present a problem. However, the magical interview was at Hurst Green Primary school, a good three miles down the A38. It would not do to arrive on a warm summer's day, hot and sweaty. Rolling up in a taxi seemed too pretentious, but then he realised that the T1 bus passed close to his flat and right by Hurst Green. He could drive to Thornbury, leave the car and keys through the garage door if necessary and catch the bus to Bradley Stoke. That would be perfect, or so he thought. On his to-do list, he added, check T1 Timetable and fares. He was nothing if not studious and carefully efficient.

Whilst Will, as he now thought himself, was busy planning, a young Year Three teacher at his current school put aside her completed marking in her shared flat in North Bristol. Abbie Thompson was fair-haired, petite and pretty rather than beautiful. After three years as a teacher, she had increasingly been intrigued by William Hayes, her mentor in her first probationary year. Abbie felt resentment when others called him Silent Bill behind his back. Yes, he was undeniably quiet, but she found him kind and helpful. He was older, but she thought this unimportant as she looked at the treasured annual staff photograph and thought again of ways of starting a relationship with a man, she knew to be single.

William was totally unaware of Abbie's increasing adoration. He would have been astounded to realise that anyone could be attracted to him, at least not since Emily at university. and fate would ensure that he might never be aware.

Chapter Seven: A Shock Encounter and Baby Eyes

Jenny Clutterbuck waited patiently for the T1 bus, which would take her to Bristol, a city she didn't know in either the present day or her own time, 2056. The bus stop was a few metres from the old coaching inn where breakfast was being served for travellers in the Premier Inn across the courtyard. The laminated menu had several versions of the full English breakfast, but she decided on black coffee and toast. The waitress frowned slightly, most customers opted for a very full breakfast to both fill up for the day and get their money's worth. She did, however, put on her best professional smile and noted that the customer was alone, probably a widow and had taken good care of herself, probably a gym member. There was something likeable about this customer who declined the Big Breakfast so graciously.

Whilst drinking her coffee, Jenny decided that she was in a serious quandary. In the next few days, the double-decker would crash with serious injuries, including her own and three deaths. She had poured over the information from her usual sealed envelope and realised that if she had the name of the person, she was sent back in time through the Time Portal to save it, it would be relatively simple. A matter of finding and preventing the victim from getting on the bus, but this was very different. Was she supposed to save everyone on the bus? The question of how she could do this had filled her thinking time before and after sleep. Answers were more difficult than questions, and Jenny was no nearer solving the serious issue. She could wait for the portal to bring her back to her comfortable, if lonely, future without succeeding in her mission. But that was not her way

The cost of transporting Jenny back thirty-two years was eye-watering, and the decision to send her was not taken lightly. She prided herself on the simple fact that she was a successful, if increasingly reluctant, time traveller. This intervention was important, and she had been chosen for her resilience and persistence. Opting out and returning without trying to save the future world-changing victim was not an option. The accident was not to happen until later, so she had several days to act, but how?' Jenny decided to travel the same route to Bristol, perhaps identify some of those on her list, have coffee and return to her base at the Premier Inn.

Having checked her timetable, she had gone early to the bus stop to avoid missing the bus. As she waited, she marvelled at the passing array of what would be seen in her time as old classic cars. She was amazed at their noisy engines and the occasional roar of motorcycles, which in thirty years' time would be reduced to police and first responder medical teams. Special permits were needed for members of the public.

There was no one else at the bus stop, and Jenny embraced the early morning warmth of an outstanding summer's morning. A day ripe with promise and hope. Jenny sighed and pondered deeply that this month would be severely life-changing and for some, life-ending. She was their only hope, and the responsibility lay heavily despite the sun's benevolence. Looking up, Jenny could see aircraft vapour trails slowly marking their journey and was surprised to see no drones buzzing low across the sky. She had become accustomed to parcels being delivered by drone. Letters were almost unknown as e-mails dominated, as the cost of labour and postage had soared. The postal strike of 2034 had virtually ended the Royal Mail as it was then called.

Jenny was very conscious that she had so much knowledge of the everyday future that she would, or rather could, be a valuable commodity to the commercial world. But then no one took notice of the elderly and grey-haired, the invisible.

On time, the double-decker Bristol-bound bus seemed almost grateful to have once more reached the top of the long and winding hill. The driver, Frank Nelson, had reached the top of the ridge many times, but each time was an achievement of concentration. From here, the journey was straightforward without peril. Frank noticed a lone woman waiting to board his bus. He glanced in his mirror, indicated and turned into the designated bus stop. The door opened with a sigh, almost one of relief for the bus, happy to be out of the steep, twisting road. Frank smiled at the new embarking passenger, and as she placed her bus pass on the card reader, she took the opportunity to take in her appearance. He was mildly surprised that she was old enough for a pass designed for the elderly. Unless she had stolen the card, an unlikely scenario, or been loaned it by a friend, she must be at least sixty, but he would have estimated perhaps fifty-four.

As Jenny turned to find a seat, he glanced at her fresh face and minimal make-up, the casual clothing gave an elegant, independent air. Her warm, friendly smile was that of a regular passenger, and Frank realised that he had picked her up before, but not here. He cast his mind back and quickly pictured her stepping aboard in Thornbury at Rock Street. Her cheerfulness was welcome as many ignored him as they boarded, full of their own thoughts and agendas for the day. Frank's secret desire to go on stage as a drag queen had given him much experience in quickly judging make-up and dress.

Frank frowned slightly as his new expensive boots, which he had much desired, pinched slightly. They were wider than his normal trainers and would sometimes catch annoyingly on the foot pedals. Perhaps vanity had foolishly overcome practicality, but he reassured himself that they would wear in and improve, but it was a difficult task as he sat for most of his day behind a wheel.

Jenny decided on staying downstairs as the bus slowly moved into the traffic bound for the stream of traffic on the A38. She briefly thought it a coincidence that she had recognised the driver; his loud red and white Gloucester rugby shirt was indeed memorable. She supposed that he was possibly the one to be driving the huge vehicle on its ill-fated journey next week.

Despite the bus having a capacity of around eighty, the downstairs seats were half empty, but as usual, passengers had taken all the window seats, leaving Jenny to have to choose a seat next to someone, potentially on her dead and injured list. It was very un-English to engage in conversation with strangers, and the exchange of names was not usually a done thing. With some relief, Jenny noticed a mother sitting near the front of the bus, near a small pram. Glancing at the rest of the passengers, she realised that she could not easily match or find her eight specified list members. She did not wish to call them dead or injured; it was too dreadful to contemplate.

The mother with the toddler on her knee was different. Unless there were others upstairs of Chinese ancestry, this could be Joy Chen. Jenny guessed that she was in her early twenties with short black hair and an open smiling face as she talked quietly to the child. The two obviously adored each other. Jenny sat down next to the mother and child, and Joy Linjin Chen smiled a silent greeting. The toddler looked curiously at the newcomer and, like his mother, smiled.

'What an absolutely beautiful baby,' Jenny said, hoping beyond hope that this was not Joy Chen; perhaps she was upstairs, without a toddler to confuse matters.

'Thank you, he's had a sleep, so he's in a good mood, and he loves travelling by bus, as we have to. We don't have a car, unfortunately.'

Jenny was a mother and grandmother, and she loathed the idea of a child being hurt.

'And what's your name, young man?' Jenny said, tickling him gently under the chin. He responded with a chuckle, liking the new lady.

'This is Chang, Chang Chen,' Joy said proudly.

Jenny felt her heart sink as she realised that there was now no doubt. Chen. There could not possibly be a mistake. The statistical chances of there being another woman of the same name upstairs were alarmingly slim.

'What a lovely name, a strong alliterative name, and it seems to suit him,' Later, this young boy's life could be changed dramatically. Jenny tried hard to keep calm and continue to smile, but it was so very hard. This was definitely and absolutely her last venture into the past; it was unbearable carrying such a burden of knowledge with her.

'Thank you so much, Chang means good or to prosper and flourish.' Joy said she loved the way in which her adorable son attracted praise.

A small tear appeared on Jenny's cheek, which she dabbed quickly away with a tissue.

Joy frowned, 'Are you alright?'

'Don't mind me, I'm just a sentimental old lady. I have a grandson, but he is far away, and I miss him so much.' Far away in miles and time, she thought. This toddler had altered her perception of the purpose of her intervention. She had already realised that without knowing the actual identity of the single person who would change the future in a positive way, she could not easily act. The whole bus, with all passengers, would have to be saved. Implications for the future, as the lives of around sixty people would be changed, were immense and beyond her careful remit. The knock-on effect could be potentially devastating. What if one person upstairs was a serial killer who would go on to kill many times, as she had saved him accidentally, whilst ensuring that all passengers were safe? I cannot play God, Jenny thought.

'Are you going shopping with your mummy in Bristol?' Jenny asked, hoping that Chang's mother would say that they were going to the large Tesco in Bradley Stoke and they would alight before the scene of the crash. If this were a regular journey for mother and child, then Joy and Chang may avoid the devastation with bodies being hurled around. But of course, this slim hope was extinguished before it had a chance to develop. Joy Chen was definitely on the bus on its fateful journey; she was on the awful list.

'No, unfortunately not. I work as a teaching assistant at a school in Thornbury, but I am registered as a translator for the police when they have the need for a fluent Mandarin speaker. I was born in Hong Kong, you see. Usually, my mother looks after Chang whilst I am at school, but she is ill this week, so I have to bring him with me. Not ideal, but we have to do the best we can.'

The best we can! Joy Linjin Chen's thoughts went back to the struggles she had faced in her young life and indeed continued to face. There was conflict with her conservative Chinese parents, although her recently deceased father had quietly supported her, often against her mother in earlier teenage arguments. Joy felt herself in a halfway land between Hong Kong Chinese and modern multicultural England.

Joy reflected on her struggles to be accepted at school; she was different, being Chinese and certainly perceived as too intelligent, not one of the crowd. For her parents, education was paramount, and Joy was given full support. In her A-level exams, she had achieved high grades, and in order to please her parents, especially her dad, she had successfully applied to the School of Oriental and Asian Studies in London. Settling into her student accommodation at Dinwiddy House near Kings Cross station she had at first felt an outsider, a country bumpkin in a cosmopolitan world. However, this was soon overcome. The university had fewer than 4,000 undergraduates representing 140 countries, and for the first time, her Mandarin was useful apart from communication with her parents at home. She met many interesting people, many well placed for high-powered careers and minor European royalty.

But it was not one of the elite who caused Joy's downfall. In her last year at the very specialised university, she had become a regular at the local coffee bar, Talk and Roast, a nearby haunt of students. A young Barista called Lee Yu Tan, a Chinese student from Singapore, attracted her attention, and Joy was far from displeased with this. Soon they briefly became lovers, and much to the disappointment of her parents, Joy became pregnant and a single mother as Lee returned to Singapore, unaware of his child.

The two women, separated in age by four decades, continued to play with the child, both deep in their own thoughts. Do the best you can. Easy to say, Joy reflected, but she faced financial insecurity and her mother's unspoken, bitter disappointment. Chang made up for so much as Joy loved him without reservation, but he was nevertheless inhibiting her career.

Jenny played a simple face-hiding game with Chang and tried hard to see what his mother could possibly add to the future, which was so important. Whatever it may or may not be, this delightful baby with sparse black hair and smiling oriental eyes must be protected.

As the double-decker finally drove into its final stop in Bristol, Jenny and Joy said their goodbyes and the older lady thanked the driver before alighting to find a cafe for coffee and a chance to ponder her impossible task.

A nearby coffee shop from an international chain had trendy seating and various books scattered around on tables and shelves. They were not the sort of books anyone would steal, but gave customers, especially single ones, something to browse whilst drinking their cappuccinos or Lattes, something to flick through and feel mildly intellectual.

Jenny carefully concentrated on keeping her sashiko bag firmly on her shoulder whilst balancing a tray with an espresso and a fruity flapjack. She manoeuvred herself between tables to a far corner. She put down the tray and placed her precious bag on the arm of the chair, and unloaded the tray. Once done, Jenny looked around at the busy coffee shop with its insistent pop music and busy buzz of conversation. The noise of the coffee makers was loud and intrusive to Jenny. By 2056, they had been replaced by largely silent models. It was not a relaxed atmosphere, and Jenny regretted her choice.

Suddenly, Jenny felt an icy grip on her heart as she saw at a table near the window her husband, Steve, her life, her one deepest love. She knew in her logical mind that he was to die, drowned in a fishing accident in the North Sea, his body never to be recovered. Jenny's stomach reeled as she tried to make sense of this impossible chance encounter.

Of course, in 2024 he was alive and, as she thought, with her and their young family in Yorkshire, but why was he here in Bristol? And more to the point, in a close personal conversation with a young and pretty brunette. Their heads together, they laughed, and Jenny thought her heart would break. This was unbearable. Lifting her coffee, she tried to remain calm, but her hand shook so much she had to put the mug down with an unwanted clatter. Steve, his conversation disturbed, looked across at the unexpected noise and frowned. He had caught sight of Jenny, but it was a much older version, one he had never seen before. The old lady looked shaken but somehow strangely familiar.

Their eyes met, and every fibre of Jenny's soul screamed at her to go across and hold him for one last time, a chance to say goodbye, a chance which the cruel sea had deprived her of. All her training had drilled into her that she had to avoid, at all costs, meetings with close family and friends.

When Jenny thought that he was two hundred miles north, it was an easy order to obey, but he was here, alive and with another younger woman. She frantically searched her mind for a reason for him to be in Bristol. She didn't dare to allow her mind to use the words, a secret affair. Jenny knew Steve, he would never betray her, never but never was a long, long time.

The young girl looked across at Jenny, the cause of the clattering of crockery.

'Is it someone you know, Steve?'

Steve tore his eyes away and smiled at his companion.

'No, I don't really know anyone here in Bristol, but I had the strangest feeling that I had met her before; she almost reminds me of my wife.' Steve was bemused but stood, putting on his jacket.

'It's time for me to go to Parkway to catch my train home. Today has been a delight, we must arrange to meet up again, and we have so much in common.'

With that, he gave the girl a hug and a kiss on the cheek before leaving the cafe to quickly be enveloped by the busy shoppers. He was gone.

Jenny had tried to recover her shattered composure and suddenly noticed that her beloved was leaving without a chance for her to do the unthinkable and speak to him. His glance at her had been that of a stranger, and that was gut-wrenching. She stood as the girl sat down, returning to her coffee. It was too late, and her love was gone from her forever, leaving so many undesired questions and a heart-thumping anxiety. All her memories were overshadowed and seriously undermined by this one in ten million encounter.

Jenny felt suddenly dizzy, and the world went grey and foggy as she fainted, knocking over two tables and several coffees to the startled cries of nearby customers.

Chapter Eight: Blood, Handcuffs, and Aftershock

Doctor Rosangel Chlebek was a fine driver, careful and assured. She enjoyed driving, and it gave her the opportunity to have her own thinking time away from her beautiful chattering children, Eve and her older brother, Billy. Her usual morning journey in her pale blue Citroen C5 was busy with Bristol-bound traffic. At this routine time of day, she often followed the double-decker but refused to try to pass in unsafe places. That's the way accidents happen, she thought. A bit ironic as she worked in the Accident and Emergency department of the Bristol Royal Infirmary.

Doctor Rosie, as she was often called, was a popular leader in her department, cool, calm, and unflappable. Having recently turned thirty, she felt confident in her career path and indeed comfortable in her personal life. Despite coming from very different cultures, her own Polish heritage would seem, at first, at odds with her husband Sachin's background in his homeland of India. But it worked, they dovetailed together, and she loved him deeply. He was a researcher into cancer treatments at the same hospital, but worked different hours, so a car share was impractical. Rosie considered travelling each day by bus from her home on Castle Street in Thornbury but enjoyed her half hour, but she enjoyed her half-hour drive alone. Listening to smooth classical music.

Rosangel had a fiercely independent streak, and even after marriage, she kept her Polish surname, something which her husband respected. He loved finding out details of his blonde-haired, brown eyed wife and had been amazed to discover that she had once played cricket at school. His own dream had been to open the innings for India at Lord's, the home and cathedral of cricket. Sadly, that would never happen, but he played for the local club team in Thornbury, and he was a fine off-break spinner and a useful lower-order batsman.

Sachin and Rosie had been amused when they discovered, due to a talkative younger sister, that their son, Billy, had a crush on Miss Chen, the teaching assistant at his school. He was entranced by her oriental, dark-haired good looks and fascinated by her ability to speak Chinese. Joy Chen was his hero, and he decided to one day learn Mandarin.

The drive to work was never a chore for Rosie, and she revelled in the gentle warmth of an English summer's day with its loving caressing breeze. She had visited Sachin's home city of Chennai; she had understood then what a hot summer's day really meant with its oppressive, sultry heat.

Rosie had a busy, active life, and after her shift was over, she would visit IKEA to research new duvets and later attend the school PTA or Friends of School, as they liked to call themselves. It was a good, supportive group, and she enjoyed working to help the school. A recently acquired half allotment would give her relaxation time and the opportunity to introduce her children to the joys of fruit and vegetable growing. Her own family had had a full allotment in Newhill, her hometown in her native Derbyshire. Getting changed and ready for her shift at The Bristol Royal Infirmary, she took a deep breath before plunging in, wondering what the day would bring.

Walking through the crowded waiting room, she noted a grey-haired old woman in handcuffs sitting next to a ridiculously young policeman. Blood splattered her dress. A bit early for that, Rosangel thought. Probably a domestic dispute over the Coco Pops.

The usual residual drunks seeking a bed for the night complained loudly, demanding attention. Two of them were regulars, well known to staff, on first-name terms. A crying young boy sat in a temporary sling with an obviously broken arm, awaiting an X-ray. Rosie greeted Sally, the hard-pressed receptionist and picked up the clipboard with her first patient to check out.

Reading as she walked, she noted the words shock and in large capitals, NO NHS RECORD. Frowning, Rosie slid aside the rich blue curtain to discover a well-dressed lady of about mid to late fifties sitting up on the bed. The nurse was taking her blood pressure.

'Good morning, my name is Doctor Chlebek. Tell me what has brought you to us today?'

'It's nothing, doctor, I had a bit of a shock and fainted for a few seconds, but the cafe insisted on calling an ambulance, Health and Safety policy apparently, I'm absolutely fine now. I feel a fraud; I'm wasting your valuable time. I'll just get my bag and go.

Rosie glanced at the sashiko bag. 'Japanese, if I'm not mistaken.'

The nurse gave Rosie a note recording Jenny's blood pressure and indicated with her eyes that the doctor should join her outside the cubicle. Rosie followed.

Indira, the nurse, whispered, "All seemed fine," but the unusual fact was that the computer had no record of the patient.

'We have double checked, but she says her name is Jenny Clutterbuck and she is a visitor from Yorkshire, staying for a few days, but the only record for that name shows a twenty-eight-year-old, and whilst she is in good shape, she is certainly a lot older than that. There are no clear injuries. When she fell, a coffee table in the cafe broke her fall. She seems to have fainted after a shock, but lack of iron may have caused that, or she stood up too quickly.'

'Thanks, Indira. The lack of record is a mystery, but she doesn't seem to be an illegal immigrant, perhaps just a glitch in the computer system?'

Rosangel and Indira pulled aside the curtain and entered the cubicle.

'Tell me, why do you think that you fainted?'

'I saw someone I thought I knew, an old flame, and I stood up to go and talk to him, but I got a little bit dizzy and passed out for a few seconds. I'm perfectly alright now.'

'Our computer doesn't seem to have your medical records; can you think why that would be?'

Jenny was prepared for this awkward question. She liked this fair-haired doctor with the slight accent, Ukrainian or perhaps Polish and hated to lie to her but fell back on her story.

'I'm afraid that I've no idea, I usually go to my own doctors in East Yorkshire, perhaps the mistake is at their end.' She looked steadily at the lovely brown eyes of the doctor and relied on her having a waiting room full of patients to tend to, and she herself was not injured or in danger.

'OK, I will discharge you, is there anyone with you?'

'No, I'm travelling alone, visiting Bristol for the first time.'

'Well, Jenny, I strongly recommend that you go to your own doctor at home to be checked out for anaemia. Ask them about your NHS records whilst you are there.'

Thanking them, Jenny left and walked steadily to the well-signposted exit and took a breath of air outside.

In the cafe, she had initially felt like a fool. Her strict orders were to remain anonymous and unnoticed. Do not draw attention to yourself. Those orders were built into her psyche, and fainting in a crowded cafe could not be described as being discreet. Everyone had been kind and considerate. The barista had called an ambulance at once before getting Jenny a glass of water. Customers helped her to a chair. Jenny noticed at once that the young girl who a few minutes earlier had been in deep conversation with her beloved husband was one of the concerned. Reckoning that the ambulance, which she didn't consider necessary, would be only a few minutes away, she took the opportunity to ask the question, one whose answer she dreaded.

'I noticed the man you were talking to earlier looked just like someone I once knew, an old friend of my sons,' she added for authenticity.

'That was Steve Clutterbuck, is he the one you think you knew?'

'Yes, that does seem familiar. How do you know him? I thought he lived in East Yorkshire.'

'Oh, he does, he has been doing some family history research, and genealogy is a hobby of mine, a passion really. It seems that Steve traced me and that we are second cousins on his mother's side.'

Relief flooded through Jenny, and she began to cry with deep sobs.'

'Here, take these napkins, are you sure that you are, OK?'

'I've never felt better in my life, and thank you, thank you all for your help. I'm sorry for any damage, I'll pay for that and any coffee I spilt.'

At that moment, two ambulance workers entered the cafe.

On the short journey to the hospital, which Jenny felt was totally a waste of time, but the professionals insisted kindly but firmly, she relived the words of the young girl. A remote cousin, not a secret lover. Searching her mind, Jenny recalled that Steve had once flirted with the idea of genealogy as a hobby, but it was short-lived. He had obviously travelled by train to share information and family photos, but Jenny could not recall him doing this, and Steve would not have done this secretly; there was absolutely no need for secrets. Jenny had tried to thank the unnamed girl, but she could not possibly understand the reality of time travel and that Jenny and Steve were married, with an apparent forty-year age difference.

Jenny would have loved to talk to her truest love, but felt grateful that she had at the very least had a brief opportunity to see him once again, even though jealousy had coloured her view of the sighting. As she walked down the hill following the signs to the nearby bus station, she felt the agony of unexpected loss so far in the past and yet so far in the future. Jenny felt the warm, salty tears running down her face. This was surely the cruellest of interventions, one which the best-laid plans could never have predicted. He had looked into her eyes as he had so often with love and passion, but today it had been without recognition. That was the most painful thing, but it was all Jenny had to hold on to. She would recollect that moment so many times and transfer his look to his more usual glance, the one she adored.

Outside the huge modern hospital, she found that the T1 didn't go to Thornbury from there, but a taxi was available. She felt the need for a meal, a shower, and a comforting sleep. Another appraisal of her intervention pack might reveal something she had missed, but she really doubted it.

The day of the dreadful crash was getting nearer, and she was certainly no closer to solving the puzzle of who she was meant to save. Probably not Joy Chen, or should she say possibly. Nothing about this intervention was certain.

Chapter Nine: A Chance Meeting or Two

Whilst Jenny sat back in the taxi, avoiding the banal banter of the very West Country driver, she drew a deep breath of relief at both being discharged from a potentially awkward situation of having no NHS record and finding that her husband was still hers alone. The shock of seeing Steve as a young man and with a pretty girl was subsiding, but only slowly. It had been an incredible coincidence and could never be repeated, but she was determined to fix the glorious memory in her mind to be savoured during the twilight hours when she was alone and needed comfort.

The taxi moved smoothly up the A38 towards Thornbury. Jenny decided that it was too early to go to the motel room, and a visit to the small market town on a fine summer's day might be interesting and settle her mind.

The driver was droning on, trying hard to engage Jenny in mindless conversation about the virtues of Bristol as a city, but it was obvious that the thoughts of his passenger were far away. He sighed and gave up just as he carefully overtook a T1 bus going in the same direction.

On board, Madison Marsden sat looking out of the window upstairs, not even bothering to take out her usual notebook to observe fellow passengers. A couple of boys around her age from her school tried their best pick-up lines, but she was not at all interested. They were good-looking and knew it, used to success with their banter, but Maddie was accustomed to repelling unwanted overtures. Boys were certainly not her thing. Now, girls were another matter, and she was pleased when the two lads decided that they were wasting their precious time, leaving her to her thoughts.

It had been a tough day; she had overslept and missed her bus, admittedly her fault, not having set the alarm the previous night, but she had had to endure a warning talk from the deputy head. It was a new school for Maddie, and she was a largely unknown factor for the school; a transfer was unusual at this late stage of the term. It was obvious that she was erudite and capable of intelligent discussion when she cared to join in. Few of the teachers bothered to discover her recent losses; otherwise, they may well have seen beyond the record of lateness, the absences and indifferent attitude.

Maddie wanted desperately to be a writer, like her adored grandfather, but school was something of a hindrance, apart from the opportunity to meet like-minded girls. A new friendship, perhaps leading on to a close relationship, would certainly be welcome, but playing rounders or learning about maritime climates in Europe seemed a waste of time. She decided to get back on track and walk through the shopping centre, swarming with pupils from her old school, to the ubiquitous coffee shop in the High Street to observe customers and potential characters for her writing. Her parents didn't seem to mind, and she could pass an hour there before returning home for her evening meal and the token fulfilling of too easy homework.

Collecting her large fruit tea, she found a seat at a small table for two near the door in the crowded cafe. It was warm, and the patio-style doors were opened to allow the entry of a welcoming breeze. Maddie smiled to herself as she remembered that in an earlier incarnation, this cafe had been a video shop in the days when videos were a major source of entertainment. She recalled the frustration of never being able to find a suitable film amongst the blockbusters, adventure dramas with their incessant explosions and cartoons. Maddie preferred gentle, thoughtful films, well-acted and with a message. Science fiction and time travel were acceptable to her, but there were few without the Star Wars intergalactic battles, computer-generated and with a minimum of acting skills. No, the age of videos was gone like the dinosaurs of Jurassic Park, and she enjoyed the current use of the building as a coffee house; it gave her the opportunity to observe and note the quirks of human characters. Her grandfather, Daniel, would have approved.

Meanwhile, Jenny left the taxi and paid with her bank card with a smile. The walk in the fresh air through the sixties style shopping arcade made her realise that she was walking in the past, familiar but very different from her life in 2056. She became increasingly aware that she needed fresh clothing and entered a clothes shop which to her seemed a memorial to past fashions but nevertheless might be fun. Jenny enjoyed spending a few minutes perusing the racks of dresses and chose two simple dresses and two blouses. A set of underwear completed her purchases. The cost of time travel interventions was counted in billions, so her master's at TRIPE, Time Research Interventions Portal (Environmental) could well stand the cost of her purchases in the cause of being able to mingle successfully with the past, albeit the relatively recent past.

As Jenny left the modern shopping arcade, she entered the High Street with its wonderful array of centuries-old buildings. For Jenny, this was one of the delightful bonus advantages of her interventions. She noted the plethora of various charity shops and decided that, as she had a few days before the predicted bus crash, she might need a light summer coat to protect her from summer showers. A brief visit to the PDSA shop resulted in purchasing a pale blue raincoat light enough to withstand a shower or two. Having been reassured that all the second-hand donations to the shop were carefully steam cleaned, she paid what she saw as a ridiculously low amount, even by 2024 standards. She put her spare change, still a novelty for her, in a donations tin, thinking of her two dogs, Dottie and Cassie, waiting for her return in 2056.

Next door was a coffee shop, and Jenny suddenly felt hungry. Since coffee and toast at breakfast, she had only had, or rather not had, a fruity flapjack that had been spilt on the floor when she had fainted. Her stomach needed refreshment and coffee, and a cake would be welcome as an appetiser before an evening meal.

The more she thought of it, the hungrier she became, and she entered the door of the cafe, although the large windows were rolled back. The place was crowded with a buzz of conversation as most tables were occupied, some with dogs adoring their masters or lying patiently waiting for the walk home. There were only two people before Jenny in the queue, so she took the opportunity to peruse the glass case with their enticing mouth-watering cakes. Jenny was torn between a lemon drizzle and a chocolate cake. By the time it was her turn to order, she had decided.

'One large hot chocolate and a slice of chocolate cake, please.' Diets could wait until 2056.

Carefully balancing her tray, Jenny turned, glancing around for a spare table. There were none at once apparent. She noticed a young girl sitting alone at a small table for two, looking around and scribbling in her notebook. Her wild mass of fair curls made her instantly recognisable. It was the girl from the T1 bus. Jenny decided to take a gamble and wove her way towards the table near the door.

'Do you mind if I join you? Most of the tables seem to be occupied.'

Maddie looked up, slightly perturbed to be interrupted, but natural politeness kicked in.

'No, of course not, I'll just move some of my stuff.' Maddie decided to finish her fruit tea and make her way home. It was becoming too crowded and noisy in here.

'Homework? 'Jenny asked as she settled her tray before the mug of hot chocolate slid away from her. Two accidents in cafes in one day were not her idea of being discreet.

'No, I'll do that later.' As she spoke, she realised that she had seen this added guest before and began to work out where. It was recent and... Of course, the bus.

Jenny was desperate to start the cake, but instead took a sip of hot, or rather quickly cooling, chocolate. The cream on top made it difficult to avoid a new moustache, but a napkin dabbed gently at her mouth helped.

'You missed a little, left side corner.'

Jenny smiled as she dabbed again to remove the final errant cream.

'Thanks, I think coffee or tea, like your choice, would have been wiser and certainly more dignified. I believe that I saw you on the T1 bus today.'

Maddie grinned, 'It's my height and hair, of course, I'm difficult to hide in a crowd, even when I want to.'

Jenny smiled encouragingly, hoping that this was not the Madison Marsden who would soon be on a doomed double-decker. She went on.

'Forgive me if I am being an old nosey parker, but I'm guessing that if it's not homework you are doing, then you must be either a spy or a writer.'

Maddie laughed; she liked this open, friendly old lady with the easy manner. Usually, she would have resented the intrusion, polite though it was.

'You are half right, my application for MI5 was rejected as I couldn't melt into the background, so I am trying to be a writer, like my grandad.' At this, a shadow went across her face as she was reminded of his recent, much-lamented passing.

'That's wonderful, I won't ask you the obvious question, what is your book about or is it poetry?' Either was possible.

'Neither really, I'm building characters ready to use as a future resource. My grandad taught me that. he wrote several books, waffle and mediocre fluff he called them, but I enjoyed reading them; they are a permanent reminder of him. I read his books and can hear his voice in my head.' She surprised herself by speaking so openly to a stranger in a coffee house, someone she had never met before.

Jenny could see the hurt the girl was feeling, but went on, 'What was his name? I'm looking for a new book to read.'

'Finney, Daniel Finney, but he used his middle name, Caleb, when he was publishing a book. Caleb Finney.'

Jenny thought to herself, well, it is still possible for the girl to be a Marsden, so she was about to ask directly, realising though that she may be crossing an invisible but definite line. She did not want to appear too intrusive.

Maddie went on, 'If I'm lucky enough to get a book published, I will use a mix of our names, it will be

M.C.Marsden. The C will be for Caleb, a Yorkshire name, but as I will be the only one to know that, it won't matter that it's a boy's name. A sort of tribute to my grandad.'

Jenny continued to smile, 'That's a beautiful idea, and I'll watch out for you on Amazon or in the Booker prize list, what the M is for?' But her heart was heavy, this intelligent, likeable girl may well be dead or injured in a few days' time

'My full name is Madison Olivia Marsden, but I expect it will be some time before I actually get published if at all.'

To cover her sadness at the name being confirmed, Jenny said, 'Excuse me a moment,' and she went back to the counter and got an extra fork and a knife. Returning, she cut the cake carefully in half.

'Perhaps you could help me with this huge piece of chocolate cake, it's too big for my diet.' Maddie began to politely decline, but Jenny insisted, saying that she was not really hungry. But in reality, she felt ravenous.

'My name is Jenny; Jenny Clutterbuck, and I'm a sort of writer.'

Maddie swallowed some of the delicious cake and licked her lips, 'Sort of...?'

'I am or was a journalist on a Northern paper, but I'm retired now.' She realised that she had imparted too much information; her name could easily be put on the internet with immediate results, a rookie mistake.

'Do writers ever retire?' Maddie asked, thinking of her grandad. 'What do you do now? You seem much too young to retire.'

'You are too kind, but I hadn't realised that you had a white stick and a guide dog under the table.'

Maddie laughed. She liked this old lady and found chatting to her easy.

Jenny would have liked to say, I'm a time traveller but instead opted for an improvised cover story, the sort she was becoming skilled at in her interventions.

'I'm freelance now, I write articles for magazines, well, anyone silly enough to buy my work. At the moment, I am researching a piece on young people's concept of the future, their hopes and fears for the long and short term.'

Maddie smiled, 'So I am a guinea pig for your research?'

''I suppose so, and the half slice of cake is your pay, you really must hold out for more, get a union.'

Maddie felt intrigued by her newfound companion, and they spent the next half hour chatting about the future. For Jenny, it was a strange conversation as she knew what would happen in the near to medium future. Maddie was perceptive but had the experience of a sixteen-year-old.

Climate change was high on Maddie's thoughts, and she correctly identified melting ice caps and rises in sea levels, but was not aware of the full devastation to come. Miami, Venice and New Orleans would be largely under water whilst the Maldives would be totally gone forever. Large chunks of Vietnam, the country so hard fought over so long ago by Vietcong and American troops, were shrunken by floods through the Mekong River.

Madison predicted hotter summers with dire consequences for some African countries, which would be almost uninhabitable. Somalia and Sudan would collapse, and Chad went much earlier, unable to withstand the additional intense heat.

Politically, Maddie was on less certain ground due to her inexperience. She expressed the viewpoint that Israel would continue to dominate and spread its mighty military presence far beyond its borders. Jenny did not inform her that the Israel of 2056 would be a shadow of its former self, on the verge of economic collapse and driven back to an enclave, losing and not gaining territory. The Arab economic powerhouses dominated and threatened the very borders of Israel.

Both Jenny and Maddie enjoyed the conversation, and after a fresh tray of two teas, they decided that Jenny had enough information for her article, and it was time for them both to reluctantly leave. Jenny thanked this delightful girl and wished her well with her writing and future endeavours. She hoped that she would see her again before she left to go north and home.

Outside, the afternoon was still warm, so Jenny walked up the High Street to find somewhere to eat. Ignoring the wonderful aroma from the Fish and Chip shop, she found a small Thai restaurant in a corner near the old Medieval Lane. Sitting at a small table alone, she ordered a Thai Green curry, spring rolls and a small glass of white wine. She decided that she would catch the T1 back up the hill, which seemed too long and steep to contemplate walking. It was time to assess her eight targets, after a refreshing shower and before, hopefully, a dream-free sleep.

Chapter Ten: Disappointment

Jenny lay on the double bed in her lonely room; the size of the bed seemed to mock her. She was alone and had not felt that so sharply since the long, desperate hours since her husband Steve's drowning whilst fishing. She had reported him missing on his non-return, and police had found his equipment on the shore, but with no sign of an angler. It was easy to conclude that he had been swept out to sea by a treacherous marriage-ending wave, but they kept professional options open whilst allocating a family liaison officer to be with a distraught Jenny.

Time had passed desperately slowly as they waited for news, any news, but none came. Having her children with her had been a comfort, even though they were upset by their mother's tears. The body was never found, although Jenny had refused to call it a body; he was and always would be Steve, her Steve. The coroner declared it to be an accidental death, but it was years before Jenny accepted that he was actually gone, never to return. The North Sea did not give up its victims easily, although the police had calculated the tides and searched south along the long Holderness coast where a body may wash ashore, but it never did. Case closed.

Jenny sighed deeply, remembering those days of waiting, each hour an agony of diminishing hope. Seeing Steve again had been both wonderful and agonising as he did not recognise her; had she changed so much? It had been a mind-crushing moment in which she hoped that somehow, he was alive, and of course, in 2024, he was alive but untouchable to her. The thought of him being with a young woman was particularly devastating, but she knew in her heart that he would never betray her.

Steve had always joked that if anything happened to him, she should remarry. Not to do so would be a waste of her endless reservoir of love. But Jenny had not, could not. The double bed seemed to silently mock her as she lay on the left-hand side, as she always had done. Without really thinking about it, she was still reserving a space for Steve. To sleep in the centre of the bed would seem wrong somehow.

The choosing of some new clothing had been a pleasant distraction, and the meeting with Madison

Marsden had been delightful, although underpinned by the horrendous thought of her being in a bus crash.

Jenny looked again at her list of eight victims, although in reality they were set in stone in her memory. It seemed cruel to assess people with minimum knowledge, but she tried, though in her heart, knowing that it would not help in her quest. She decided to divide the group into two: those she had met and named, and those she had not. In the easier met list was definitely Madison Marsden, and Joy Chen, although she suspected that Frank Nelson was probably the driver in the loud red and white rugby shirt. Not confirmed, but probable. That left four on the not met list. Could she afford to treat the elderly couple, Amanda and John Buckley, as one unit, as people tended to? Of course, she had forgotten Rosangel Chlebek, the doctor at the Bristol Royal Infirmary; it was highly unlikely that there were two with the same name. So that whittled the not met list down to three if the Buckleys were coupled together. They and William Hayes had fairly common English surnames, so they were probably white. That narrowed it down to around forty million, give or take. No problem then.

Perhaps it might be better to try to match the list to the two roles she knew were given. Firstly, and most importantly, who was considered important to the year 2056 to help society. Ages might help a little. John Buckley was 71, therefore was probably retired and not likely to do much on the grand scale in the next few years. How quickly we throw the elderly onto the useless pile, Jenny thought. John's wife was ten years younger and possibly still working, although Jenny had little idea what that may be. Not potentially a real contender though.

The youngest on the list was, of course, the sixteen-year-old, Madison. She was intelligent enough to enter a profession which led to groundbreaking developments, yet the girl had professed her ambition to be a writer. Would a TRIPE intervention with its huge costs have been used to save a young Shakespeare from an early death? The loss of his plays and sonnets would have been an incredible loss. So was Madison destined to be a great writer? She was put on the possible list.

Instinct told her that the man she had met briefly in his role as driver was Frank Nelson, and he could be the driver of the doomed double-decker. Could he be the one she was meant to save? No matter how hard she tried and with all due respect to bus drivers, Jenny discounted him on a professional level, if not an age level. Perhaps it was in some other way that Frank would be seen as essential to the future. This was so hard, Jenny thought, playing God with people's lives, but all this was hypothetical. More information was needed.

The remaining two on the 'met' list were perhaps easier to assess. Joy Chen was a single mother with a low-paid job as a teaching assistant and the added occupational role of police translator. Perhaps this was a clue to her perceived usefulness. She may have been instrumental in the conviction of a Chinese drug baron whose imprisonment would save hundreds from the horrors of drug use.

Rosangel Chlebek was a doctor in Accident and Emergency, work of vital importance to the NHS in the present, but for the future? Perhaps if she were working in cancer research and helped discover a cure, she would be truly worthy of an intervention, but she was unfortunately not in that medical sphere.

William Hayes and Iris Chandoo were mysteries to her, both in their thirties, William slightly older, but

William in particular would be hard to find. Iris, on the other hand, had an unusual name and would therefore possibly not be of English extraction. In a multi-cultural society, this was of little help. Either of these could be her intended intervention target.

Jenny decided that a break from staring at her list was called for. She got up from the bed and put on the kettle, preparing a potentially brain-refreshing cup of tea.

Sitting in the one chair whilst waiting for the kettle to boil, Jenny decided to take her list and try to guess, and guess it most certainly would be, which one might be recruited as a time traveller in the future. She herself had been approached at the age of thirty-six, so she estimated that she could rule out the older ones on the list. Once again, the Buckleys were the first and easiest. Would TRIPE find a seventy-one-year-old or indeed a sixty-one-year-old worth the cost of a massive investment, not to mention the need for a certain physical capacity?

Of the rest of the list, Frank Nelson was forty-two and borderline too old, but certainly not to be put aside. Jenny stood to pour the steaming water from the kettle into a cup, regretting not buying a packet of biscuits to go with her welcome cup of tea. She was not about to use intelligence to break down the list. Whilst Jenny had been a primary school headteacher when recruited in 2032, she was not arrogant enough to pigeonhole people into IQ groupings. Besides, her main remit was to intervene and save her target. TRIPE's future recruitment was no business of hers, although it was interesting to speculate. If she had to bet on one future time traveller, she might guess Madison; she was bright and young. The two unknowns were Iris and William, but, given the present incomplete information, she might guess that her intended intervention target was one of them, or possibly Rosangel, or maybe Madison. Jenny thought that she would be a useless picker of horses in a race.

The discounted couple on both Jenny's lists were, of course totally unaware of their age-related dismissal. They had returned from their meeting about their offer to host a Ukrainian family and their responses were wildly different.

At the UK Homes for Ukraine agency office in Bristol they had been seated and offered coffee before the shock news was given to them. Months earlier they had both agreed to sponsor a refugee family from the war-torn

Ukraine and had undertaken online training and an e-learning course. A match had been found and both sides agreed, and all looked straightforward. James Rowland, the agency representative in Bristol, had looked at the file before him and drew a breath before continuing. He noticed that Amanda had put aside her coffee, it was not a speciality such as served in coffee houses. A simple spoon of cheap coffee. A splash of milk and a quick stir. Obviously not to her taste. John on the other hand was sipping nervously at his cup oblivious to the taste, wondering what the meeting was about. In John's mind all was settled and the suitable match agreed.

James had thought it a good match, a retired couple with a large house and garden, willing to share with the young Ukrainian couple and their young child. However, it had all gone wrong as these matters often did.

'Thank you both for coming to see me today. You must be wondering why I've asked you to come into the office, but a phone call wouldn't have felt right.' James said, looking carefully at the two sponsors sitting before him. 'I'm afraid that circumstances have changed quite dramatically?'

'Has the match been cancelled?' John asked, putting down his coffee cup.

'You make it sound like a football match,' Amanda said, almost, but not quite with a sneer,

James went on, 'I'm afraid it is true. Your matched family have had something of a tragedy. Here,' James checked his file. 'Petro and Nataliya's flat was hit by a Russian drone attack a few days ago, and both are in hospital, not life-threatening, I hasten to add.'

John was shocked, 'What about their children? Are they OK?'

James checked his file again, although he didn't really need to. 'Both children were at school and are staying with grandparents for the time being.'

Amanda began to rise, 'So our match is off, and we are wasting our time here.'

James was alarmed by this sudden move. 'No, please, Amanda, there is more.'

Reluctantly, Amanda sat down again, but her annoyance was obvious in her body language, arms folded, and legs crossed, closed to further discussion.

John glanced at his wife, slightly put out by this ill-mannered display.

'Go on, James, we are disappointed that the match has broken down, but obviously delighted that their injuries are not life-threatening, and the children are safe.'

Amanda, meanwhile, was quietly seething. It was all set; Petro was tall and ruggedly handsome, and the expected £500 a month to augment her fashionable wardrobe had been taken away from her. Typical that John could only express concern for the Ukrainian family.

James opened a second blue file on his desk and opened it to reveal a printed form and a photograph stapled to the front.

'Taras and Olena Marchenko went through the sponsorship process and were matched well with a family in Chepstow, but unfortunately, the family had to withdraw at the very last minute as flooding had hit their house badly and they are having to live in a friend's house for the time being.'

'So, you think that putting the two broken halves of the match together might work?' John said, understanding the problem and potential immediate resolution.

'It's all a bit of a rush, John, I'm afraid. The Marchenko family are already here in the UK and understandably concerned as to their home for the next 6 months.'

'What would you like us to do to help with this dreadful situation?' John asked.

James began to see hope in John's positive response. 'May I suggest that I leave you for a few minutes to look at the Marchenko file and make up your mind whether to go ahead? Could I get you more coffee?'

'Not unless it tastes better than the last one,' Amanda replied, reaching across for the form.

John cringed at his wife's embarrassing remark. As James left, with a feeling of distaste for the woman, he wondered if she were really hosting material.

Amanda read out the details on the form. 'Taras and Olena Marchenko. He is 34 and she is 30, living in Kyiv. He is a plumber, and she is a school librarian. Well, at least we could get our plumbing fixed for free.'

'Are there any children, or are they alone?'

'No two girls, Sofia, who is six and Mila, aged four.' She passed the photograph of a happy family group in their well-decorated flat before the Russian invasion. They say they want to ensure the safety of their girls and set up a new life in the UK.'

'Most understandable, we would want to do the same, if we had children, of course.'

Amanda raised her eyebrows and looked with scorn at her husband. 'You know well my feelings on that matter, at least the children are not screaming babies.'

'We were already to accept a Ukrainian family, but circumstances have changed, but it's just a different family, that's all. What do you think?'

Amande was pleased to see the handsome smiling father in the photograph. 'Well, I suppose we could still make it work.'

At that moment, James returned and looked hopefully at John. he expected Amanda to refuse; she seemed the refusing kind. To his surprise, it was Amanda who replied for them both.

'Well, James, we would be pleased to help. When would the Marchenkos arrive?'

James was pleased with the reply and looked across at the older man.

'John...?'

'It would be good to help a family in need, and to be honest, James, I love the idea of two children in the house at Christmas. We agree wholeheartedly, where do we sign up?'

'There's no need, you have undertaken the necessary formalities and online training courses. I could bring Taras, Olena, and the girls to you tomorrow if that is not too soon and if they agree. The match must be a two-way process.

Amanda was about to make a cutting remark about gratitude, but held her tongue for once. John could almost read her mind and was glad of her silence.

'Tomorrow would be fine, James. We look forward to meeting our new Ukrainian family, if they agree, of course.'

Chapter Eleven: <u>Steak and Onion Pie with Puff Pastry</u>

Jenny Clutterbuck felt tired, and her mind was swirling with the seemingly impossible task given to her. It was increasingly obvious that she would have to save the whole double-decker from its fate. There were only a few days left before Thursday, July 10th, and she felt that she had made little progress, apart from identifying and talking to some of the potential crash victims. Her head was spinning with thoughts ugly and difficult to unravel. She needed a break and perhaps food. The Thai meal had been tasty but small, perhaps a drink in The Ship opposite the motel and a perusal of the dessert menu. That seemed like a good plan to help her sleep.

After washing her face and putting on one of her new blouses, she felt immediately better. Outside the pub in the beer garden, couples and groups were enjoying the late evening sunshine, laughing and carefree. Jenny certainly envied them. In other circumstances, this would be a pleasant and relaxed excursion into 2024. But next Thursday loomed. Inevitable and horrendous.

Inside the ancient wooden beams of The Ship, testimony to the age of the pub was built around the time that Spanish galleons were approaching the English coast in vast numbers. Jenny wondered if the builders had any idea of the impending danger. Perhaps sometimes ignorance is indeed bliss.

Finding a small table for herself, Jenny looked at the menu and was surprised by the low prices, although no doubt in 2024 they seemed steep for desserts. Having had her chocolate quota that day, she decided upon apple crumble and a half pint of local cider. Looking around, she wondered if any of the diners would be boarding the T1 next Thursday. Impossible to tell, so she put that problem away into a compartment of her mind labelled Things to do – Later.

In Eastville, Frank Nelson opened his front door to be assailed by the glorious smell of his evening meal. He liked routine, and over the years, his wife Lillian had refined his likes and dislikes, and she knew that he loved steak and onion pie with a rich gravy and puff pastry. Food of the Gods, Frank thought as he entered the kitchen, kissing his wife and giving her a squeeze. She was, he decided, just the right side of plump; cuddly was his special word for her. Lillian had deep, come-to-bed eyes which melted his heart and rich auburn hair. Her voice was steady and soft in its delivery. An English version of Sophia Loren, not as she was now, but in 1969 when Miss Loren was at her most desirable in Frank's humble opinion. But could Sophia cook a fantastic steak and onion pie with wonderful gravy, topped with puff pastry? Perhaps she could manage a pan of pasta, but it wasn't the same. No, Lillian won his vote every time.

'How was your day at the shop?'

Lilliam loved the way he always greeted her with a kiss and asked her about her day before telling her about his.

'Same old, same old, although we did have two young shoplifters stealing chocolate and a deodorant spray of all things. When I shouted at them, they scarpered but dropped the deodorant and ran. They were only youngsters and probably too scared to come back for a while. How about you?'

'The usual, although I do have some news.'

'Well, it had better stay for a few minutes. I'm just about to serve up one of your favourites, steak and onion pie. Go and wash up, it will be ready in two minutes.'

Frank laughed, 'I could tell that it was steak pie, I followed the gorgeous smell from IKEA up the Fishponds Road, salivating all the way. Besides, it is Thursday, and Thursday is always pie night.'

Using her oven gloves, a present from last Christmas, Lilliam brought forth a wonderful pie steaming hot from the oven. Plates were retrieved hot from the microwave, and two meals were set out, one much larger than the other. For a brief moment, Lillian wondered if she was feeding her husband too much and too well. He seemed to be putting on weight, and that would not be good for him. She couldn't bear to lose Frank to a sudden heart attack; life without his routines and laughter would be unthinkable.

At that moment, Frank came downstairs, and Lillian glanced at his waistline. Perhaps a diet was called for; Fish and Chip Friday may have to be replaced by a nice summer salad. Perhaps next week.

Frank sat and looked at the well-filled plate and began to eat with enthusiasm. He had married the perfect cook, he decided.

'So, what is this new, Frank? Have they finally had the good sense to sack you and get a real driver in to replace you?'

'Nothing so dramatic, you know that the bus company could never manage without me, I'm their key driver.' Lillian smiled; she did love her husband so much.

'No, are we planning on doing anything next Thursday, at the tent? It was to have been our day off, but we may have to reschedule.'

'Nothing in particular, if it's nice, I thought a trip to Slimbridge. As you know, we need to go fairly regularly to make full use of our membership. It is always a pleasant visit and the birds are wonderful, we are very lucky to have such a marvellous place so close. What have you got in mind?'

'Well, Mike Henderson came and asked me if I would swap shifts. If I do his Thursday shift, he has Friday off and he can take his wife for a long weekend in Reading.'

'Very romantic, does Joan know about it?'

'It's not that kind of romantic weekend, and yes, she certainly does know. It's the christening of their first grandchild on the Saturday.'

'How lovely, I hope that you said yes.' Lillian asked, knowing full well that her soft-hearted husband would agree without hesitation.

'No, I refused, I said that it was more important for you to go and see the spoonbills and swans.'

Lillian dropped her fork, 'What! You didn't, please tell me you didn't do that. Joan would never forgive you or me by association.'

'No, of course I didn't, I owe Mike a favour and I'm now on a promise for a few pints as well. It does mean that I'll be doing the old T1 route next Thursday, you don't mind, do you?'

'I will agree if you can tell me the name of the baby,' Lillan said, knowing that she was on safe ground. Men would never ask the obvious question.

'His name is Mohammed Zebedee Macbeth, so I win. You didn't think I would know, did you?'

'You are a very poor liar, Frank; I'll phone Joan later to congratulate her and ask the baby's name. I suspect you were making it up, especially as I know for a fact it's a girl.

Frank laughed, 'You win as usual.'

Lillian replied, 'I could switch the rota at the shop, perhaps we could go down to Weston-Super-Mare, a long walk by the sea would do us good. Fresh air and a chance for you to stretch your legs, sitting in the bus all day as you do.'

Frank put down his knife and fork, having eaten all his meal, enjoying every mouthful.

'That sounds great, Lillian, perhaps we could get fish and chips down there, and a walk would build the appetite, not as good as your fish and chips though I hasten to add. What's for pudding?

Lillian replied, 'Strawberries and cream,' but thought a diet was needed. However, how to tell Frank was a potential problem; he did love his routines and her home cooking.

After washing up together, Frank declared strawberries and cream to be his all-time favourite in summer, but rhubarb or apple crumble were difficult to beat. Lillian washed the dishes whilst Frank dried as they chatted. The dishwasher was for Sundays, the rest of the week for social chatting by the sink. Afterwards, they would take a stroll around the small back garden and admire the blooms which were at their glorious summer peak. Their pride and joy was the collection of roses, which they tended with loving care.

That evening, Frank looked at himself in the long mirror. He had noticed Lillian glancing at his waistline, and it was true that he had put on a few unwanted pounds recently. Perhaps it was time to reassess his secret career aspirations. He could never get away with the figure-hugging, flamboyant dresses of the show business drag queens. It had always been an impossible ambition, not shattered but slowly eroding with time as his figure grew and let him down. Perhaps a diet, as Lillian wisely suggested on occasion. It was time to talk to her and look carefully and seriously at his lifestyle and aims.

Sitting together before the television, Frank suggested that he make a nice cup of tea; it was always a nice cup, never a mediocre or poor-quality cup. Besides, it was always a mug, unless his in-laws were arriving.

Whilst he was in the kitchen, Lillian turned off the banal reality programme, knowing that there was something on his mind.

Lillian sat on her recliner chair and waited for Frank to come in with two hot mugs, his being a bright red and white Gloucester rugby one and hers a Downton Abbey one, a souvenir of a visit to Highclere Castle last summer. Frank sat down on the right-hand side of the sofa and was mildly surprised that the television was off. Before he could question it, Lillian began.

'What's on your mind, Frank? We've been married for long enough for me to be able to read you like an open book. I know when something is troubling you. Is it something at work, or the blackfly on the roses, or is it me?'

Frank looked across at his wife and marvelled at her perception. he had always considered himself extremely lucky to have met and married her, but he tried to cover his difficulty with humour, as he usually did.'

'I noticed that you might have blackfly, so I thought that a spray would help after your shower.'

'Frank,' she replied in a voice that warned at once that she was in no mood for jokes.

He tried to cover his unease by sipping at his tea to give himself time to think. His mind went back to when he was teaching Lillian to drive their old Mini Cooper, and she had stuck her tongue between her teeth to concentrate. He remembered smiling and thinking that this was the most adorable girl in the world, or at least in Gloucestershire.

'I have always been truthful with you, I have never knowingly lied to you, that's something I promised myself when we got married, but there are some lies that don't need to be said. I don't think there is anything you don't know about me, including my time in the army and even before that.

'But.....,' Lillian said, becoming increasingly alarmed by the way the unexpected conversation was going.

But I have never told you my deepest, darkest ambition, I've kept it secret for so long, even from you, my one true love.'

'Frank Nelson, spit it out, you are beginning to scare me.' She put down her mug and went to sit by her beloved husband on the sofa.' Is it something medical, please God, not cancer. Jess and I would be devastated.'

Their daughter was the most perfect thing in her life, but was about to leave home for university. They would be empty nesters reassessing their lives together alone after eighteen years. Had he met someone new, someone younger? She began to wonder how she would tell their daughter; it would break her heart; they were a very close family, or so she thought.

'No, no, it's nothing like that, this has been going on for years since I was at secondary school, but I have had to hide it for so long. I noticed that you were glancing at my stomach and realised that my weight gain was becoming obvious. I have always tried to look after myself, but I'm almost middle-aged and more prone to being, shall we say, portly.'

Lillian suddenly thought of the dangers of diabetes for the overweight, but he wasn't really overweight. Nothing a few salads and more exercise wouldn't cure.

'No, Lillian, it's not that.' He took a deep breath, time for a revealing truth, one that might alter Lillian's perception of him. He felt his heart racing. Lillian was the only person in the world he could tell his dark aspirations to.

'You know that I enjoy watching Strictly Come Dancing and all those ridiculous reality drag shows...?' He faltered slightly.

'Yes, we both do, but what has that got to do with your weight?' She was confused and could not make head or tail of the meagre scraps of information which her husband was so reluctantly giving her.

'Frank, please tell me, straight out, you've not become a Conservative, have you?'

'Good God, no, it's not as bad as that.' He paused, unable to look Lillian in the eyes. This was a much-dreaded pivotal moment.

'I know that I'm often seen as a bit of a comedian, usually to cover awkward situations, but I have always wanted to be one of those drag queens on television, cracking witty jokes with their flamboyant, outrageous dresses and wigs. I know it's all over the top, but I would have loved to be one of them rather than a bus driver, which I am good at. It would be a challenge, but I don't know how to begin, and the extra weight I am carrying would make slinky dresses an impossible dream. If you don't take chances, you might as well not be alive. I know it's ridiculous....'

Lillian interrupted, 'Frank, I have loved you for all the time I have known you, and only Jess has come close. Our minds are as one, and I have known, or rather guessed, your ambition for years now. It makes no difference to me. I know full well that you are in no way gay. If that's what you want to do, I will support you and sew on all those sequins if called for, as long as you are happy.'

Both felt floods of relief, he that his ambition had not been met with revulsion or ridicule. She lost all her worries about secret medical issues.

Lillian became decisive and, not for the first time, took control.'

'Right, here's what we will do, we'll find out how you can get on those reality shows, start small, local talent shows, that sort of thing, we'll have to think of a name for you and organise dresses and wigs, that's the easy part. A diet and exercise will get you back in trim, it shouldn't take too long.'

'Thank you, Lillian, your words have certainly helped enormously, but I have increasingly become aware that this is only a pipe dream, never to become real. I can only imagine what your mother would say. No, I'm destined to be a bus driver for the rest of my life.'

'And a bloody good bus driver, you are the best, and you know I will support you whatever you wish to do. I love you, Frank, whether you are Fifi La Rue or just plain Frank the bus driver, but I do think a diet and more exercise would do us both good. We could start with our visit to Weston next Friday, it's a long flat sea front and we could park at one end to make the most of it.'

'But no fish and chips at the end of it,' he added with a smile, 'I've got to give up this silly dream of mine to be creative and entertain crowds. I'm 42 and I don't want to be seen as a failed fat drag queen. But I do need something else, something to put my energies into.

'What about a dog?' Lillian suggested and at once realised that whilst both of them were at work all day, it would be unfair on the dog.

Lillian thought for a moment, 'What about writing a book, you have always said that you come across all types on your route, and you are certainly capable of humour.'

Frank thought for a moment, it wasn't the worst idea in the world, he had never thought of himself as an academic, far from it, but he was computer literate, and Lillian could proofread it and give him honest advice and help. He began to warm to the idea, a notebook on his knee whilst driving was a very bad idea, but he could scribble out characters based on his passengers when he came home.

'It may be worth a try, you're a star, queen of ideas as well as steak and onion pies, I'll go and make us a fresh mug of tea, we've let this one get cold.

'I don't think so, Frank, or should I call you Fifi. She stood and held out her hand to him. 'We can start our exercise routine tonight, and I know of a wonderful way to work off some weight, the best way there is.' Come on, it's an early night for you, my boy.'

Frank stood and followed his wife towards the stairs, wondering if there was a better wife on the planet or any other planet for that matter.

Chapter Twelve: Day Return to Hull

Friday. Beginning of the most welcome weekend for many, the gateway to relaxation and enjoyment away from the pressures of work for two days, but for time travellers or interventionalists, there was no off-duty weekend. Friday posed fresh problems.

The regular travellers on the T1 bus into the city of Bristol would probably not be on board for the next couple of days, and their identification would be even more difficult. Today had to be used wisely, but as Jenny sat at breakfast, ironically at the small table where she had indulged in apple crumble and local cider last night, she felt drawn in a different direction. Thankfully, she had only had half a pint of cider, otherwise, the breakfast being placed in front of her would not have seemed so welcome. She could not remember the last time she had eaten a full cooked breakfast, but decided that this could be a long day, and the plan in her mind was growing, gnawing at her mind.

Jenny's only connection to her target passengers was the double-decker itself, so she resolved to have a shower, change into one of her new dresses, and have a cooked breakfast so she was prepared for the day, whatever it may hold. The Big Breakfast looked enormous even on the menu, so she ordered a lighter bite menu of sausage, egg, bacon, mushrooms, and beans. She declined the beans and added an Americano coffee and toast to the order. This would be more than sufficient.

Jenny wondered about the sausage. In 2056, there were so many regulations regarding the contents of sausage that they had left them virtually fat-free but tasteless. She ate slowly and enjoyed the taste of such an early meal whilst glancing at her watch, the vital link to her return to her own time exactly a week from now. The all-important watch had no direct link to the portal in Swindon in 2056, but the countdown was set. She could not see how she could make progress in her task over the weekend. And the illegal plan began to grow in her mind, no matter how hard she tried to submerge it in a real dilemma.

Leaving the dubious sausage, Jenny drained her coffee and returned to her room on the upstairs of the nearby motel. Glancing out of the window, she noticed that a groundsman was mowing the wicket ready for the next cricket match. After brushing her teeth, she picked up her faithful sashiko bag and went out into the July sunshine. It was early and there was still a slight chill in the air, enough to make her wonder about the wisdom of not wearing her light PDSA charity shop bought coat.

Boarding the double-decker, she decided to go upstairs after quickly scanning the passengers downstairs to see if she recognised anyone. To her disappointment, she did not, even though the driver was different, a friendly, capable-looking woman. Understandable as this was a later bus and the usual driver, the one she guessed was Frank Nelson, would have been driving the earlier one.

Upstairs, Jenny held on carefully as the double-decker moved away into the traffic, and she took a seat near the back to ease observation of all passengers. The route was becoming familiar, and as the bus reached the fatal roundabout, she bit her lip in concentration as she tried to picture how the giant vehicle, designed for stability, would come to end on its side, causing injuries, distress, and death to some. More to the point, how could she prevent this from happening? The long-term impact of what she was trying to do would have severe ripples in consequences and implications for all the passengers. Time travel interventions were not meant to cause so many changes to the future, but her orders were clear. Someone on the double-decker had to be saved for the future good.

When the coach entered the bus lane near Bristol, it went easily past the line of traffic before stopping at a Megabus designated starting point outside a McDonald's with dubious-looking characters hanging about outside. Buses regularly pulled in to deposit the majority of their passengers. Few stayed on to the final stop near the harbour and Bristol Crown Court. Mel Chandoo was one of these, pleased that this should be the last of her bus journeys and she could start work again on Monday, travelling to the Bristol Royal Infirmary by her own car. The sun shone, and she was happy to see her duty as a juror almost complete.

Jenny Clutterbuck was unaware of Mel and walked steadily past the motorbike delivery riders, beggars, and drug-influenced dropouts from society. Not a problem in her own time, where drug use was severely restricted.

Jenny had a plan, or rather a two-part plan, the first being definite and the second very unwise and against all her training. She made her way to the coffee house, stopping only to purchase a newspaper, something she and all in her future time had not done for many years. It felt so strange and old-fashioned to handle what seemed like an antiquity with its day-old news. In her time, 2056, news was instantly and electronically available through television and individual devices. Somehow, she found the feel of the paper comforting. Besides, the newspaper would allow her to drink her coffee and read to cover her being alone. Most of the other customers were couples.

To Jenny's disappointment, the table where her husband had sat was occupied by a retired couple, but as she picked up her tray of coffee, breakfast had made a scone or flap jack very unnecessary, she was pleased to see the old couple stand and pick up their shopping bags getting ready to go. Jenny moved across to the particular table she wanted and, carefully setting her tray down, removed the old couple's tray to another table. She sat in the very chair where her husband Steve had sat. She closed her eyes for the moment and relished the thought that this was as near as she would get to her much-loved unless the second part of her plan was put into action. A plan she would never be able to justify, a plan she knew was wrong in so many ways.

Jenny glanced at the door, willing Steve to come in, but that was very unlikely; the moment of wonderful seeing him again had passed. Forbidden. It was hard for her to see him glance in her direction, but without recognition. She had aged, but his too-early death had meant that he would not. Jenny sighed and felt that this self-torment had been a terrible idea. She opened the newspaper, one of the more intelligent purveyors of news, information, and analysis of events, to take her mind off her dilemma.

There was no mention of the total collapse of Syria, Somalia and Sudan as the warming of the earth made life intolerable in already hot areas and the Russian invasion of the Ukraine seemed to be perceived as a major threat to world peace whereas in her time it was looked back on as a skirmish compared with the seemingly endless war between two of the world's three superpowers, India and China. The third, the United States, had long gone into almost total isolation; its vast military was a defensive organisation designed to keep out immigrants, illegal or otherwise. A long succession of American presidents followed the mantra, America for Americans, and the country looked inwards to be self-sufficient. Jenny was surprised to see adverts for air travel to the long-gone Miami for holidays in Disneyland. Passports had become almost unknown for Americans as they saw little virtue in foreign travel. More important to secure their borders and pull up the drawbridge. The border with Mexico and even Canada was a massive, iron-clad clad impenetrable wall. In 2042, the United Nations, that toothless debating society, had moved from New York to Oslo in the Norwegian warmth.

Jenny became engrossed in an article about the future of Northern Ireland, or tried to in order to detract from the decision which she knew she must shortly make. Reading the newspaper was like doing a quiz when she had all the answers written down. Ireland had become the United Provinces of Ireland after several referendums and many new Troubles until national pride settled the unified country down as one.

She was amused to see so many references to the United Kingdom whereas in 2047 Scotland, Wales and the newly united Ireland, often known as the Provinces, broke away from England to form a Gaelic Republic which was the basis for a marvellous tourist industry but a gentle decline without the economic engine room of the core country, England. Without the burden, which was unspoken of, the billions being poured into supporting these three ailing nations, with their new capital in Glasgow, England, flourished economically. Brexit had long been forgotten as a dreadful mistake, but new treaties had been formed with the Northern Alliance. England, Denmark, Norway, Sweden, Iceland, and the Netherlands formed a powerful union with a Viking longship as their logo. Finland had been offered the opportunity to join this thriving trade block but had declined to be independent.

Jenny's thoughts swirled with the complexities of her mission and the personal sacrifices it entailed. She had never imagined that her dedication to the greater good could lead her to such a crossroads, where duty and desire collided so violently. The weight of her decision pressed down on her, each step towards the coffee house feeling heavier than the last. Her mind raced with memories of her life with Steve, the warmth of his touch, and the innocent laughter of their children. Yet, she knew that indulging in these memories could jeopardise everything she stood for. As she sat down with her coffee, she felt the sting of loneliness sharpen, like a blade against her heart. The bustling life around her seemed oddly distant, a stark contrast to the solitude of her purpose. Jenny sighed deeply, trying to reconcile her longing with the reality of her mission. She knew she must act soon, with precision and resolve, to ensure that her journey would not be in vain.

Jenny sighed and folded up the newspaper, and thought that in her time of 2056, it would be seen as a historical artefact for her grandchildren or to be donated to the local Haltemprice school. It was frowned upon to take items back or, in this case, forward in time, but this was the last intervention and could do little, if any harm. There were strict rules to be obeyed without question. Betting on lottery tickets or buying shares in new, small, and up-and-coming companies would yield millions in the future, but Jenny had no interest in wealth. She was comfortable with her income from the time travel and her state and teacher's pensions.

Jenny had let her coffee go cold and prevaricated, should she order a fresh one? The barista had looked warily at her when she entered the coffee house, half expecting, or rather fearing, another fainting incident.

Taking a deep breath, the reluctant time traveller made up her mind, well, sort of. Picking up her sashiko bag, she left to the barista's relief. Outside, the July temperature had lifted, and it was pleasantly warm. Looking round,

Jenny saw a taxi rank and asked to be taken to the railway station. To her surprise, the Indian driver asked which one. Her plan had come apart before it could be put dangerously in place. Probably for the best, she thought.

'I'm afraid that I don't know,' she admitted. 'I'm new to Bristol.'

'Well, madam, where do you want to go by train?'

Key question that hits at the heart of the problem. She knew that she wanted to go to Hull and take a taxi to her home, to see Steve for perhaps the last time, and cuddle her adorable toddlers for one more time. But this was impossible. She would be a stranger to them, albeit a vaguely familiar one to Steve. Jenny pictured herself explaining her role as an older lady in time travel. Perhaps he would believe her unlikely story, but then there was the enormous issue of the probability of meeting her younger self, the one living and sleeping with Steve. That would be a catastrophe in all senses.

The taxi driver was patient, recognising her confusion.' Bristol Parkway is the direct line north to the Midlands and Northeast, whilst Temple Meads is for London and the southwest. I suppose they are both the same, really,' he smiled.

'I want to go to Hull for the day, I think.'

The driver wondered whether a trip to Southmead hospital would be better, as he was obviously in a very confused state, but he had a living to make, and time was money to him.

'Then you want the cross-country service from Parkway. If you are sure, get in and I'll get you there in no time.'

Jenny was full of doubt, but nevertheless got into the back of the taxi, which sped along the M32 and turned off to Bristol Parkway.

Getting out, Jenny thanked the driver and gave him a generous tip. She went in and joined the small queue in the booking office.

'A single day return to Hull, please.'

On presenting her card, her tickets and receipt were presented to her.

'What time is the next train, and do I change?'

'The 11.44 is the next one and you will change at Sheffield, arriving in Hull at 16.15' he replied glancing at his computer screen.

Jenny was shocked, and she left the booking office in a daze. She had forgotten that the trains of 2024 were slow. Sitting on a nearby bench, she rapidly calculated that by the time she arrived at her old home, it would be later, much later than she had anticipated. There would be time to perhaps see her husband and children from a distance if the opportunity arose, but they would probably not be outside, or if they were, it would be in the back garden. Looking at her precious watch, it confirmed her return to the time portal in a week, but the dial, which told her the current time, was useful to calculate that she could not get back to Thornbury and her task much before midnight.

This was a poorly thought-out mistake, a bad mistake, a long, slow journey there and back with the small possibility of seeing her young family. Tears pricked at her eyes, and unusually for her, she was indecisive. Retrieving a handkerchief from her sashiko bag, she dabbed her eyes. What next? She felt she was failing whichever way she turned; the problem of the crash next Thursday was no nearer being solved. If she were not careful, the watch would automatically draw her back to 2056, and the task would fail.

Jenny stood and was not sure of what to do next. Walking slowly out to the line of taxis, she asked to go to Bradley Stoke to the Willow Brook shopping centre. From there, she could get the next T1 back to Thornbury to reassess her plans. It proved a short drive, and she left the taxi to go into the large, at least large by 2024 standards, superstore. Next door was a small coffee shop. Perhaps she needed a shot of black coffee to revive her mind and regain the initiative.

Afterwards, Jenny was to say that she never felt the blow in the back, causing her to fall forward onto the pavement. She did not see her assailant, or were there two? Jenny felt her sashiko bag being snatched roughly from her shoulder, and her watch was quickly removed. She tried to resist, but the sudden attack had taken her totally by surprise. The loss of her bag was awful; it meant so much to her, but the fast-disappearing watch was potentially life-threatening. Jenny tried to get up but felt that her head was grazed and bloody.

She was hurt and trapped in the past, caught between two times, her only means of returning home gone.

Chapter Thirteen: An Impromptu Posse

For William Hayes, this had been a good day, a very good day in fact. After speaking to his headteacher about his exciting upcoming interview next Thursday, it was agreed that he should visit his potential new school. A preliminary visit was necessary as part of the preparation for the interview. It was especially vital as the meeting between the headteacher and a possible deputy may well make the interview a formality. The partnership between the two was of paramount importance.

William did not get on with his current headteacher, and this feeling was mutual. If boring old Silent Bill were to get the deputy headship, then there would be a vacancy to be filled by someone with more flair and attractiveness. John Millington looked at William and decided that it was unlikely that he would sparkle enough to be deemed deputy head material. But he would do his best to support his application both as a reference writer and by allowing him to take the day off to visit Hurst Green Primary School. He knew the head of that school well enough to give him a ring to verbally support William Hayes, anything to get rid of the conscientious but dull member of staff.

William had appreciated the unexpected support, and the concept of a day away from his school was certainly alien to his sense of duty. In the morning staff meeting, John Millington had announced that William would be absent the next Friday as he would be visiting a school in Bradley Stoke with an interview the following week. There were raised eyebrows followed by muted expressions of congratulations. Silent Bill was part of the furniture and had been for years. This was a real turn-up for the books. Sitting in the corner of the staffroom, Abbie Thompson felt a sudden emptiness in her stomach; the idea of William leaving was deeply depressing for the young teacher. She found him very desirable and attractive and in no way boring. He might well leave before she managed to contrive a way to tell him how she felt about him. He needed to fail this interview. Abbie needed more time. The interview was only a week away. It may be too late for her to express her feelings openly; at the moment, he was ignorant of the way she looked at him in meetings with barely concealed adoration.

When Friday arrived, William or Will as he had decided to become if in the unlikely event that he became deputy head at Hurst Green, opted to drive his Ford Fiesta for the short distance from home to Hurst Green despite its gearbox problems. On the day of the interview, he planned to drive the ailing car to Thornbury to leave the car at the Ford garage and catch the T1, which would get him to the interview with time to spare.

The grinding noise from the gearbox was not good, and it was becoming increasingly difficult to change gears. The car limped towards Hurst Green school for his appointment with the headteacher. The car park was full, so he parked nearby and walked towards the locked gates. A small intercom was necessary to announce his arrival. Nervous moments. What should he say? Pressing the button, he took a deep breath and said, 'Will Hayes, I have an appointment with the Headteacher, Mr Warren. The gate clicked and opened slightly. A voice invited him in and to go straight to reception. For a brief moment, Will wished he were back in his classroom, safe from the possible humiliation that interviews usually brought. Stepping forward, he unconsciously checked that his tie was straight and brushed his thick hair back. First impressions.

At the door, he was met by a stocky man of average height who smiled and held out his hand. Will was surprised to find that Mr Warren was a man of colour, light brown rather than green or purple. There was no earthly reason why he should be taken aback, but it was unexpected. The man had a round, friendly face with deep brown eyes and short, slightly wavy hair. He wore a blue shirt with a navy-blue tank top, which gave a smart-casual look.

'Mr Warren, my name is,' and here he hesitated for a brief moment, 'Will Hayes.'

They shook hands, and Will noticed the firm grip and cheerful welcome.

'Please call me Curtis, Mr Warren is my father.' He laughed a rich, deep laugh at his own well-worn joke, and Will decided at once that he liked this man.

'Come through into my office, Will, we'll have a chat over a cup of green tea. Coffee is frowned upon at Hurst Green. Too much of a stimulant. It keeps the teachers awake. I hope that's OK with you.'

Will wasn't sure but politely accepted as he sat in the office chair.

Curtis called through to the outer office, 'Sue, would you be so kind as to provide two cups of your wonderful green tea for me and my special guest.'

Sue Bradshaw came into the office and was introduced to Will. She was young with shoulder-length hair and green eyes. Like the headteacher, she was friendly, open and welcoming. She spoke to the guest in a soft but unmistakable Bristol accent.

'We do have coffee for visitors, if you would prefer. Curtis likes to pretend that he is an eco-warrior.' Cutis laughed and smiled warmly at his secretary. There was obviously a comfortable bond and understanding between the two.

Will noticed the lack of formality. Curtis had promoted Sue from office assistant to secretary due to her efficiency and rapport with parents and staff. As a single mother with two children in the infant's department, she was surprised but forever grateful. Being a lone parent was economically draining, but Curtis always rightly denied that he had promoted her out of any sense of sympathy.

Will smiled at the likeable young secretary, 'No, green tea would be fine with me, I probably drink too much coffee.'

Sue left, and Curtis began his talk with his potential new deputy head. He noticed that he seemed quiet but friendly and dressed appropriately without being too formal.

'As you noticed, I am a dusky brown like a fine toffee, my father was from Trinidad, but my mother was from West Cork in Ireland. A dangerous mix, but I get by, I've been here as head for four years now, and the previous deputy left for promotion to a school in Somerset. We were all very proud of her, and we are looking for someone to fill her shoes, not literally, I might add.' He laughed at this impromptu joke, and Will decided that he really wanted to work here. People were obviously important here at Hurt Green, and it felt like a real team.

Curtis went on as the green teas arrived. Sue put the two mugs down and whispered to Will, 'If you don't like it, I can get you a coffee instead.'

She left with a conspiratorial smile for Will. He returned the smile and picked up the hot mug with the Hurst Green logo, still basking in the earlier description of himself as a special guest. Curtis sat back, relaxed in manner, and explained that the school was one form entry but was full due to its popularity. There was an Ofsted due, but the last one had a good outcome. Curtis said that he wished to have an outstanding verdict on the school.

'The teachers deserve it, they are talented, young in the main, and very enthusiastic. I sometimes have to throw them out at night as they work long and hard for our children.'

At that moment, there was a small knock at the door, and on being told to come in, two girls entered. Will estimated they were about eight and obviously shy of the unexpected stranger. One was clearly Indian with beautiful dark eyes and pigtails, whilst her companion was blonde with slightly dishevelled shoulder-length hair.

Curtis addressed them with seriousness; they were given his full priority attention. Children first, Will thought approvingly.

'Lakshmi, Anne-Marie, how can I help?'

Both girls began to talk at once.

Curtis intervened, 'You've got two mouths, but I've only got one set of ears, Lakshmi, you first, you are the tallest and I think the oldest, so you start.'

Will was impressed by the head's knowledge of his children.

Lakshmi remembered the reason for their being there and spoke quickly, glancing accusingly at her classmate, a close friend for several years until now.

'Miss Wilton sent us to you, Anne-Marie called me a name, and I didn't like it, so we argued, and it got a bit out of hand.'

Curtis listened and spoke seriously.

'Girls, I thought that you were friends, but I'll tell you what, this gentleman may be joining Hurst Green next term, so I will let him listen to you both and decide.'

Will's stomach gave a jolt; this was obviously a test for him, and he drew breath before asking the obvious question.

'Lakshmi, that's a lovely name if I may say so. What bad name did Anne-Marie call you?'

Lakshmi looked at Anne-Marie, who blushed and looked at her shoes.

'She called me,' and here she hesitated, glancing at her headteacher, 'She called me the N word.'

Both men groaned inside; they had painted themselves into a potentially difficult, far-reaching corner, but Will realised that he had to go on.

'And what is the N word? I am new here and don't understand.'

Lakshmi was reluctant to say it out loud, so she offered to whisper it to the tall stranger. Will agreed, and she stepped forward to cup her hand to his right ear.

'She called me a nincompoop, twice.'

Will felt a wave of relief.

'Anne-Marie, another beautiful name. Do all children at the school have lovely names?'

'I don't really know.'

'Did you call Lakshmi a nincompoop? Is that true?' He spoke the word aloud for the head's benefit.

'Yes, but...' and her voice trailed away, unable to find a good defence.

Will spoke in the manner of a county court judge about to pronounce sentence.

'Well, girls, my old Yorkshire grandmother used to call me a nincompoop, and I know for a fact that she loved me, so it's not perhaps as serious as you think, Lakshmi. But I don't know what it means. I do know that my Granny would never have called me a bad name even when I sneaked open the biscuit tin and took a custard cream without permission. If I were you, I would go to the library together and get a dictionary to find out what it means, and then say sorry to Miss Wilton for disturbing the excellent learning in her class. Is that fair?'

Both girls from very different backgrounds looked at each other, relieved that this awkward situation had been resolved. They left holding hands and smiling, sharing the knowledge that the stranger might be joining the school, perhaps as their own teacher.

'Well done, Will. I'm sorry to have put you into a potentially difficult situation. I had no idea that the N word was involved. Thank goodness it wasn't the other N word. You handled it very well.'

Will took a sip of his cool green tea to cover his pleasure at apparently passing a test, one far more difficult than an interview.

Curtis stood and said, 'Let's go on a tour of the school and I will introduce you to the staff, and when we get back, perhaps, we can get a hot drink to replace these cold ones.'

For the next forty-five minutes, Will's mind was in a swirl as he entered each classroom, and every time he was impressed by the easy, friendly manner in which the children greeted their head. There was obvious mutual respect, and Curtis knew all the children by name. The teachers were, as Curtis said, young and all shook Will's hand, showing their universal welcome to the potential newcomer. In the last classroom, Miss Wilton's, Will was delighted to see Lakshmi and Anne-Maries with their heads together working on a maths problem. They glanced up and Lakshmi said, 'A nincompoop means a foolish person, but I have forgiven Anne-Marie, she is my best friend forever after all.'

Back in his office, Curtis was about to ask Sue for a fresh mug of green tea when she appeared as if by magic with mugs in hand,

'Good anticipation, Sue, thank you.'

Will wondered if there would be any more unexpected tests. Curtis paused before becoming serious, an unusual state for him.

'I'll put my cards on the table, Will. We have had twenty-four applicants for this post of deputy head, some good, some not so good.'

Will felt disappointment surge through his body, failure again, and he would so much have enjoyed working here and with a head he liked and respected. He waited to be let down lightly. His application was going to be rejected even before he arrived for the interview next week; it had all been a waste of time, which had raised his hopes beyond all expectations.

'The thing is, the governors and I sifted carefully through the applications, and they fell into certain categories. The obvious ones were wanting to use Hust Green as a convenient stepping stone for their upwardly mobile career paths. Our children deserve better than to be used like that. Then there were the chancers whose qualifications and experience were light; their applications were obviously not specific to our school. A few thought that they could jump straight from university into a management job here. They usually had hyphenated names, oddly enough. The third category was the fly-by-nights who moved schools every one or two years, not giving any continuity or stability. Then there was you, Will.'

Silent Bill lived up to his name mainly because he wasn't sure what to say at this moment. Where was Curtis leading, and which category was he going to be put in?

'The governors and I are in complete agreement, depending on our meeting this morning. I'm going to ask you a question, which is none of my business, but I will ask anyway. Do you have any other interviews lined up before ours next Friday? You don't have to answer, of course, I will respect that.'

Will almost laughed out loud at the preposterous idea that he could possibly have more than two invitations to interview.

'No, Curtis, and if I did, I would withdraw from any other. This is a great school, and I am honoured by being asked to interview. I would love to work here even if only as a teacher, let alone a deputy head.'

Curtis visibly relaxed and smiled. He hadn't realised how tense his shoulders had become.'

'Wonderful, I feel that you and I can forge a fine partnership to drive the school forward and make it a truly outstanding school. There is just one thing thou, the perceived wisdom is that there should be a man-woman partnership in senior management.'

Will's heart sank; it had been going well, better than he could have hoped. Were his hopes about to be dashed at the last minute?

Curtis smiled broadly at Will's obvious concern. 'If you could wear high heels and a nice dress for an interview, it would help,'

Will breathed a huge sigh of relief. Yes, a working partnership with this man would make going into work a real pleasure.

'I was actually thinking of my usual white blouse and black skirt.'

'I think we're going to get on fine, Will.'

A shadow crossed William Hayes' face as he remembered, 'What about the interview?' His track record was pretty miserable in this respect.

'There are three candidates to be interviewed, your good self, a young lad from Essex who is obviously job hopping, fast tracking to the top, and a very inexperienced lady from Taunton. The job is yours for the taking, and I hope that this time next week, you will be our new deputy head.

Will found difficulty keeping his excitement in check; leaving his current school would present few problems; he knew he would not be missed. He was blissfully unaware that one young teacher would be distraught on hearing of his unexpected success.

It was lunchtime when he walked towards the gate through a sea of playing children draining off their pent-up energy before their midday meal. He liked the maroon sweatshirts and sky blue polo shirts; everything about the school seemed positive.

Before he reached the gate, he noticed that many had discarded their sweatshirts in the July warmth. Lakshmi and Anne-Marie were sitting on a bench in close conference. They looked up to see the stranger in the office leaving. Lakshmi called over to him.

'We've decided that we would like to have you at Hurst Green. Good luck.'

Will waved and almost felt himself float out towards his car with happiness. This had been his best morning since, well, he couldn't remember a finer morning. As he got into the ailing Ford Fiesta, he decided to make the short drive to the Willowbrook shopping centre to get some lunch. He had the whole day off and didn't want to go back to his school, which would certainly put a dampener on his day.

He had declined the offer of lunch at Hurst Green and suddenly felt hungry. There was a Wetherspoons in the shopping centre and he had a craving for pie and chips with perhaps a half pint of lager. He intended to sit and go through every glorious moment of his meeting and analyse everything said. It had all been very dreamlike.

Will's contentment was shattered by a cry of distress, and he looked across to see an older lady being pushed in the back by two obvious muggers in black hoodies, despite the warmth of the summer's day. Will thought that this was a scene more appropriate to a dark alley, not in broad daylight outside a shopping centre. He was outraged that this cowardly attack should take place as one of the assailants grabbed the blue bag from the lady's shoulder and the other dragged the watch from her wrist. She valiantly tried to resist, but was shocked, and the two ran off.

Will acted quickly; he was not going to let these two thugs spoil his day as well as the old lady's. Ignoring the prone and bleeding figure, he ran and chose quickly the nearest one as being the easiest to catch. At the least, he hoped to get the bag back. Anger gave speed to his legs, and he felt that he was fitter than his fleeing opponents. The one with the bag was handicapped by its weight, and after a short chase, William caught him by his hoodie and twirled him round. Will was not a violent man, but he put his principles to one side and punched the youth square on the nose. He hadn't realised how much it would hurt his knuckles, but the thug reeled back with a bloody nose and a stream of curses. He ran away holding his possibly broken nose.

Will looked round like a lion seeking a second prey on the Serengeti. His hand hurt, but adrenaline spurred him on. The lady was still down, although several passersby went to her aid.

What Will saw next amazed him, and it was a scene that became legend. The second mugger, the one with the watch, ran in the opposite direction.

Kate Jenkins was on her usual Friday shopping trip and at 71 needed the aid of a walking stick. She was slow but had seen everything unfold before her, and the young hoodie-wearing mugger ran towards her, making his escape. At that moment, she decided not to be one of the invisible grey women, and as he passed, she didn't step back but pushed her stout wooden walking stick between his legs, causing him to stumble and struggle to keep his balance. He fell but got up quickly, desperate to make his escape.

Mugging old ladies was not as easy as he had thought. In telling the story to family and friends later, it was suitably embellished each time, but in reality, it didn't need to be. Kate said that he went down like a five-legged giraffe with an extra wooden leg on ice. As he ran, Kate went to retrieve her stick and noticed a watch left behind, balancing precariously over a drain. It was in severe danger of slipping through the metal bars before the usually gentle maker of cakes could act.

A young boy from the local secondary school assessed the situation and deftly picked up the watch.

'I think this is yours; you did a good job on him; I don't think he will be back for a while.'

Kate took the watch and took out her purse, ready to reward him, but he refused and went to catch up with his friends.

Jenny Clutterbuck was certainly shaken by the theft and began to cry at her sudden predicament. Several people stopped to help and give advice, but she had lost her bag and, more importantly, her precious watch. A chair was brought out from a nearby cafe, and a first aid kit was opened to clean the wound and apply a large plaster across her forehead. Her hands were dirty and stinging from the fall.

An old lady came up to her to see how she was.

Kate said, 'Don't worry love I saw everything I'm your star witness, but I dealt with that little bugger. I taught him the error of his evil ways. He dropped this by the way,

I assume it's yours.' She handed Jenny the watch, and the relief was tangible.

Jenny began to thank Kate profusely, but she went on, 'I didn't do anything, this gentleman did most of the work, he gave the other lad a good right hook, and I believe that he's also rescued your bag.' Nice bag, Sashiko, if I'm not mistaken.'

Jenny Clutterbuck tried hard to thank her rescuers, but Kate said, 'I've got to go if you're sure you are OK. I have to go shopping; my husband loves a good fresh salad for his tea.' And with that, she went off leaning on her trusty walking stick.

The small crowd began to melt away, but Will was concerned; a head injury could be serious, and he offered to phone for an ambulance. Jenny graciously but firmly refused. Will was not easily deterred. To leave this obviously shocked lady would be unforgivable.

"If you don't want me to call an ambulance, could I at least get you a cup of hot, sweet tea?"

'It should be me buying you a cup of tea in thanks for what you did for me. It looks as if your hand needs some attention. The two of them began to walk towards the cafe.

Jenny limped slightly, and Will flexed his right hand to check for damage.

'Well, we are a fine pair of walking wounded, aren't we?' Jenny smiled weakly at her tall rescuer. 'My name is Jenny Clutterbuck, by the way.'

'I won't shake hands if you don't mind. My name is Will, Will Hayes

Jenny stopped walking and looked closely at her taller companion in some astonishment.

'Will, do you ever catch the T1 from Thornbury?'

Will hesitated, 'Not usually, but I will be doing it next Thursday, car trouble, and I've got an interview that day, so the T1 it is.' Will answered slowly whilst wondering if this strange question could mean a form of concussion.

Chapter Fourteen: An Uneasy Confrontation

The air outside the Bristol County Court building seemed particularly sweet to Mel Chandoo. After a full ten days of jury service, the judge had thanked them for their time and diligent efforts. The foreman of the jury, Terry Gilligan, had pronounced a guilty verdict, and Mel felt a wave of relief. She had decided early that the Bulgarian lorry driver was guilty of his eight charges of sexual assault on children and young people; he had conducted a reign of terror using his lorry as a means of committing his widespread, deplorable, and unspeakable crimes.

As a psychoanalyst, Mel was professionally trained to assess individuals, and the evidence was strong against this opportunist, a bringer of terror and trauma. Mel thought the detailed and methodical police work was to be highly commended, and she had spoken eloquently against the defendant. Mel saw her role as being to stand firmly on the side of the innocent young victims whose lives had been ruined by the surly Bogden Petrov, lorry driver and part time rapist. One or two of the jurors weren't sure, but they were the ones who took few notes and whose attention span was not great. The foreman, Terry, had argued for dismissal of the case, although the evidence was strong and the police case watertight. DNA was hard to argue against. When the counting of votes took place, it was eleven to one, and everyone looked to Mel for leadership. She said quietly that the young victims needed them to do the right thing and make the streets safer for a long time. Finally, the jury foreman realised that he was beaten by logic and Mel's compulsive analysis of the evidence. It was, in the end, a unanimous decision.

The judge had summed up the case and commended the way the jury had managed the complex and appalling case. Some of the evidence had been harrowing, and every parent on the jury had felt horror as they imagined their children enduring the terror which this man had inflicted. Sentencing was to take place later, but the judge told the defendant that he could expect a long custodial sentence, one which he was never to complete, as he later opted for a cowardly suicide in prison.

Mel took a deep breath outside the court offices and, for a moment, wondered whether to call in at her office at the nearby Bristol Royal Infirmary, but decided that she deserved time away from the workplace and the stifling jury room. Although she would not be exempt from future jury service, she felt for the first time free and began to look forward to the weekend.

Mel considered having a cup of tea in her usual nearby cafe, but decided that catching the next T1 bus to Thornbury was a better choice. A hot bath to wash away the stench of evil surrounding the horrendous case, followed by a large glass of red Côte du Rhone, would help. In the past, she may well have phoned Joel McCarthy, her married friend with benefits, but had recently decided that she wanted more than casual occasional sex. She wanted children, and as she crossed the busy road to the nearby bus stop, she began to reorganise her life, to plan to meet a suitable single man with whom she could settle down. At that moment, a voice behind her broke into her thoughts.

'It wasn't personal, you know, back there, I mean.'

Mel felt her heart sink as she recognised the harsh tone of Terry Gilligan, the jury foreman. A man who had enjoyed his moment of power in an otherwise boring existence. She turned, not wanting to be part of this obnoxious man's conversation. Mel thoroughly disliked confrontation, but this seemed somewhat inevitable. She turned and sighed, but was determined not to walk away from this man's obvious racism.

'You spent every opportunity to remind me that I was not white, the fact that that bastard in there was a white Bulgarian seemed to make it alright to defend him. How could you possibly stand up for him?'

'You've got it all wrong.'

'All wrong, all wrong, I don't think so.' Mel replied.

Terry had not expected such a fierce retort and was momentarily taken aback. Mel was now in full flow, and she released her anger about all the racist abuse she had experienced or seen.

'My parents came from Trinidad because they loved this country and spent their working lives serving and paying taxes, paying their way. The only, the one and only time my dad didn't support England in any sport was when England played the West Indies at cricket. He thoroughly enjoyed those matches and saw it as his old country versus his new. He loved cricket and saw this as a win-win situation, and he loved the skills of the players, whatever their colour.'

Terry tried to intervene, but there was no stopping this thirty-year-old lady whose verbal attack was causing some passers-by to glance across at the obvious altercation. He wished he had never spoken to her to apologise. Mel went on.

'We don't feel the need to wave the flag of St George and chant abuse at anyone. My family and I are deeply proud of this country. How many foreigners fought and died in the two World Wars to defend this country? How many people work in the two main hospitals in Bristol? Well, I will tell you. There are 14.000 workers in the NHS there including myself. If you disregard the Scots and Irish or even the Welsh, are you aware that only 3.500 are what you would call white English? If you have a heart attack right here, right now I can guarantee that you would most likely be treated by what you would call, unwanted immigrants,' Mel was exasperated, she didn't want to speak to this man but felt that he needed to hear what she had to say even though she had made up the NHS figure. She paused with shallow, angry breath. Terry took the opportunity to respond.

'Listen, you've got it all wrong. I have two daughters, and the idea of them being assaulted by anyone, white or otherwise, appals me, but I could not in all conscience let that man in there be railroaded without a fair trial. I deliberately played Devil's advocate to ensure that the justice system was honest and impartial. I take your point about the NHS; I admire their workers 100%, and I work in a care home looking after the old and the lonely. I play trumpet with the Salvation Army to raise money for the homeless, whether white, black, or lilac striped. You were a very well-spoken leader in that jury room, and I felt, as foreman, that I had to offer a balanced viewpoint as you had made up your mind very early on. Like you, I am deeply proud of this country, our country, and its NHS and justice systems. It may be far from perfect, but it's better than most countries, and we have a duty to ensure that it remains so.

Mel had not wanted this exchange, but began to see that she was probably guilty of jumping to too obvious conclusions about the jury foreman.

'I just wanted to apologise if I have offended you and to thank you for what you do working in the NHS. Believe me, it is truly appreciated.' Terry held out his hand, and Mel instinctively took it. He was right; she had been arrogant in her pigeon-holing of the man.

'I'm sorry, you are right, but we can both agree that the defendant was very guilty, and we achieved the right result, but by different avenues.'

Terry smiled, 'All's well that ends, as Shakespeare famously said. Well, I have to go before the parking charges become sky high. After today, I feel the need to cuddle my daughters and keep them safe. By the way, the West Indies are playing at Bristol in early September. If I were to see you there, I would be pleased and proud to buy you a drink, even if you are supporting the wrong team.' He grinned and began to walk away.

'No, Terry, the drinks would be on me, goodbye, and give your daughters a special cuddle from me.'

Mel walked slowly to the bus stop. She had misjudged the man and was glad that he had given her the opportunity to understand him better. After a short wait, she boarded the double-decker and went upstairs on the left-hand side. She felt tired but had much to think about and was glad that tomorrow was Saturday. An opportunity to relax and reassess her life. When Terry had spoken of going home to hug his daughters, Mel realised with sudden clarity that she had to ditch the married Joel and concentrate on finding a suitable partner and husband. She had felt a pang of jealousy at the thought of Terry and his daughters. She realised that she wanted children; now they seemed essential to her well-being.

The bus picked up more passengers and began to fill up with workers going home, happy that it was the weekend, and shoppers laden with bags. At the large shopping centre in Bradley Stoke, several passengers disembarked whilst more shoppers got on. Mel felt the need for a hot bath and more than one glass of red wine. Maybe a glass of golden Jamaican rum, to savour.

Glancing outside, Mel's attention was caught by a small crowd surrounding an old lady sitting on a chair. Mel frowned, wondering what the incident was, but at that moment she felt a flash in her brain and realised with a strange certainty that the well-dressed lady receiving first aid would be in her unusual dreams that night.

Chapter Fifteen: A Saturday walk, Almost all Downhill

Saturday. The usual Saturday feeling of two days away from work, which most enjoyed, was not there for Jenny Clutterbuck. Her hands stung from the slight grazes as she had fallen and hit the ground after being almost mugged. As she awoke, her mind was swirling, and she decided to lie in bed for a little while longer. A glance at her oh-so-precious watch, her only link to the portal in 2056, showed her it was 7.09 am, but the sun was shining fully into her motel room already.

Too early for breakfast, but Jenny decided to treat herself to a cup of tea in bed. Her mind went back to the many years when her husband Steve had brought her a mug of fruit tea, usually raspberry, and returned to bed with her. This had been their precious quiet time before the children awoke, and they could chat about the day to come. But this Saturday, she was alone and had never felt more so.

Yesterday had been a disaster, saved only by the brave intervention of an old lady with a stout stick and by William Hayes and his wonderful recovery of her sashiko bag. As Jenny sat up, sipping her tea, she marvelled at the amazing coincidence of meeting William. Pre-ordained? Jenny had long since stopped trying to make sense of the universe and tried to enjoy each day as it came. This intervention had led to two incredible coincidences, and seeing her long-dead husband in 2024 in a Bristol cafe was deeply unsettling. Her mind wondered if her other self was being brought a mug of fruit tea in bed in their home in Haltemprice.

Jenny felt an odd pang of jealousy. Was it possible to be jealous of herself? It was too mind-boggling, and she yearned for her home in 2056 and her children and wonderful grandchildren in a future secure time, safe from the vagaries of complex time travel. This was to be her last intervention, but it was one which left her with mental anxiety. Her task felt impossible, and it was Saturday when the regulars on the doomed double-decker would be enjoying their weekend without the need to travel to Bristol.

This was to be a wasted day. One to get through without being able to move on with her role as saviour of one major figure for the future. She went through her list, one that was embedded in her mind. The eight passengers highlighted, but of course, there were others on the bus. Were they injured or just too unimportant to warrant a name? Like the soldiers of the Battle of the Somme. Missing in action.

Jenny felt her mind wandering, and she tried to focus on her list. She had not met John and Amanda Buckley and Iris Mel Chandoo and assumed that the bus driver she had come across when she caught the T1 at the same time was Frank Nelson with his red and white hooped rugby shirt.

Running through the list, she recognised that without those potential thieves, she would not have met William Hayes. He had insisted on taking her into the nearby cafe for his remedy for shock, hot, sweet tea. Normally, she would have refused, but even in her dishevelled state, she realised that this was an opportunity to learn something about William.

As she had sat in the warm cafe, she had quietly observed the tall William Hayes. It was obvious that he was still fuelled by adrenaline after chasing one of the muggers and punching him in the manner of a Clint Eastwood or some other hero. But there was something else, she was calming down, still grateful for the retrieval of her watch and bag, but nevertheless her heartbeat was slowing back to normal. Her multi-purpose watch confirmed this. But William was still excited, and Jenny sensed that he had something on his mind. For his part, William was bursting with the news that he would hopefully become deputy head at Hurst Green next week, all being well. He had no one to tell, but this calm, smiling lady seemed open to his story. She had asked if he travelled much on the T1 bus, but he put that down to confusion. There were no visible signs of a serious head injury, so he offered to buy them both a cake to go with their tea. Jenny accepted his kind offer but adamantly refused to let him pay. There were no words to express her gratitude to this normally quiet man.

William realised that he was hungry but restricted himself to two slices of coffee and walnut cake to be shared, of course. He couldn't wait to tell someone about his meeting that morning at Hurst Green. Jenny sipped her tea, and it tasted delicious, too sweet, but nevertheless wonderful and restorative.

'I was very lucky that you were there to confront my attackers. My watch and bag are very precious to me, more than you can know. Are you always here around now?'

'Amazingly, I would normally be teaching at this time, but I was visiting a local school, Hurst Green, and I have an interview there next Thursday.' Will's hand hurt; he hadn't realised when watching films and men punching each other so easily that it would involve pain for the one punch. A broken hand? Will didn't think so, but was reluctant to have it checked out in the hospital. Going to an interview with a hand in plaster may give a false and negative image. Besides, a long wait at Southmead hospital for a probable negative result didn't appeal, but strangely, talking to this old lady was pleasant, and he needed to tell someone about his wonderful meeting with the head at Hurst Green.

Jenny sensed this and asked an open question. 'An interview, how exciting, tell me all about it.'

Will Hayes didn't need to be asked twice. He told her everything about his usual failure in interviews and living alone and the magic of being told that he was in all probability going to become a deputy head in a fine school, working in partnership with a progressive, friendly head whose values matched his own.

Jenny listened encouragingly, and Will felt strangely drawn to this older lady. She was very easy to talk to, but when he said that the chances were that all he had to do was turn up and do a reasonable interview, and he would get the job, she visibly winced.

'I'm sorry, I'm prattling on about myself to a stranger whilst you are injured. Are you certain that you didn't hit your head too hard when you were pushed down? I could easily take you to the hospital.'

'No, it's just my grazed hands, and the kind girl at the cafe here did a good job of cleaning them with antiseptic wipes. I'm fine, mainly thanks to you.'

'You said that your watch was precious to you. Was it a gift from a loved one or a family heirloom?' Will asked, although the watch didn't look old, quite the reverse.

Jenny smiled at the idea of the people at the Time Research Interventions Portal (Environmental) being loved ones, although she was fond of her mentor, Professor Thomas Goodwin-Rowe. He had been the one to recruit her as a time traveller in what seemed an age ago. Jenny's mind recalled that there was a possibility that one of the eight on the ill-fated double-decker may well be recruited later to be a time traveller. Was William Hayes on that possible list? She thought it unlikely, this likeable man seemed rooted in the present and his probable exciting new job.

'No, my watch is to give me information about my health, heart rate, blood pressure, that kind of thing,' she said, hopefully vague enough to deflect attention from the all-important link to her future. Time to change course. 'My bag, on the other hand, was a gift from my husband, Steve. He's gone now, died in a tragic fishing accident, drowned. He bought me this bag in Takayama in Japan many years ago, it is irreplaceable and travels everywhere with me.'

'I'm sorry to hear that, it must have been hard for you to lose a loved one in so sudden and terrible a way.'

Jenny hadn't liked to add that in 2024, Steve was alive and well.

The sun was well up, time to shower. As she washed her hair, she wondered what all her known passengers on the bus on Thursday were doing right now. Jenny felt a list coming on, potential world changers and the more intriguing list of potential future time travellers. Drying herself on the large, slightly rough white bath towel, she picked up the large pad on the table. On a whim, she took the remote and switched on the television.

The news was being read by a young woman, a human being, and not the AI-generated presenter Jenny was accustomed to. She missed the warmth of the human touch, although the AI version was visually perfect, she knew the smile was manufactured. Pictures of war and destruction in the Middle East and the resultant refugee crisis had calmed down in the late 2040s when Israel had collapsed economically without the support of the United States, which was taking an increasingly isolationist stance. Syrian, Egyptian, and Saudi tanks had entered Jerusalem, and the new state of Palestine was proclaimed. The flood of refugees away from the region had gradually settled, and Saudi influence was strong. Conflict was ended, but this was all to come as was the year of three American presidents with two assassinations. And the movement northward of the centres of population due to global warming. A news item followed on the struggle of polar bears in warmer climates. Jenny sighed. The last wild polar bears, those wonderful creatures, had become extinct in the early 2050s, a sad loss.

Jenny switched off the television as her watch bleeped on the bedside table, the message flashed that she needed to take a walk for her health. She realised that much of her time in 2024 had been sedentary, in cafes or sitting on buses. Her ruminations on the eight passengers could wait until later.

Jenny had a limited choice of clothing, but her faithful loose lilac blouse and jeans seemed best for the day. Comfortable trainers completed the outfit, although she contemplated a charity shop bought green sweatshirt, but the sun outside persuaded her to put this aside.

Having had a cup of tea she decided to skip breakfast, her watch would disapprove of her increase in weight, A walk down the hill to Thornbury might be the exercise she needed, and she left the motel, putting her sashiko bag on her shoulder she embarked on her journey to the small market town, down the long winding road.

Woodland to the left with an ancient stone-walled boundary and open fields to the right with Jacob's sheep grazing was an attractive backdrop, but the trees cast shadows, and Jenny regretted not wearing the green sweatshirt. Light clouds briefly covered the sun, and Jenny shivered involuntarily. She tried to maintain a steady brisk pace, and her watch approved. As the road ended its final twist, Jenny was dismayed to see that the road began to rise towards the entrance to the medieval market town. Travelling on the bus, she hadn't noticed the slope, and her pace slowed. Jenny felt too warm with her exertions and was glad when she entered the High Street. Her watch gave not just the time but also her health status. The number of steps was noted and compared with the last week. Heart rate was high as a result of the walk, and Jenny was pleased to have overcome the hill, although she decided not to repeat this. The reverse journey on foot uphill was at once discounted.

In the partly pedestrianised High Street, she had seen several colourful notices proclaiming that today was the annual town carnival on the nearby playing fields. Plan for the day. Find a cafe, rest her aching feet, spend time ruminating on the possibilities for the dreaded Thursday, and try to avoid the inevitable cream-filled cakes.

Having settled herself at a small table for two and tried her black coffee, Jenny took out her pad and pen. Taking a moment to ponder, she wrote at the top of the page, Potential Interventionalists. She went through the familiar list of those she had met and those she had not, at least not yet. Writing the word Possibles she added Madison Marsden. Young, intelligent, and a budding writer, her imagination would possibly leave her open to new, incredible concepts. A definite one for the positive list. William Hayes, her knight in shining armour from the previous day, was also obviously intelligent and lived alone without family attachments. His name was written under Madison's.

Instinct told her that Frank Nelson was a man too grounded in his own time and might not be able to adjust himself to travel through time. Jenny chided herself for such a stereotyped verdict but moved on. Joy Chen's life was filled with her wonderful son, the baby Chang. She would certainly not wish to travel anywhere without the laughing toddler, let alone the past. Joy was discounted.

Doctor Rosangel Chlebek's profession meant that it was unlikely that she would welcome a secondary career as a traveller in time, certainly intelligent enough, though.

That left John, Amanda Buckley and Iris Mel Chandoo as unknowns. So, her possible list was Madison and William. This mind mapping was, to a large extent, irrelevant to her. Her primary role was to save one individual, without knowing which one to focus on, she could see little choice but to prevent the bus from crashing and therefore save all, including the chosen one.

Jenny wrote. Possible Causes of a Crash.

At that moment, a shadow caused her to look up and see a tall middle-aged man holding a cup of coffee.

Chapter Sixteen: <u>Casual and Key Meetings</u>

'May I join you? I'm afraid that this is the only table with a spare chair, unless anyone is joining you, of course.'

Jenny looked up, in her mind surprised, but graciously offered the stranger a seat at her table. She quickly closed her pad. Looking around, she noted that the cafe was indeed full of customers, mainly older couples and families shopping. There was a friendly buzz of noise. Could this be John Buckley, one of the unmet on her list? Surely too much of a coincidence.

'I see that you have almost finished your drink, may I replenish it in return for this spare seat? I would have felt silly drinking whilst standing,' he said with a charming smile.

Jenny accepted, after all, this was Saturday, and it was difficult to take actions which would move her forward in her task, unless this was indeed John Buckley, a statistically improbable likelihood.

Whilst the stranger went to the counter to order a black coffee for Jenny, she took a moment to assess him. He was middle-aged, she guessed, and well dressed in a double-breasted black blazer with grey trousers, crisply ironed with dark leather shoes immaculately polished and strangely red laces. This was a man who took care of his appearance, a man on the lookout for a partner, probably divorced, which would probably rule out the married John Buckley. But happily married? Jenny had no idea, not yet.

Placing the coffee carefully in front of Jenny, he introduced himself.

'Hi, my name is Joel, Joel McCarthy, don't worry, I don't usually try to pick up beautiful ladies in coffee shops, I just called in for a well-earned drink after opening my shop, travel agents. My assistants will work there until 1.00. We close early on Saturday. This is my day off.'

Jenny worked hard to avoid blushing at this charm offensive but noted his use of the phrase, well earned, opening up a shop to allow others to work was hardly what she would call arduous. However, he was an attractive man, and Jenny felt pleased to have his company, even though it was not John Buckley.

The time traveller introduced herself whilst putting her notepad carefully into her blue bag.

'I'm sorry, I didn't mean to disturb your work, please carry on and just ignore me.' A difficult task on a small, shared table. 'I'm guessing that you are a writer, you have that look about you,' Joel laughed easily.

'Yes, that's right.' Jenny lied; it was far easier to lie than to tell the improbable truth. She thought of Madison Marsden, researching characters in a nearby cafe. That would explain the notepad.

'What sort of books do you write, anything that I may have heard of or read? Do you use a pseudonym?'

Jenny answered quickly, far too quickly. 'Time travel' and could at once have kicked herself. Much too close to the truth.

'Mmm. Not my area of expertise, I'm afraid, I'm more a romantic historical tear-jerker myself.' And here he looked directly into Jenny's eyes, and this time she did feel herself blush like a schoolgirl being asked out on a first date. What would Steve have made of this charming man, obviously well used to gaining the attention of women? He would probably have called him a soft southern ponce, not being one to mince his words in the usual Yorkshire way.

Jenny could not help but glance at his well-manicured fingers and noted with some surprising pleasure the absence of a wedding ring. The faintest of pale skin where the ring would have been, testimony to a probable earlier marriage.

Doing a quick calculation, Jenny worked out that in 2056, her time, Joel would be in his mid-nineties. It caused her to smile to herself just as Mel Chandoo came into the cafe, Joel had his back to her and did not see her turn round to immediately leave after seeing Joel, Jenny's coffee companion.

Jenny was unaware of the identity of the newcomer who seemed to recognise Joel, but it was her reaction to seeing Jenny that surprised her. Mel had half recognised the older woman from the mugging incident yesterday and felt a sharp pang of migraine. Jenny frowned. There was obviously history between the two. It was certainly Joel himself and not the lack of seats that had caused her to leave, but Jenny felt that she had looked at her and recognised her, causing her to put her hand to her head. Her scowl at Joel disclosed a dislike. Was this his wife?

Meanwhile, Joel, unaware of the mini drama behind him, was prattling on about his first marriage,

'On the last Tuesday together, Maggie told me she liked the little oranges, satsumas, better than the larger ones I bought. It caused an almighty row, let me tell you. We went quickly from arguments about oranges to a full-scale divorce in a matter of months. Glad to be rid of her, to be honest.' He used the word honest easily, but Jenny sensed that he did not understand the concept. In his world, truth was an inconvenience to be used and manipulated to his needs.

Jenny forced herself to draw her attention back from the younger customer who had left quickly to this arrogant, shallow man.

'Sorry. Oranges? She felt duty-bound to ask.

'I was telling you about the reasons for my divorce. She started taking up lots of bad habits.'

Jenny didn't want to know but asked anyway. 'What sort of bad habits?'

Joel was happy to have Jenny's full attention again. Something behind him had obviously distracted her.

'Oh, the usual, dinner late to the table, wanting to watch her own programmes on television, leaving the dishes in the sink overnight, that sort of thing.'

Superficial, selfish, and narcissistic, Jenny thought as she quickly finished her coffee. Her first positive assessment of the man had put the idea in her mind that she should perhaps be open to a new relationship, back, or should it be forwards in 2056. The concept that a self-centred mannequin like this could ever replace her Steve was preposterous, but she decided that there could be other options in her future; she was not an old woman, and certainly didn't feel it. Steve had not contemplated an early death, but he had once said that if anything happened to him, she should remarry. It had been seven years, and she could not dwell on her beloved husband's body, lost forever in the wild North Sea. Perhaps Steve had had a premonition, as his will and life insurance were up to date, but Jenny had decided that if Steve had had a premonition, he would never have gone fishing that awful day.

Jenny stood and put on a smile whilst thanking Joel for the coffee, suddenly glad to be leaving, although if truth be told, her feet would have appreciated a longer rest after her long walk. Outside, she breathed deeply, and the air felt clean like drinking in champagne after the muggy atmosphere of the noisy café.

Jenny was entranced by the obviously old buildings and walked slowly down to the old water pump, now merely a decorative floral feature. There were hanging baskets and flower decorations everywhere. A small sign on the pump outlined the town's success in the Britain in Bloom competition. The results were an outstanding testimony to the community spirit of the small town. A bench outside the old bank building gave her a chance to further rest her feet, and she contemplated taking off her trainers but wisely decided against it. Jenny felt herself begin to doze in the warm sunshine and did not see or hear the purposeful approach of a young woman.

For the third time in this intervention, she had been surprised by an approach from others. The potential mugging was almost a disaster, and she had not been as streetwise as usual. Joel joining her at her table in the cafe was unanticipated but non-threatening, but the newcomer had walked towards her whilst Jenny dozed. It was time to retire and stay in 2056. She felt less aware and cautious of those around her; the sense of danger was less sharp. Usually her guard was well honed, a shield against potential trouble, but this vital attribute was certainly failing her.

Jenny looked up and was surprised to see the young woman with short curly hair and beautiful toffee coloured skin. Large dark blue or black glasses certainly suited her, the woman from the cafe, the one who had seemed to recognise her and the one who certainly recognised her coffee companion.

'Would you mind if I joined you?' Mel asked tentatively.

'Of course,' and Jenny moved slightly, although in truth the bench was wide enough for four.

Mel sat and drew breath as she worked out what to say. It would no doubt seem incredible, and she was reluctant to open herself up to ridicule and scorn. She glanced at the friendly, smiling face of Jenny and decided that this was someone who found ridicule to be alien to her nature. As Jenny wondered how to begin a conversation, Mel began.

'I recognised you from the cafe a few minutes ago and from outside the shopping centre at Bradley Stoke when you seemed to have had an accident of some kind. I was on the bus and saw you for only a few seconds. Are you alright?'

'A very amateur attempt at a mugging, but all's well that ends well, as the Bard said. My injuries were mainly grazed hands, slight shock and a blow to my pride. I thought that I could look after myself much better than that. Two very kind shoppers rescued me and my belongings.'

Mel continued whilst trying to work out what to say, if indeed anything needed to be said, but Jenny exuded an air of reassurance. 'I'm glad that you survived, a mugging these days may well have involved knives,'

Jenny winced at the idea and realised that the situation may have proved far more of a disaster than she first thought. In 2056, knife crime was virtually eradicated by a vigorous all-party campaign, well-coordinated and backed by a firm judicial system. Criminals did not dare carry a knife in public or as an aid to crime; the risks were too great, and the consequences were harsh.

'I was well looked after and nothing was stolen in the end,' Jenny said. 'But tell me, you obviously recognised the man at my table in the cafe, I sensed that you were not happy about him. My name is Jenny, by the way.'

'Hi, my name is Mel, and I was not happy to see Joel obviously trying to pick you up, although he usually goes for younger types, sorry I meant...'

'Jenny laughed, 'Don't worry, I know exactly what you meant, no offence taken. I'm old enough to have come across men like Joel before and hopefully wise enough to recognise a first-class prat when I see one. There was no danger of my being entranced by his charm.'

'That's good,' Mel said, 'I wouldn't want anyone else to make my mistake, he is married, whatever her told you. We had a short affair but nothing serious.'

'He said that he was divorced, but I guess that he used the same line with you, especially as you are much younger and prettier than I.'

Mel apologised again for her earlier gaffe, and Jenny found herself liking this younger lady. She had a hunch and asked. 'Is Mel short for Melanie. I quite like that name.'

'It's actually Iris Melanie, but I ditched the flowery first name and stuck to Mel. Simply Mel.'

Jenny had been right; this was indeed Iris Melanie Chandoo, one of the unknowns on her list. Her heartbeat accelerated. Perhaps this would not be a wasted Saturday after all.

Mel explained, finding it remarkably easy to talk openly in the warm sunshine to this fair-haired picture of casual elegance and indeed confidence. 'Joel and I broke up recently, well, I actually broke up with him. he was a friend with convenient benefits, but I knew he was married. His wife is also having affairs, that does make me seem a woman of a certain type, doesn't it,' and she gazed down the street and over to the hills on the opposite side of the gentle Severn valley. The mighty river with its enormous tidal range, bettered only by a river in Canada. The Romans had called it the Sabrena, and they would have known about the famous Severn bore, the surge upstream of a tidal wave.

'You seem intelligent and independent, and you ended the affair, good for you, I say. He wasn't worthy of someone like you. You did well to break it off in my opinion, although I have to say that I am not here to judge you.'

Mel felt warmed by Jenny's words, and this gave her the heart to bring up the main reason for approaching Jenny as she dozed on the bench.

'That's all history now, but I did want to talk to you about another matter'

Jenny was mystified and looked at Mel with her head slightly to one side. Where was this going, she wondered.

'Me, but we've only just met, whatever can you mean? I am intrigued.'

Mel drew a deep breath before continuing. 'Do you believe in dreams?'

'Well, I dream, doesn't everyone? But what do you mean by believing in dreams?'

Mel looked down at her shoes, unable to meet Jenny's gaze. This was more difficult than she had imagined.

'I have very vivid dreams, ever since I was thirteen, and they always come true, not always in the manner I expect, but my dreams of the future are always accurate in their own way'

For Jenny, this was a totally unexpected turn of events. If she accepted that someone could dream the future and that Mel was destined to be in a dramatic bus crash, she could surely be in a unique position to save herself.

'What do you dream of, and can you control your dreams?' Jenny asked.

From this question, without scorn or reservation, Mel realised that the opening out of her most secret thoughts had proved easy or at least easier than she had feared.

Mel sighed and said, "My dreams always occur at night, and no, I cannot control them. However, yesterday was quite unusual. When I saw you sitting on that chair with a small group around you, I felt an indescribable surge of emotion. A vivid image of you in a futuristic world appeared in my mind. It seems irrational, I know, and it only lasted for a few seconds, but last night I had a very vivid and unsettling dream about you, despite the fact that we had not met before. That had never happened to me previously. When I saw you again in the cafe with Joel, I experienced a sharp and unexpected headache. You possess a remarkable aura.'

Jenny calmed her breathing before asking, 'What was your disturbing dream about Mel? Tell me, I probably need to know.'

Mel looked directly into Jenny's eyes, 'I saw death amongst some kind of wreckage, but I sensed strongly that you were trying your best to save lives.'

A light cloud moved across the sun, and Jenny was not sure if it was that sudden cool shadow or Mel's words that chilled her, but she shivered involuntarily.

Jenny realised that Mel was a remarkable young woman with a rare gift, and the reluctant time traveller thought that this may well be a future time interventionalist. An awesome thought, but what was the next step?

Jenny shifted her position slightly on the hard wooden bench and smiled at her companion.

'If anyone could overhear our conversation, they would think us mad or at least worthy of medical assessment.'

'A bit ironic really,' Mel replied, 'I work as a psychoanalyst at the local hospital. If we were indeed referred, I would probably be the one designated as the assessor.'

'Let's hope that it doesn't come to that, then, too complicated to contemplate.'

Mel fell silent for a few moments, and Jenny wondered whether to reveal her final task as an interventionalist.

Finally, Mel said that she had never felt such a strong aura about anyone before. She asked in an open and frank manner,' You are, I believe, not a Thornbury resident, but where are you from, or should I ask when are you from?

Chapter Seventeen: Disclosure, and Too Much Information

In all her previous interventions, Jenny had never been confronted by such a direct and difficult question. She paused, trying desperately to think of a correct response, the truth, a lie or humour to laugh it off. Perhaps pretended to have misheard the question.

She decided to ask a question in answer to the question.

'Can you give me an example of your dreams coming true?' she asked quietly, 'I do believe you, but I'm still getting my head around the concept. It is most unusual after all. There are hundreds of predictions made about major disasters, but it is the one that comes true that people remember. The rest are merely forgotten.'

Mel smiled, she had never been asked to prove herself as a dreamer of the future before, as she had learned to keep her gift, or was it a curse to herself?

'That sounds like a school exam, question: Dreams of the Future, discuss.'

Jenny apologised, 'I'm sorry we've only just met and here I am asking you to show me proof of your unusual ability like a real sceptic.'

'That's O.K. Perhaps I need to prove it to myself, and well done, you deflected away from my original question very neatly with some skill.'

Jenny smiled; she found herself liking this intelligent and unusual woman more and more. She suspected that Mel's skills as a psychoanalyst were of the highest standard.

'Should I be lying on a couch with you nearby with a notebook rather than sitting on a hard wooden bench?'

'No, this bench is fine and to be honest, I'm enjoying this warm sunshine and your company, but I am both intrigued and concerned about my dream about you from last night.'

Jenny saw that the younger woman was both serious and troubled. 'Perhaps we can put last night aside for the moment and look at one dream which was a glimpse of the future.'

Around 2010, I'm not certain of the date, but it was the Grand National at Aintree. I've no interest in horse racing apart from this major race, which most people have a small flutter on, as they say. I'm disturbed by the number of horses killed or injured in the race, to be honest.'

'Did you have a bet on a horse, and it won?'

'Quite the contrary, I never bet on anything really and never try to profit from my dreams. It's actually an ability which I'd rather not have.'

Jenny believed Mel to be honest and sincere. 'So, what happened in the race, in your dream and in reality?'

'I could see a horse called King John's Castle very clearly, although I had never heard of it before. Apparently, it was named after a real castle in Limerick in Ireland. I saw that it was a lovely grey, but the word stubborn kept coming to mind, and I knew for certain that it would not win or even finish. I saw it watching and knew that it would not fall or, thankfully, be injured or worse. This was not a foretelling of death.'

Jenny tried to work out the possibilities but had to ask. 'What happened?'

'When the other horses moved forward steadily to the starting line, King John's Castle just stood refusing to move despite all the efforts of the jockey and the attendants. The horse just refused to follow the usual herd instinct, just stood and watched the others gallop away. Could the horse have had a premonition? Is that possible?'

Jenny looked at the possibilities, carefully weighing each in her mind.

'Whatever the reason for the horse's declining to move, it was impossible to predict, and yet you dreamt it happening the night before. Have you had many dreams like this one?

Mel replied, 'Many, most of them inconsequential or forgettable, but my dream about you was sharp and seemed important. It gave me a headache when I awoke. Some dreams drift away from me quickly, and I have learned to allow this, if only for my sanity. I have never tried to profit from my dreams. But what about you? Your skill in evading my question has been excellent. I would ask again, where are you from, or should I say when?'

Jenny did not answer at once, she recognised that Mel's skill as a psychoanalyst was finely tuned to asking probing questions. She felt on the horns of a real dilemma. To reveal herself as a time traveller was against all her training and indeed common sense. She watched two ladies enter the craft shop opposite. It was a delightful little shop that she had visited earlier. The marvellous crafts were all beautifully handmade, and she discovered that the makers were on a rota to man the till, thus reducing costs. The prices, to her eyes, were spectacularly low, but she was comparing them with prices in 2056. Jenny recognised that the time, efforts, and labour did not cover the cost to the purchaser, and she had had to remind herself that she was on a serious life-threatening intervention and not a shopping trip.

Mel gave her companion sufficient time to consider her response, acknowledging that it was a challenging decision requiring thoughtful deliberation.

Finally, Jenny tore her thoughts away from the craft shop and looked at Mel.

'You said that your name was Mel, short for Melanie and that you used Mel rather than Iris, which was your given first name, but you didn't give me your surname.'

Mel was about to fill in this information, but instead went back to their earlier conversation and realised that indeed she had omitted her surname. It had not been deliberate or intentional, she just hadn't.

Jenny spoke carefully in a softly non-threatening way, 'Your full name is Iris Melanie Chandoo. Don't worry, I'm not a stalker or criminal or a tax official in any way. You must trust me as I trust you.'

Mel was taken aback at this weird change in course that the conversation had just taken; she quickly pondered on ways that Jenny could possibly know her surname, and she was forced to discount each one.

'How could you possibly know that? It's an unusual name, West Indian in origin, so you didn't guess. Have you seen my picture in the newspaper?' As she said this, she realised that she had rarely, if ever, been in the newspaper, had Joel mentioned her by name? This was possible but unlikely as his charm offensive would not have included a lover's full name.

'Do you have dreams, like me? I have never met anyone like me before.'

'Sorry, Mel. I sleep the sleep of the dead, or preferably like a baby. Your name wasn't revealed to me in a dream.'

Mel recognised that stage magicians did marvellous tricks, but when revealed, they turned out to be simple manipulation of expectations plus speed of hand. They made the impossible seem possible, and Mel wondered if she was being tricked, but then for what reason, and it had been she who initiated this strange meeting and conversation.

'This isn't a party trick or even a trick of any kind, as far as I can see. Last night I had a disturbing and strong dream about you, having seen you briefly on a bus. You could not possibly have known that I would approach you this morning. You asked me to trust you, and I feel that I do, even though you are a stranger to me.'

Jenny took a deep breath and started what she knew she should not start, a disclosure.

'My name is Jenny Angela Lane, and I was born in Scarborough on October 14th, 1996. I married Steve Clutterbuck in 2018, and I have two children: George, born in 2020 and Rebecca, born in 2022. She waited carefully for a response, but when it came, it was totally unexpected.'

Mel said quietly, 'Battle of Hastings.'

Jenny was confused by her lack of reaction to the date, which would make her twenty-eight.

'Sorry, Battle of Hastings?'

Mel explained; 'One of my clients told me that the famous battle was fought on October 14th, and it sort of stuck in my mind. Did you say 1996, or did I mishear?'

'No, I was indeed born in 1996 and married in 2018, I retired in July 2051 as a primary school headteacher.' Jenny waited for the torrent of questions or incredulity. Neither came immediately.

Mel looked carefully at Jenny, 'That would make you twenty-eight. With all due respect, you look well for your age, but I would have said late fifties.'

'That's kind of you to say, but I am actually almost sixty, at least in my own time.' Here came the crux of the issue.

'And your time is...?' Mel asked slowly.

'I'm what they call a time interventionalist, I was sent via a portal from 2056 to help change a life, a very important person's life.'

Avoiding the temptation to ask who the important person was, she asked, quite reasonably, for some proof to verify this incredible story and story it must be. It could not really be true, yet Jenny seemed a genuine person and without guile.

'Who will win the next General election?'

Jenny smiled, 'It would not be good to have information like that, it's too powerful.'

Mel sensed reluctance and probed further. 'OK, who will win the FA Cup in 2025?'

'Sorry, Mel, I have no real interest in football. I'm from Yorkshire, so cricket is more my passion. Any, could you remember who won the FA Cup thirty-two years ago?'

'Very true, but then I have no way to check that you are telling the truth, or at least what you believe to be the truth. Anything in the future could be a clever prediction, unable to be checked, whilst the past gives no clues as to your validity.'

'I agree, like your dreams, my time travel is very difficult to prove, although yours is somewhat easier. I can tell you about the next three presidents of the United States, but I will be proved correct in the fullness of time. Time we certainly don't have.'

'That sounds dramatic, should I ask?'

'No, you shouldn't ask, but I will tell you anyway. This is my final intervention into the past, your present, I can hardly be sacked. But you must remember that each of my actions could have far-reaching and unexpected implications. Being sent back in time is mind-boggling in terms of financial cost but also the possibility of changing the future in an unexpected but deeply significant way.'

'Your being here must be important then. I have a swirling mind full of questions, questions which I never thought that I would be asking, ever.'

Jenny tried to reassure Mel as she had gone through the same questions and doubts herself when she was first recruited. She certainly wasn't sure why she had chosen to take the least trodden path and opted to reveal herself.

'I don't know about you, but I feel the need for a cup of tea and possibly a slice of cake, my treat.'

'We need somewhere we can talk without being overheard, there is a pub up the High Street with tables outside. It's certainly warm enough to sit outside, and we won't be overheard by passers-by.'

So, Jenny and Mel left the bench and, crossing the road, walked up to the nearby White Swan. On the way, Jenny commented on how quaint the houses and shops were, the architecture of a previous age, built to last. Mel went into the pub and ordered coffee and two flapjacks whilst Jenny found a table away from other customers. She wondered if she had indeed done the right thing. By Thursday, time would tell, for good or bad.

Mel returned, and they spent a few moments sorting out the refreshments.

'I hope that the flapjacks are O.K. The pub usually specialises in full English breakfasts, so the choice wasn't extensive.'

'This is absolutely fine, thank you. Now, what questions do you have for me? I'm sure that you are still not 100% sure that I'm not out of my mind.'

Mel laughed, and Jenny liked the way that her eyes wrinkled when she did so, laughter lines, a good sign. She felt comfortable and was increasingly sure that her companion was destined to become a time traveller herself one day. Perhaps better to keep that to herself for the time being.

'In my professional opinion, and bear in mind I have known you for such a short time, I would assess you as being of very sound mind and for a sixty-year-old, you are in very good condition. You are perceptive, clear-thinking, and capable with obvious intelligence. I believe that you actually believe yourself to be from the future even if you are not.'

'I like the bit about being in a good physical shape, don't forget I was actually twenty-eight in your time, 2024, making me into a terrible shape for my age.'

Mel sighed deeply, 'I'm having real difficulty with this whole idea and my clinical training questions everything. You ask what questions I have, well, I have so many I don't know where to begin.'

Jenny understood Mel's reluctance to immediately believe what she was hearing. A sudden thought crossed her mind: why had she not thought of this before? She reached for her blue Japanese bag and reached in for the copy of the Thornbury Gazette newspaper, dated next Thursday. Handing Mel the newspaper, she watched as she read the headline about the T1 crash in Bradley Stoke. Three dead and several injured. Mel read the article twice and carefully checked the date. This was a very elaborate hoax, if indeed that was what it was, but Mel knew that it wasn't; her mind raced as she laid the newspaper on her lap.

'Let me help you,' Jenny said, 'I was recruited by my old university professor in May 2032 and underwent training before going on my first intervention into the past in February 2033. In answer to your probable next question, no, it is not possible to travel into the future, at least not yet, but the scientists are working on it. We can only travel back in time by about thirty years. I was sent to save someone involved in that crash next Thursday.'

'You say we, how many time travellers are there? I can't believe that I am asking such questions.'

'The honest answer is that I don't know. The whole TRIPE operation is top secret; it could be a handful or up to fifty for all I know, and before you ask, TRIPE stands for Time Research Interventions Portal (Environmental). I know it seems ridiculous, but then I didn't think that one up. I'm just a small cog in a very expensive machine,'

'Can you control how far back you can go, up to the thirty years? Is it accurate or even safe?'

'The portal can be programmed fairly accurately, and it is getting better all the time, sorry about the pun.'

'Don't apologise, you're the most exciting thing ever to enter my life.... and dreams.'

Jenny smiled at the thought of being described as exciting. She had had her moments with her husband Steve, but her time-travelling exploits had usually called for her to be anonymous and distinctly unexciting. Had she made a mistake in being too honest?

She stood and picked up her sashiko bag.

'Let me buy the coffees this time, it will give you time to organise the order of the four hundred and ten questions which you are keen to ask.'

'Thank you, just coffee for me this time if you don't mind.'

Jenny sighed, the fruity flapjacks had been delicious, and she felt that another would do her no harm. She could certainly resist anything, like Oscar Wilde, except temptation, but it was hard. As she queued for her coffee, she wondered if she was doing the right thing, but instinct told her that Mel Chandoo was a special person. She had to be very careful how she handled the next hour.

Placing the welcome hot coffee in front of Mel, Jenny slightly regretted the lack of flapjacks.

Sitting down, Jenny asked Mel what her first questions would be.

'Will you answer me honestly?' Mel asked, looking carefully at Jenny, although she thought she felt that she knew the answer already.

'I will try my best, but I cannot answer specific questions about the time portal or about the future, not major events, at least.'

'I'll start with, why are you here? Who do you have to save? If what you have said is true, this must be a very important person. It can't be me, I'm definitely average and unlikely to be important in the future.'

Jenny sipped the hot coffee before answering, 'I have a list of eight people, some of whom I have met, like yourself. Most will be on the T1 bus to Bristol when it crashes next Thursday.' She watched for the reaction, when it came, she was pleasantly surprised.

'What can we do to prevent this from happening? Is it not possible to just inform all eight and tell them not to get on the bus? Tell the police or something.'

'And what would you tell the police, that you are a dreamer of the future or that I am from the future. Can you imagine their response?'

Mel's thoughts were not selfish and didn't involve saving herself. This was definitely a good sign.

For the next hour, Mel resisted the urge to ask questions about life in the future and concentrated instead on the immediate life-threatening task ahead. 'What is your plan? I assume that you have one.'

'As a matter of fact, I don't, my experience of preventing major crashes is somewhat limited, I was a primary school headteacher. Our curriculum didn't cover that eventuality. I was sort of hoping that you might have some ideas.'

'Then we need a list of options and go for the best one. We can work together on this.' After a slight pause, Mel asked.

'I'm on the list, am I a casualty?'

Jenny was serious as she answered.

'I'm sorry, Mel, I just don't know, but three people will die, and I don't know who. The newspaper was thin on details, although it assumed that the casualties were locals.'

Mel sighed. This was becoming more bizarre and certainly scarier by the minute.

'I'm sorry, Jenny, my mind has reached saturation point, I need to go home, have a nap and hopefully not dream and try to make sense of all this.'

'I understand completely, Mel, I too feel drained, and I know that you have lots more questions to ask. A couple of hours ago, I wasn't even aware of your gift as a dreamer of the future, and you certainly weren't aware of time travellers. It all seems very Doctor Who-like, doesn't it?'

They agreed to meet for a meal together that evening and to plan for what to do to ensure the safety of the double-decker on Thursday.

Mel asked, 'Where are you staying, or do time travellers need somewhere special to rest?'

Jenny laughed, 'It's the Premier Inn next to the Ship pub, room 17, nothing mysterious about that, I'm afraid.'

Mel thought quickly, 'The Ship will be crowded, it being a Saturday night, we need somewhere we can eat but talk in private, I share a house with a couple of friends, so that's not an option. The White Horse, just nearby up the A38, has just opened as an Indian restaurant, so it will possibly be less crowded. I'll pick you up at, say, 6.00. That will give us time to eat and plan.'

It was agreed, and they stood before hugging warmly like old friends. Mel left to briskly walk down the High Street and round the corner to her nearby small house.

Jenny sat down again and contemplated another drink, but felt at bursting point. Had she done the right thing in revealing so much to Mel? She relaxed and felt that Mel was absolutely the right person, and there was a shared bond between them.

It would be good to have someone to share her task with, something she had never had to do in all her previous interventions.

Definitely the time to retire.

Chapter Eighteen: Candy Floss, Crushed Grass, and Donkeys

Having made a semi-urgent visit to the toilets inside the pub, Jenny stepped out into the gentle warmth of July and stood as the High Street seemed full of families, mostly with balloons, as if leaving the carnival or excitedly moving steadily up to the entrance to the carnival in the park.

She decided that her brain needed and deserved a break; it felt overloaded, and tonight would be full on with planning and questions. A visit to the local carnival and catching the T1 back up the hill to her room for a rest seemed a very good plan. Her stomach said food, it was after midday, but she heroically resisted. It was obvious which way was the right way to the carnival, and Jenny walked slowly up the High Street before turning right down a narrow alley to join the queue to pay her entrance fee and enter the Mundy playing field.

It felt like a lively, happy place, full of laughter and relaxation; the troubles of the world were left behind for a time. Families sat in groups enjoying a glass of beer whilst the children ran excitedly around, fuelled by sugar sweets and candy floss. It felt like a good place, an ordinary place in a small town, untroubled by bombs, starvation or enslavement. The town had a long-settled history at peace, although its young men had marched to war twice in the last century and some in later years to join the world's perpetual conflicts. A market town at play and, to Jenny, it eased her troubled mind.

Tonight, she would meet up with the remarkable Mel Chandoo and discuss serious plans, but for this afternoon, she decided to put all this aside and enjoy the moment.

Making her way to join the small queue for the hot dog and beefburger stand, she closed her eyes for a moment. The strong smell of fried food mixed with the aroma of crushed grass took her back to happy times with her family, with Steve and the children, George and Rebecca. It was hard, so very hard to realise that all three were alive and well at that moment in time in their family home in Haltemprice, East Yorkshire.

'What can I get you, my love?' The stall holder asked for the second time. The old lady was obviously in a world of her own. he was patient, but time was money, and there was a line of people waiting.

'Just a cup of tea and a hot dog, please, no fried onions, thanks.'

Having been handed the food, she walked away, carefully balancing the polystyrene cup of hot tea. She looked around for somewhere to sit and managed to find a patch of grass unadorned by families. Carefully sitting, trying to do so elegantly without spilling tea over herself was an art in itself. Finally succeeding, she sat and looked round, feeling totally alone, an island of loneliness in a pleasant sea of contentment. For a moment, she relished the hot dog, which was very welcome, but the scalding tea was difficult to manage, and the grass was not designed for such cups.

The nearby smell of fried onions, together with sausages and beefburgers, was intoxicating, and Jenny contemplated the luxury of a follow-up cheeseburger, which she had always been partial to. Her mind went back to when she and Steve had decided to join The Sealed Knot, the English Civil War reenactment society. They had both had a strong interest in history, and they loved the authenticity of the battles and living history.

Jenny smiled as she remembered how Steve had adamantly refused to join a Royalist regiment, being a staunch republican, but Jenny hadn't really minded either way. So it was that they had joined the local East Riding regiment, Lieutenant Sir John Lilburne's Regiment of Foot. She had loved making the cloth uniforms and dresses for herself and Rebecca. The children were too young to go on the battlefield, but they loved taking part in the living history camps, open to the public. The regiment was full of knowledgeable enthusiasts, and the camaraderie was pleasant. Weekends were often spent driving to the latest battle re-enactments around the north of England with the heavy uniforms and dresses packed in an estate car full of camping equipment.

Jenny had loved the evening campfire with the singing of traditional folk songs and easy humour of well-run jokes. She remembered so many of the characters, many out of place in their own world, but content to be part of the regiment in 1643. Injuries were rare as safety was paramount. Muskets and cannons were loaded with gunpowder, but obviously no iron balls. The site and sounds were, to the public, very realistic with the volley fire and push of pikes thrilling.

Each morning, the smell of fried food and crushed grass was common to each campsite, and for a moment, Jenny looked back at those times with their happy memories. It was strange to ponder the fact that as she sat sipping fast-cooling tea in 2024, the world of the Sealed Knot had not happened yet for her. She and Steve had joined in 2039; time was sometimes a difficult concept, and societies which reenacted the past confused Jenny somewhat.

Jenny's eyes began to close, and she lay back into a light sleep, as tiredness fuelled by tea and a hot dog overtook her. Her dreams were of the stirring sounds of drums urgently calling the regiment to battle and the sound of ragged musket fire. In the background were the sounds of the carnival, donkey bells, organ piped music and children's laughter. It was easy to drift off. Jenny felt safe.

Meanwhile, in the Buckley household, the arrival of the Ukrainian family had caused disruption to the staid routines of John and Amanda. John had not realised how he and his wife were such creatures of habit, and cancer had certainly restricted his abilities, much to Amanda's unspoken annoyance.

The big arrival day had been unsettling and should perhaps have been anticipated. James Rowland, the link partnership coordinator, had formally introduced the family and looked carefully at Amanda to gauge her reaction. She was the obvious reluctant partner, yet she seemed welcoming enough. John, on the other hand, was delighted but quite shocked by the small amount of luggage.

Whilst Amanda went to make tea for them all, John was pleased that they had agreed to sponsor a Ukrainian family and wondered what horrors the family and especially the two children had witnessed.

Taras Marchenko was 34 with a deep set of gentle brown eyes, a dark, neatly trimmed beard and a thatch of thick hair. He explained that he and Olena had decided that Kiev, their home, had become too dangerous for the two girls.

'I was a plumber and worked part time with the Kiev fire brigade, so I wasn't called up to the army,' he said in clear but slightly halting English. All the time, he looked towards Olena for help, reassurance, and love.

Olena Marchenko had long, straight, light brown hair and a happy, open face with a warm smile. She explained, 'Taras has good English but understands more than he can speak. I worked in a school library and my English is probably better.' John wondered if the positions were reversed, how he and Amanda would cope if they were forced to go to a peaceful Ukraine, speaking very little Ukrainian. Thank goodness that English was such a universal language; even Americans could speak a mangled version.

Olena sat on the sofa with two very shy girls sitting close by her. Sofia was six, wearing a simple blue checked dress, she was a mini version of her mother with the same colouring, long brown hair, and seemed the more confident one out of the two children.

John thought that Mila, the four-year-old, was the personification of cuteness. She climbed onto her mother's knee and cuddled close. Unlike the others in the family, she had blond hair and a fringe, brown eyes, and an adorable smile. He had hoped for a boy to take to cricket and teach chess to, but nevertheless, he realised that Christmas would be special this year. Amanda had never wanted children, and as he sat looking at the children, he realised that there was a huge gap in his life. Too late now, but for a while, these children in their home would be a very welcome addition.

'I have made arrangements for the girls to visit the primary school across the road. Is Mila old enough for school, Olena?'

'Not quite, John, but a playschool would be good for her English and to learn the customs of your country. It seems so wonderfully safe here. In Kiev, we were frightened every time a plane appeared in the sky.'

Amanda came into the room with a large tray of tea for everyone and went back to bring in a plate of biscuits, which she placed on a smaller side table. Mila went uncertainly across to her father and to be nearer the tempting biscuits.

John smiled at the girl, then addressed her sister. 'Sofia, please pass the biscuits to everyone, that would be most helpful.'

Glancing at her mother for confirmation, Sofia stood and carefully went across to the plate, taking it round to everyone, taking care to ensure that Mila took only one. John frowned in a mock-serious way. 'Sofia, it is an old English custom that children should take two biscuits, one for each hand.'

The older girl smiled. She liked this old man and was happy to see him smile back in an understanding way. Mila did not need a second invitation and held a custard cream and bourbon biscuit in her small hands, alternating her nibbles between the two.

Olena sipped her tea before making a prepared announcement. 'John, Amanda, Taras, and I would like to thank you both from the bottom of our hearts. You have a beautiful home, so quiet and lovely. But we do have one request.'

Taras looked across at his wife before adding. 'Most Ukrainians are Christian Orthodox, but my family have always worshipped as Roman Catholics, and we would like to continue that for our girls. I notice the church across the road, is it catholic?'

Amanda frowned, not sure of the distinction but fairly sure that there was no Christian Orthodox church in Thornbury. John reassured the newcomers, 'Don't worry, there is an excellent Roman Catholic church in Castle Street. I'll take you there to introduce you. A bit ironic that Henry V111 and Anne Boleyn stayed at the castle there. He was the one who split England away from Catholicism, the church across the road is the Church of England, but welcoming to all.'

Taras and Olena seemed relieved. In their war-torn homeland, Roman Catholics were in the small minority within the Christian community.

John added, 'There is also a small Roman Catholic school in Thornbury, too far to walk, which brings me onto my question, Taras, do you drive?'

Taras looked at Olena before answering, 'Yes, of course, but on the right side of the road.'

John replied, 'I'll add you to my car insurance, and you will be able to use our car. I no longer drive due to my failing health, and Amanda is not keen on driving these days. This arrangement should work well.'

Olena added. 'You are too kind, John; we are very lucky to have met you, both of you. I'm sorry that you are not well.'

James finished his tea and declared, 'Well, it's time for me to get back to the office. You all seem happy with the partnership, and you have my number if there's anything I can help with or any problems, although I don't foresee any in your case.' He stood, shaking hands with the adults and then left, happy to have made a successful sponsor match.

'Girls, you have not finished the biscuits on the plate. This won't do at all. Please help yourselves. If you don't, then I will have to, and that will not help my waistline,' John declared.

Olena tried to politely protest, but the two girls were already taking extra biscuits, one for each hand, as was the English custom. Mila meandered towards John. Her mouth littered with crumbs, she leaned softly against his knees before attempting to climb up. She had decided that she liked the old man.

'What about you, Sofia. What do you like doing best at school?' He expected a bland answer, but the older girl was clear, 'I like reading and history, but I don't know much about your English history yet, but I hope to learn. I have heard about your English cricket and would like to see it myself.'

This was music to John's ears, and he planned to look at the fixture list to see what the next match in Bristol at the County ground was.

'Don't rush the girls, John, it's all a bit overwhelming for them at the moment, no doubt. Perhaps you could all go to the Thornbury Carnival and Taras could practice driving on the left.' She looked at the young Ukrainian and inwardly melted into his soft, gentle eyes, but sadly realised that he had eyes only for his wife.

So it was that Tomas drove them all carefully down the hill to a car park in the centre of Thornbury before going down to the catholic church. Amanda decided that she would stay at home, as carnivals and catholic churches were certainly not her thing. John sat by the Marchenko family after introducing them to Father Padraig Kelly, the priest, and listened politely. The family were warmly welcomed into the community, and Father Kelly looked forward to his flock being swollen in church services.

Later, they walked up the High Street towards the carnival, the two young Ukrainians revelling in the peaceful town with its old buildings untouched by bombs and drone attacks. Leaving home had been a hard decision, and they wondered if it was indeed the right thing to do. However, they followed behind John, walking up the street, a young girl in each hand. Sofia and Mila had adopted him as an unofficial dido, or grandfather. In his turn, John was in his element, and every fibre of his being regretted Amanda's decision so many years ago not to have children. He had missed out on so much, but was determined to take full advantage of this sponsorship and being a temporary grandfather.

On the carnival field, Jenny awoke from her food and sun-enforced sleep feeling foolish. She was drooling slightly and had managed to get grease stains on her dress. Worse was that as she sat up, she realised that at her age, trim though she was, getting up was not an easy manoeuvre. She turned onto all fours, embarrassed when she felt strong arms on either side of her as Tomas and Olena, seeing the situation, came quickly to her aid.

'Thank you so much,' Jenny said, 'I think that I would have been down there for a long time.'

'We are glad to help,' Olena said, carefully brushing grass from Jenny's dress.

She noted the Eastern European accent, and as the family left to go to purchase large ice creams, she saw the familiar blue and yellow stickers on the rucksacks of the two girls, who went to watch the donkeys. In between licks of soft ice cream, they pleaded for rides on Richie the mottled donkey and Snowdrop, the almost white one. Both had appealing, gentle eyes, difficult to ignore.

The Ukraine. Jenny felt a shadow cross her mind as she was reminded of that awful history-changing day, when a nuclear weapon was used in war, for the third time, as Kiev was obliterated for tactical purposes, to shorten the war, they claimed. Jenny recollected that it had indeed achieved its aim, but not with its original intention. The world had recoiled with shock and horror, and the Russian leadership had responded by deposing Vladimir Putin after decades in power. A more moderate government in the Kremlin had secured a peace settlement, satisfactory to all, and aid had flooded into Ukraine from all around the world, and cities were rebuilt, and the country was again at peace, but at a dreadful, terrible cost.

Jenny remembered the day of infamy when the nuclear explosion had shaken the world's confidence. October 17th, 2027. She looked across at the young family enjoying their ice creams and hoped that they would not return to their home country before that date. It would be so easy to warn the family, but the ripples of this simple act of kindness would probably escalate, and the implications would no doubt be enormous.

Thank God she had not been sent on an intervention to prevent the nuclear attack. A bus crash in England seemed a minor event compared with that horror, and she made her way back to catch the bus up to the motel to prepare for her meeting with Mel Chandoo.

Had it been a mistake to reveal herself to the dreamer of dreams? It was certainly against all the rules of interventions, but Jenny felt it to be somehow right. At that moment, she could not have itemised logically her reasons. She had to trust her instincts.

Too late now to change her mind anyway.

Chapter Nineteen: Poppadom's and Planning

Mel Chandoo drove into an empty space outside the Premier Inn with practised ease. Looking up, she saw Jenny Clutterbuck waiting with a wave and a smile. Both were grateful that the other was there. Mel felt herself full of doubts, but trusted Jenny, who moved around to the passenger seat.

Jenny adjusted her seatbelt and looked across at Mel. 'I thought that you may not come.'

'I did think that you may have been a figment of my imagination, or more likely a dream,' Mel said whilst carefully reversing the car, ready to move north on the A38. 'But if I hadn't come, I reckon that I would spend the rest of my life wondering, especially if the bus did crash on Thursday, and you were proved to really be a time traveller.'

'I'm sorry, Mel, I have certainly burdened you, and given you too little and at the same time too much information. Your head must be swirling with questions.'

Mel looked left and right as she found a gap in the traffic past the cricket ground, and settled for the short drive to the White Horse.

Mel continued, 'Of course, the rest of my life may be less than a week if your prediction is correct, I could be one of the victims, you said yourself that you didn't know who the dead were.'

Jenny realised the implication of what the perceptive young psychoanalyst had said.

'So, on Thursday, you intend to board a maybe doomed double-decker? You don't need to, you know, your jury service is over, and I assume that you would normally be travelling by car to your hospital job. If I had not disclosed being an interventionalist, you would not even have contemplated being on the T1 next Thursday. I say maybe doomed, but the only certainty I have is that the bus will crash.'

The enormity of what she had said hit Jenny hard; already, her actions had changed the future, at least for one. This was so unfair, and she was reinforced in her determination not to travel in time again.

'Hang on, we are here, and judging by the car park, we should be able to find a secluded table.'

Inside the old pub, newly refurbished and essentially a curry restaurant despite the signs outside proclaiming it to be a traditional inn, the owner and manager, Narayan Kaur, greeted the two women warmly. The new venture had been open for just six months, yet had not yet taken off in popularity, and customers were always welcome. Curry restaurants were certainly in demand, especially in cities such as Birmingham, where Narayan was born, in the

Sparkhill area. Perhaps it was time to ditch the traditional inn sign and replace it with a more Indian sounding name.

Mel smiled and asked for a table away from other customers, if possible.

'Certainly, come this way.' Few tables were occupied, even on Saturday night, so the request was easy to accommodate. Picking up two menus, he led the way, wondering about the relationship between the two women. He may have guessed mother-daughter, but the younger one's toffee coloured skin and tight black curly hair would seem to rule this out. He guessed Caribbean, certainly not Indian. Perhaps just friends or work colleagues, neighbours even. Why the need for a secluded table? Perhaps their relationship was more intimate. Still, none of his business.

Settling for a few moments, they perused the mainly Indian food menu. Jenny thought back to Steve, who disliked curry and would automatically order lasagne or fish and chips. These seemed to be two of the few items on the menus which could be said to reflect a traditional inn menu.

A hovering waiter asked if they would like drinks. Jenny ordered a glass of dry white wine and was pleasantly surprised when Mel asked for tonic water, explaining that she was driving, even if only a short distance. In Jenny's own time, drinking and driving were strictly forbidden with serious consequences.

Upon receiving their drinks, they noted that the pub was almost vacant. It appeared that locating a quiet table was no longer necessary.

Mel ordered a Samosa and a plate of chicken biryani, whilst Jenny opted for onion bhaji and lamb Rogan Josh. Both meals came with mini popedom's, but Jenny could not stop herself and ordered extra, full-sized ones.

'Sorry, I can never resist them, I know I shouldn't, but they are very moreish.'

The food came quickly, and both concentrated on eating. Jenny's hot dog seemed like a long time ago, and she said that the White Horse deserved to be better attended on Saturday evenings, as the food was delicious.

'Well, that was lovely,' Jenny said, 'But our main business is to, well, I suppose, decide what to do now. I've never been in this situation before.'

Mel wiped her mouth with her napkin and asked how many interventions Jenny had been on. The time traveller noted that Mel seemed to have accepted that she was really someone from the future, absurd though it must seem to her.

Jenny thought carefully, 'Around nine, I think, mainly to the mid-thirties. This is actually the furthest back I have personally been, but the scientists are working on extending the possibilities as they always are.'

Mel asked. 'You were in my dream, and I have to keep reminding myself that I approached you when you were sitting on the bench outside the old bank. All this is, therefore, unlikely to be an elaborate hoax; then there's the newspaper, of course. I cannot specify details, but I knew for certain that it was the future. Can you tell me something about what life is like thirty years from now? No details I can place bets on and win money, but generally.'

Jenny sensed that Mel still needed reassurance, understandable as her newly met companion was predicting possible death or injury in a few days' time. Jenny began to filter information to give as few facts away as possible.

'Well, warming of the Earth and rising of sea levels were being predicted years ago, but the climate has changed dramatically. No one has to go to southern Spain to get a suntan; England has very warm summers, but they are wet and stormy. The world population has risen to around 9.7 billion, and food resources have to be carefully marshalled. Seaweed and algae, together with high-protein insects and tiger nuts, are used extensively. Don't worry, it tastes better than I make it sound, and it is certainly sustainable. Clean water is more important than oil or diamonds.'

'What about homes, in your time, I mean?' Mel asked.

Many existing homes in 2024 have already been adapted to energy-conscious needs. New homes are smart with no electric switches, and it's all sound and movement generated with voice control for all electric items. My house has HealthCare, a voice tells me when to take medication or watch my weight or go for a walk, it is extremely energy efficient, has to be to combat the much higher temperatures and regular storms. A white Christmas is definitely a thing of the past, Victorian greeting cards are museum pieces, we haven't had a snowy Christmas for over twenty-five years.'

'A pity, I think that I would miss that, even though I'm from the Caribbean, it was or rather is, my favourite aspect of Christmas.'

The waiter returned to ask if they wished for a dessert, but they opted for coffee.

Mel said, 'I could go on all night asking you about your life in the future, and I realise that you have carefully avoided anything political, but our main problem is next Thursday. We should really talk about that and make plans.'

The restaurant had begun to fill, but not so much that they could not continue to talk in privacy.

Jenny opened her blue sashiko bag and handed Mel a pad with a list of the passengers as far as she knew it. The younger woman sighed deeply, 'Somehow it makes it seem very real to see my name on the list, and you say that you have no idea who will be killed and who injured?'

'That is sadly correct, but I have been sent back to save just one. If I knew who it was, my task, or should I say our task, would be simple. We just prevent that person from boarding the bus.'

'Surely we could stop the bus from crashing and therefore save all lives,' Mel pleaded.

'I'm sorry, Mel, I have tried many times to think of a way to prevent the bus from crashing, but that would be difficult, and the knock-on implications would be enormous. It would be a tsunami of continuous change rather than a ripple and would cause more problems than it solves. My best plan would be to identify the chosen one and then change their day.'

'But these are ordinary people, no doubt doing worthy work, but history-changing, I don't think so. Who are your most likely suspects? I can certainly rule myself out of the running. My job is important in a localised sense. You yourself can't have been sent back over thirty years to save yourself, that would be illogical.'

'And extremely expensive,' Jenny added. 'No, I am on the bus, but I'm not the one I have to save. If we do rule you out for the moment, let's look at the others. However, if we do choose and choose wrongly, then all this is a waste, and that would be horrendous.'

'So, in a way, this is a pointless exercise. Have you met any of those on the list? I should add that I know Rosangel Chlebek; she lives in Castle Street and works in A&E at the Bristol Royal Infirmary hospital. I also work at the BRI, and ordinarily I would not have come across her as there are hundreds of NHS workers, but she lives quite near me, and we met at Tai Chi lessons. I do know for a fact that she drives to work each day, so I don't quite know why she is on the list.'

'Maybe she has car difficulties and catches the bus instead,' Jenny pondered.

''That makes sense, the T1 goes close to the BRI. Have you met any of the others? Their names are not familiar to me, although I may have come across them without knowing, coincidences are like that, I suppose.'

'Very true, I have met four–maybe five on the list, not including yourself. William is a teacher going for an interview for a deputy headship in a primary school in Bradley Stoke, a lovely man who saved me from a mugging, or rather, he saved my sashiko bag after a mugging. You would like him.' Jenny added with a glint in her eye and a mischievous twinkle in her eye.

'Not me, I'm off men for a while after Joel, my friend with benefits. Anyway, one or both of us could be dead on Thursday, not a good start for a new relationship.'

'You don't have to be on the bus, no one would blame you for opting out,' Jenny added seriously.

'No, I'll be there, this is too exciting to miss, although pretty scary at the same time. I'll be on the bus to support whatever actions we decide on. Which others did you meet?'

Joy Chen is a delightful Chinese mum, single parent with a son, Chang. She's a teaching assistant and an occasional translator for the police, which is why she is probably on the bus to Bristol. I think that I sort of met the man I think will be the driver, Frank is a rugby supporter, but I have only said good morning to him, and guessed that he will be the driver on Thursday, but they do tend to alter routes, so I'm not certain.'

Mel finished the last of her coffee, 'So far, none of these people would seem candidates to be history changers, what about your fourth. You have certainly been busy whilst you have been here.'

'Thanks, but most meetings have been accidental rather than planned. I met Doctor Chlebek at A and E, after my mugging, when I was being checked out. Polish, I think, and very capable.'

'What about the young girl?' Mel asked, 'Her age gives her the potential to do something special with her life that would affect others and change history.'

Madison is a loner, very intelligent, and fiercely independent. You are quite right, that might be the one we seek, but what if we get it wrong?'

'OK, what about the others, the ones you have not met?'

The Buckleys are likely retired and unlikely to make earth-shattering, significant changes. They seem to have less potential compared to Madison.'

'So, to sum up, A young schoolgirl is likely to be your selected one, would you agree?'

'On the law of probability, I would say yes, I know that she wishes to be a writer, but sixteen-year-olds do change their minds, and time is on her side, unless she is one of the three killed on Thursday. We could save her, but get it wrong, I can't afford to do that.'

Jenny finished her coffee and called for the bill, refusing to listen to Mel's offer to share the cost.

After Jenny paid with a card, they stood up and walked outside. Once in Mel's car, Jenny said, 'Thank you for your company tonight, Mel, and for helping in planning our next steps, even though we have not completed a plan. Our task seems very challenging, if not impossible.'

They drove the short distance back to the motel, and Mel gave Jenny a card with her telephone number.

'Tomorrow is Sunday, and I have to go to visit my parents, my mother isn't well, so I have to go. Give me a ring on Monday, hopefully I will have had a dream which solves our problem.'

'You are a very remarkable young lady, Mel Chandoo, resourceful and brave; you have been very disciplined in not questioning me about life in the future too much and restricted yourself to our Thursday bus problem. Not many would have done that or even believed that I was from the future. I hope you can dream of an answer.'

Jenny exited the car and watched as Mel drove back to her house in Thornbury. She acknowledged that Mel was a strong ally, which provided some comfort, although Thursday was approaching quickly without an obvious solution.

Chapter Twenty: The Sound of Willow on Leather and Two Rosies

As Jenny awoke, she noticed that it was daylight and there was a regular knocking noise, which seemed familiar, but she could not immediately identify its source.

She turned her thoughts to the present, away from the dreaded Thursday. Jenny realised that a leisurely day at the cricket ground might be precisely what she needed to recharge and gather her thoughts for the challenge ahead.

Checking her watch by the side of the bed, she discovered it was 12:08, indicating she had slept through the morning. She recalled having an Indian meal with Mel Chandoo and one glass of white wine, which did not seem enough to cause such prolonged sleep.

Jenny concluded that this unintentional Sunday lie-in was the result of an accumulation of several days of physical tiredness and mental stress. Her body had obviously decided that she needed to rest, and rest she certainly had. Her watch said that her vital functions were normal, which was a relief. Her first reaction had been guilt, that she had wasted a whole morning, but as she reasoned,

Mel was visiting ailing parents and would not be available to help plan. There was little she could do to solve her interventionalist problem.

Last night, she had concluded that the potential time traveller was definitely Mel, or if not, possibly Madison, the schoolgirl writer. She frowned as the noise returned, not that it had gone away for long. Cricket, of course, was the sound of a willow cricket bat striking a leather ball, and she remembered the cricket ground right outside her balcony. It was a good sound, a reassuring sound, a very English sound. The sound of summer. The English had taken the game to all their widespread colonies, and the game was firmly embedded around the world.

Walking to the window, Jenny opened the curtain slightly to have her thoughts confirmed. A typical local cricket match is the true grassroots strength of the game. Jenny decided on a shower and then the luxury of some time watching the match. It may well be wasted time, but it brought back many fine memories of going with her husband Steve to see Yorkshire play at Scarborough or the mighty Headingley ground to see England. They loved to go to the Marine Drive cricket ground to watch Scarborough or Yorkshire play in what seemed, looking back, endless sunny summer days. Afterwards, they would cross the road to go onto the cliff tops overlooking the sparkling North Sea with its ozone-rich breeze.

Well, Jenny thought to herself, it's too late for breakfast, and I certainly don't feel ready for a pub lunch. The cricket match seemed very tempting, as a Yorkshire girl, she reckoned that the love of cricket was in her blood.

After a refreshing shower, Jenny dressed, nodding at the receptionist, she walked the short distance to the cricket pavilion. A board outside declared that this was a West of England Premier League match, Thornbury against Bridgwater. Entering the pavilion bar, she ordered a glass of cider and a ham sandwich.

"Who is batting?" Jenny asked the barman.

'Team or batsman?' he replied in a friendly manner.

'Team first and then batsman.'

'Thornbury are batting, and the batsmen are Sachin Agarwal and Pedro Ellis, his name is Peter, but everyone calls him Pedro, although no one can remember why.' He glanced out of the large windows and handed Jenny her drink. 'Thornbury are 170 for seven,' he added.

As the barman passed Jenny her sandwich on a plate, he said, 'I don't think that I have seen you here before, are you with the Bridgwater team?' He concluded that she might well be the mother of one of the opposing team. He took pride in being able to assess new customers.

Jenny smiled, 'No, I'm a neutral on this one, I just thought that a drink and a snack and a couple of hours cricket would be a good way to spend some lazy Sunday time.'

'Judging by your accent, mild though it is, I'm guessing that you are not from around here, Lancashire?'

'Good God no, I'm from God's own county, Yorkshire,' Jenny laughed in mock horror at the very idea of being from the enemy county. Taking her drink and sandwich, she left the pavilion and chose a small table with a coloured umbrella for shade.

The cider was cold, and the sandwich was homemade, substantial and tasty. She regretted not having a full meal at the Ship Inn. Thoughts of Scarborough's sea breezes had her thinking about fish and chips. Maybe tonight. Around her, a small crowd sat on benches and on the grass by the boundary rope. Children played while old men reminisced about past games. The older they got, the better they were.

On the next table sat an older man nursing a pint of bitter whilst his companion, a young child, a girl, ate a packet of crisps whilst taking occasional sips of orange juice. He was explaining the complexities of cricket to the girl, probably his granddaughter.

'When the batsman goes in, he stays in until he is out, then he comes back in, and the next batsman goes out until he is out, then he too comes in, it's quite simple really, Sofia. What sport do you like back in Ukraine?'

The young girl with the pleasant open face and simple blue checked dress was about six years old; Jenny estimated that she was about two years older than her eldest son, George, who was four and living in Yorkshire at that moment, what Jenny would not give to see him and have him on her lap eating ice cream or crisps.

The girl, Jenny thought, was the epitome of simple wholesomeness. She paused in her dedicated crunching of salt and vinegar crisps to answer the old man who gazed at her with adoration.

'Dad likes football, and so do I. He goes to watch Dynamo Kyiv, they play not far from our apartment. He says they are the best in all of Ukraine, but he doesn't like Shakhtar Donetsk; they play in orange, but we play in all white with bits of yellow and blue, our country's colours. When I am older, he says that he will take me to see them and I will cheer, like Dad.'

'Would you like to play football when you are older, Sofia?' the old man asked gently. He loved cricket, but the game was ignored; he only had eyes for the girl, who was probably not his granddaughter.

'No, I want to be a gymnast, I go to a club in Kyiv, Mila tries to copy me, but she is only four.'

Jenny suddenly remembered being helped up from the grass at the carnival and the Ukrainian flags on the rucksacks. She had thought the couple looked vaguely familiar. Thank God the delightful girl was not on her list.

The old man expressed interest in the girl's gymnastics but went on to explain the details of the cricket fielding positions. Jenny smiled to herself at the girl's increasing bewilderment, but she was polite and obviously loved the old man. Jenny wondered what the relationship was if not blood relatives.

'And then there are the slips and silly mid-on and backwards point and third man, but you will pick these up as you understand the game more.'

Before the cricketing bafflement became too deep, the conversation was disturbed by a dog on a lead, keen to meet and greet all and sundry with a fiercely wagging tail. At the end of the line was Madison Marsden, writer in training. Maddie was slightly confused to see Jenny and someone from her chess club sitting nearby.

'Hello John, I'm just taking Rosie here for her long Sunday walk. We try to come up the hill by the paths through the fields, it's good for both of us, I think, although it doesn't feel so at the moment.' She sat whilst the dog, a Bocker, a delightful golden mix of a beagle and a cocker spaniel, became instant friends with Sofia, who knelt to caress and stroke the young dog.

'A lovely dog, Maddie, very friendly, what is she called?'

'This is Rosie, her job is to keep me fit. I noticed that you weren't at the chess club last week, John. Everything alright?'

'We are acting as hosts to a Ukrainian family for six months, and we were busy preparing their rooms. This is Sofia.'

The girl smiled up at Maddie but was keen to return to the adoring dog. Maddie looked across at Jenny. 'Hello again, I hadn't expected to see you here today.'

'I'm staying at the Premier Inn over there, and I couldn't resist watching the cricket for a while.'

Maddie was aware that she should perhaps introduce the two adults who were sitting close to each other but not together.

'John, do you know Jenny here? She's a writer, as I want to be one day. Meet John Buckley, we play chess at the club together each week, although he is a million times better than I.'

John laughed and stood to shake Jenny's hand.

'Pleased to meet you, Maddie is selling herself short, she is a fine player, would you be interested in joining the chess club, we are always keen to recruit new members.'

Jenny's mind was far from chess. The jigsaw was now almost complete; the old man would be on the fated double-decker next Thursday. She had now met everyone apart from John's wife, Amanda.

'I'm sorry, John, I'm only visiting for a few days, and anyway, I'm a poor chess player at best.'

Maddie handed the lead to Sofia and asked her to look after Rosie whilst she went into the clubhouse to get herself a glass of orange.

She asked, 'Can I get anyone a top up on their drinks?' aware that she had brought limited money on her long Sunday walk.

Jenny replied, 'Yes, please, Maddie, an orange juice sounds lovely, John?

'Not for me, thanks, I have the bladder of a twelve-year-old budgerigar, but Sofia would, I'm sure, appreciate one.'

To Madison's relief, Jenny brought out her purse from her sashiko bag and gave Maddie a ten-pound note.

'That should cover it, I think, my treat.'

Meanwhile, Sofia wondered why John would have a budgerigar's bladder; she determined to ask him later.

'Jenny and John watched as Maddie, with a quick smile, headed towards the clubhouse, Rosie contentedly lying at Sofia's feet, her tail still wagging happily. The conversation turned towards the cricket match unfolding before them, the gentle thud of the ball on the bat filling the air. Jenny couldn't shake the thought of the upcoming Thursday as a T1 stopped outside the cricket ground to pick up passengers. John, on the other hand, was curious about Jenny's writing, wondering what stories she had to tell. Sofia, now sipping her orange juice, looked up at John and asked innocently, "Why would you compare your bladder to a budgerigar's?" Her question brought a hearty laugh from John, who began to explain the quirks of British humour. At the same time, Jenny observed the scene, her mind still partially elsewhere, but appreciating the moment of levity. The sun cast a warm glow over the gathering, and for a brief moment, the worries of the world seemed distant, replaced by simple, shared smiles and the promise of new friendships.

As the conversation wove its way through light-hearted banter and the subtle nuances of cricket, Jenny found herself unexpectedly charmed by the group's camaraderie. She noted the way Sofia's eyes lit up with curiosity, how John's laughter seemed to ripple through the group, and the ease with which Maddie navigated social interactions. It reminded Jenny of the simple pleasures in life, those moments of connection that often went unnoticed. With the cricket match carrying on in the background, she felt a growing sense of belonging among these new acquaintances, even as her mind intermittently drifted back to the puzzle that awaited her.

Almost unnoticed, a young woman with two children in tow walked past carrying a picnic basket. At that moment, a loud thud of bat on ball heralded a cricket ball heading towards the group with alarming speed. The young woman quickly put down the basket and collected the ball with some skill. She threw the ball fast and hard to the wicket keeper to a splattering of applause from the crowd and players.

'Thanks, Rosie,' one of the batsmen called. At this, the Bocker pricked up her ears and lifted her head to where she had heard her name called.

Rosie Chlebek picked up her basket and smiled at the nearby group. A slight frown crossed her face as she fought to recognise the somehow familiar face before her.

Jenny acknowledged the young doctor from Accident and Emergency with a polite smile. Rosie remembered.

'Ah, yes, our mystery lady. Did you get your NHS records sorted out?'

'Yes, I managed to sort everything out,' Jenny replied, a note of relief in her voice. The children, sensing the relaxed atmosphere, began to play nearby, their laughter mingling with the sounds of the game. Sofia took the dog's lead and went to introduce the dog, Rosie, to the two children. They were intrigued by the fact that both the dog and their mother shared a name. John extended his welcome to the newcomer with a friendly smile. As the conversation naturally shifted to include Rosangel, Jenny felt a sense of contentment, the pieces of her life's puzzle momentarily set aside to embrace the joy of new connections and shared experiences.

'You seem to have played cricket before,' John enquired, impressed by Rosangel's evident skill.

Rosangel laughed, a warm, infectious sound that carried on the breeze, 'Yes, I used to play quite a bit in my school days. It's been a while, but I guess some things just stick with you.' As she settled into the group, the conversation flowed effortlessly, weaving tales of past games, school triumphs, and the unexpected turns life had taken. The children, now wholly engrossed with Rosie the dog, giggled as the playful canine responded to their calls. Jenny, sipping her orange juice, glanced around at the genial gathering, feeling a rare sense of peace. The earlier tension about her impending Thursday mission seemed to dissipate in the warmth of the present moment. Even John seemed more relaxed, sharing anecdotes with a glint of nostalgia in his eyes. The afternoon unfolded gently, marked by the occasional cheers from the cricket match and the rustling leaves, a perfect backdrop for the budding friendships and the shared joy of simple pleasures.

A good day, an easy summer's day, which Jenny enjoyed. She listened to Rosie Chlebek's tales of her brothers and cricket stories at school in Derbyshire. Madison spoke of her love for her grandfather and her determination to become a writer. Rosie and Maddie shared stories of Polish friends and relatives, and Jenny listened with interest to Rosie's stories of visits to India, home of her husband. This doctor was currently batting for Thornbury. John noticed that Jenny was careful not to add too much about herself, but kept a veil of mystery drawn about herself. For her part, Jenny mentioned her family in East Yorkshire, but without details.

Two shadows passed through Jenny's mind: the knowledge of the total destruction of Kiev in Ukraine, the home of the delightful Sofia and the regular passing of the T1 double-decker buses coming to and from Bristol.

While the shadows of her thoughts lingered, Jenny took solace in the animated discussions around her. The cricket match provided a comforting backdrop, its rhythm a steady counterpoint to the ebb and flow of conversation. The camaraderie among the group deepened as stories were shared and laughter resonated, creating a tapestry of connection that felt both new and timeless. Sofia's curiosity about the English game of cricket led to an impromptu lesson from John, who, with the zeal of an enthusiast, explained the intricacies of wickets and overs. Rosangel Chlebek's children, now entirely at ease with the dog Rosie, played joyously, their laughter a sweet melody that harmonised with the gentle murmur of the crowd. Jenny, usually so guarded, found herself softening, the warmth of the group melting her usual reserve. It was in these simple moments of shared humanity that she found a fleeting yet profound sense of belonging, a reminder that even amidst life's uncertainties, pockets of peace and joy existed, waiting to be discovered.

Chapter Twenty-One: Conflict, Comparisons, and Confusion

Will Hayes drove into the car park of his school, buoyant and happy. His pre-interview meeting with the head teacher at his potential new school had gone far better than he could ever have hoped. The seeing off of two muggers and the recovery of a watch and bag owned by a pleasant older lady left warm memories, although his right hand still gave him pain. A pain he could cope with as he went to his current headteacher's office. He reported on his visit to Hurst Green Primary school but kept details to a minimum. Will had never got on well with the man sitting before him, and the feeling was mutual. The warmth of his meeting with Curtis Warren was in stark contrast with the atmosphere in the office. He didn't mention the fact that he had been all but promised the job after the interview.

Will's mind briefly wandered to the pleasant encounter with the elderly lady and the promising future ahead at Hurst Green. Still, the headteacher's icy demeanour quickly brought him back to the present. The headteacher, with a curt nod, dismissed Will with a reminder of his current responsibilities, a clear indication that any enthusiasm for his potential departure would not be reciprocated. As Will stepped out of the office, the weight of the unspoken animosity lingered, yet he felt a renewed determination to move forward, bolstered by the warmth and optimism of his earlier encounters.

'Oh, sorry, my mind was elsewhere.' Will said as he bumped straight into Abbie Thompson, who appeared flustered by the collision between herself and her mentor.

'That's OK, William, I should have watched where I was going. How did your meeting at Hurst Green go?' The question was asked, but she dreaded a positive answer, which would lead to her secret love leaving the school before she could pluck up the courage to tell him about her feelings.

'It went really well, Abbie,' he said, his voice tinged with excitement despite the lingering tension from his previous encounter. 'I think there's a real chance I might get the job.' Abbie's face fell slightly, but she quickly masked her disappointment with a supportive smile. 'That's great news, Will. I'm really happy for you,' she replied, her voice betraying none of the turmoil she felt inside. As they continued down the corridor, the sound of children bustling into school filled the air, a reminder of the vibrant life surrounding them. Abbie's heart ached with the thought of Will leaving, but she resolved to enjoy the remaining time they had together. Meanwhile, Will, buoyed by the prospects ahead, felt a mixture of gratitude and apprehension as he navigated the familiar halls, each step bringing him closer to a future that seemed both promising and uncertain.

Abbie moved towards her classroom, calculating how much time she would have to make a decisive romantic move before it was too late. She sighed, it was now or never, but reckoned that even if Will were successful, he would not be too far away; it's not as if he were moving hundreds of miles away. There would be no more accidental collisions in corridors, joint staff meetings, or assemblies together. Time for action.

As the school day progressed, Abbie found herself grappling with the impending change, her mind oscillating between moments of resolve and waves of uncertainty. Each glance at Will's familiar figure brought a pang of regret mingled with hope, while she meticulously planned her approach. The corridors buzzed with the energy of children, an ever-present backdrop to her inner turmoil.

With each passing hour, the urgency of her decision pressed upon her, the fleeting nature of time crystallising her determination. She knew that in the delicate balance of her emotions and the unfolding future, she had to seize the moment, to bridge the gap between hope and reality, before the opportunity slipped through her grasp forever.

The children in William Hayes' class glanced at each other as they noticed the change in their teacher. The usual solid, slightly boring teaching, efficient but unexciting, seemed to have disappeared after his day off last week. Instead, before them was a man energised and full of lively humour. They appreciated the difference and responded well, but regretted that they would be leaving his class at the end of the year.

As the bell signalled the end of the day, Abbie took a deep breath and made her way to Will's classroom, her heart pounding with anticipation. The sunlight streamed through the windows, casting a warm glow on the room where Will stood, tidying up the day's materials. Gathering her courage, Abbie called his name softly, her voice barely above a whisper. Will turned, a curious look on his face, and Abbie took the final steps towards him, her words tumbling out in a rush as she confessed her feelings, her heart laid bare. A moment of silence stretched between them, filled with unspoken emotions and the weight of possibility. Then, with a gentle smile, Will reached out, his hand brushing against hers, offering a glimpse of the future they might share. The air seemed to shimmer with hope and the promise of new beginnings, as the school around them buzzed with the life of another day coming to a close.

Will had settled into being the perpetual bachelor, haunted by memories of a long-lost love, while stuck in an unfriendly work environment. Yet, there was light at the end of a dark tunnel. In a few days, he had high hopes of promotion and a happier school. Here was a kind, friendly girl who was expressing her strong feelings towards him. He had never thought of Abbie as anything more than a colleague, but it was as if a veil had been lifted from his eyes.

'I never realised, I mean, I should have done, but I was never much good at relationships. Perhaps we could go out for a meal tonight, and I can tell you all about my visit to my new school. I am desperate to tell someone all about it.'

Abbie was relieved that her expression of love had not been rejected out of hand and delighted at the prospect of a meal together. Time for a shared bottle of red wine and her best sexy underwear. Time for bold initiatives.

'That would be wonderful, William, there's a new Thai restaurant near my house, if you like Thai food, that is.'

'I do indeed, and I know the place you mean. I'll book a table for two.' He loved the phrase, for two, and life could suddenly only get better. The tunnel's light became a warm glow.

Abbie reckoned that Thai desserts were mediocre to say the least, but she planned a more delicious, exciting dessert for William as she planted a shy kiss on his cheek.

'Abbie, this has all come as something of a surprise, but in a very good way, but could I ask you a favour? I would prefer to be called Will, William seems so old-fashioned somehow.'

As she walked away from Will's classroom, Abbie felt a mix of exhilaration and trepidation. The encounter had gone better than she had dared to hope, and the prospect of a shared future with Will filled her with optimism and lots of wonderful possibilities.

For Amanda Buckley, there were no such warm feelings, only increasing bitterness. The hosting of a Ukrainian family was not working out as she had planned, or rather naively hoped. Despite considering herself a youthful fifty-nine-ish with a good figure, which could pass for thirty-nine, she realised that the young, handsome, and very desirable Taras had eyes only for his lovely wife, Olena.

Amanda couldn't help but feel a sting of jealousy every time she saw the tender interactions between Taras and Olena. The romanticised vision she had of her life mingling with theirs was quickly fading, leaving behind a harsh reality she wasn't prepared for. The constant reminders of their deep bond only intensified Amanda's sense of isolation, prompting her to question the decisions that had led her to this point.

The focus of her frustration was her husband, John.

Amanda's bitterness grew each day as she observed the vibrant connection between Taras and Olena, which starkly contrasted with her own fading relationship. Her husband,

John, once the charismatic older suitor who swept her into an early marriage, had become a shadow of his former self. The cancer and reliance on his walking stick had weathered him into a shambling old man, devoid of the ambition and desires that once fuelled their life together. While John found contentment in the presence of the children and took joy in helping Taras and Olena adjust to their new life in England, Amanda felt increasingly isolated and disillusioned, her youthful spirit clashing with the reality of the life she now led.

Every interaction between the Ukrainian couple seemed to highlight the contrast with her own marriage, and the more Amanda tried to find solace in her own pursuits, the more she felt the weight of her discontent. The once-vibrant dreams of her younger years seemed to mock her now, leaving her grappling with the harsh truths of her life. As she watched Taras and Olena build a new chapter amidst their challenges, Amanda couldn't shake the feeling of being left behind in the shadows of her own aspirations, lost in a life that no longer felt like her own. The days blurred together, each one a reminder of the chasm between her hopes and her reality, pushing her further into a spiral of regret and longing for a past that seemed both distant and unattainable.

John had returned from the cricket match yesterday with six-year-old Sofia, whose stomach was full of juice, crisps and chocolate and a mind full of baffling cricket terms. She had loved her time with her adopted grandfather and being able to play with the delightful dog, Rosie. She told her parents all about her wonderful day and tried hard to remember the difference between mid-on and silly mid-off. John smiled but glanced at his slightly scowling wife, obviously unhappy. This was in contrast to their cricket companion Jenny, who was the same age as his wife. Jenny was a smiling, warm companion who John found attractive. The comparison was unsettling.

As the evening drew on, the tension between Amanda and John seemed to magnify, each tender moment between Taras and Olena casting a sharper shadow over their fractured relationship. John, lost in the warmth of yesterday's memories, tried to bridge the growing chasm with gestures of kindness, but Amanda's heartache festered, her envy and regret gnawing at her soul. The lovely charm of their home and the laughter of children playing did little to soothe her disquiet. While John found solace in the simple joys and the company of their guests, Amanda's disillusionment deepened, painting her world in hues of bitterness and longing. The differences between her life and the vibrant connection she witnessed in her guests became an unbearable reminder of what she once had and what she now lacked. She stood at the window, the twilight casting long shadows across the room, her mind a tumult of unresolved emotions, as she watched John with Sofia and Mila, wondering how to reclaim the joy that seemed to slip further from her grasp with each passing day.

Amanda had never wanted to figure out changing children, and she watched John's obvious pleasure as he played with the two young girls with irritation. John may have wanted children, but she certainly didn't.

Amanda's mind churned with the conflict of her emotions, the burden of her disappointment pressing heavily upon her. She couldn't ignore the growing distance between herself and John, exacerbated by the presence of their guests, who seemed to embody all that she felt was missing in her own life. Her resentment towards John's contentment mingled with a longing for a connection she feared was lost forever. As the days wore on, each gesture of affection between Taras and Olena became a painful reminder of what Amanda yearned for but felt powerless to attain. The warmth and life they brought into the house only served to highlight the coldness she felt in her own heart. She knew something had to change, but the path forward seemed shrouded in uncertainty, leaving her teetering on the edge of a decision that could alter the course of her life forever.

In a few months, they would be gone, and the house would return to the glum, dreary place with its shambling routines. It was an almost unbearable thought, and she seriously contemplated leaving a husband she found a constant source of irritation.

Chapter Twenty-Two: Brakes, Steaks, and Other Mistakes

Frank Nelson, ex-army and potentially ex-bus driver, left the manager's office feeling his anger reach a boiling point.

As he fumed over the unjust reprimand he had received, Frank had always prided himself on his punctuality and dedication, but today, a minor mechanical failure had delayed his bus route, and the manager had shown no leniency. The frustration gnawed at him, feeling the weight of his past accomplishments in the army being overshadowed by this mundane job that offered little respect or recognition. As he strode out of the office, he couldn't help but reflect on the mounting pressures in his life. His thoughts wandered to his old ambition of being a drag queen on reality television. One never to be revealed at his workplace and certainly one never to be achieved.

His encounter with the manager was just another reminder of how far he had strayed from the path he once envisioned for himself. The leather of his new boots echoed his faltering steps, unlike the vibrant energy he once felt in uniform. Determined not to let this setback define him, Frank resolved to find a way to reclaim his sense of purpose, even if it meant making difficult choices in the days ahead. The road before him was uncertain, but he knew he had to move forward with the same tenacity that had once been his hallmark.

Perhaps his wife, Lillian, was right; he should pursue a writing career, although he recognised that success on a major Rowling-like scale was unlikely. He yearned for something more creative and had tried painting, but his first painting by numbers had proved successful in outcome, but ultimately unsatisfactory.

Frank had calmed down a little when he arrived home; it wouldn't do to take his emotional baggage home to burden his beloved wife.

'How did your day go?' Lillian asked as she finished preparing her husband's steak and chips.

'Same old, same old, I warned old Hewitson, the so-called manager, about the brakes feeling soft on my bus, but he refused to listen and said that we couldn't afford brake checks every few minutes on a whim. He wasn't happy with a delay to his precious bus timetable.'

'Cost-cutting in the proper maintenance of the bus fleet is all well and good, but passenger safety is paramount.' Frank said, shaking his head. I might have to consider looking into something different, maybe even that writing you always talk about.' As Frank washed his hands, ready for what he knew would be a fine meal, he reflected on how lucky he was to have such a supportive wife.

Frank took his seat at the table, the aroma of the freshly cooked meal mingled with the comforting familiarity of home, Frank felt a glimmer of hope amidst his frustration. Perhaps it was time to heed Lillian's advice and explore new avenues, leaving behind the grievances of the day.

'You've said before that they are cutting corners. You know far more than he does; all he has experienced is driving his wife mad with his petty ways. '

'You're right, Lillian,' Frank said with a sigh, appreciating her unwavering support. 'Maybe it's time to take a leap of faith and try my hand at writing. I can't keep going like this, feeling trapped and undervalued.' Lillian smiled warmly, her eyes filled with encouragement, and Frank felt a sense of relief wash over him. As they shared the meal, the conversation shifted to the possibilities that lay ahead, the excitement of new beginnings mingling with the familiar comfort of their shared journey. It was in these moments that Frank found the strength to consider a future that aligned more closely with his passions, and with Lillian by his side, he knew he could face whatever challenges came their way.

'Of course I will have to continue driving, the writing would have to be a sideline, I doubt that I will become rich overnight or if ever.'

Frank had actually started a free university online course designed for emerging writers, working on the computer in the early hours or late at night. He had been encouraged to develop short pieces of writing, and others had written critical analysis, always anonymous but with the proviso that any criticism had to be outweighed by positives. Although initially daunting, Frank found this method very encouraging. This gave him a fresh, more optimistic perspective on his future. Still, he found the unsociable hours were making him tired and occasionally affecting his daytime job as a reliable bus driver.

Despite the challenges, the course became a beacon of hope for Frank, a lifeline to a world where his creativity could flourish. He began to share his developing stories with Lillian, who read them with enthusiasm and offered constructive feedback. Her unwavering belief in his potential fuelled his determination to succeed.

One evening, as they sat together in their cozy living room, Frank read aloud a particularly poignant piece he had written about a soldier finding solace in unexpected places. Lillian's eyes welled with tears as she listened, her heart swelling with pride. 'Frank, this is beautiful,' she said softly. 'You have a gift, and it's time the world saw it too.'

Frank knew that the road ahead would be challenging, but with Lillian by his side and a renewed sense of purpose, he felt ready to embrace whatever came his way. Together, they navigated the ups and downs, finding joy in the journey and strength in their unwavering bond.

And so, as the evening drew to a close, Frank and Lillian sat hand in hand, dreaming of a future where passions could be pursued and new adventures awaited. It was in these quiet moments, filled with hope and possibility, that they found the courage to believe in a brighter tomorrow.

In Thornbury that night, Joy Linjin Chen watched her baby, Chang, slowly falling asleep, his eyelids heavy, he had had a wonderful time playing with his mother, and he was now tired.

Silence enveloped the room, a gentle reminder of the peaceful moments that often follow a well-spent day. As a single mother, life was not always easy, and her mother said it was a dreadful mistake, but when she looked at her beautiful boy, cosy and warm and full of trust, she knew in her heart that Chang could never be considered a mistake. His father was long gone, unaware that he had a son, but Joy had regarded him as a brief fling and not a potential father figure. Perhaps that would come later if she met someone suitable, someone who would love Chang as she did. But there was plenty of time for those thoughts.

She gently kissed Chang's forehead, her heart swelling with love and determination to provide the best for him. Joy knew that her life as a single mother would be filled with challenges, but it would also be filled with moments of unparalleled joy and fulfilment. As she gently lifted him, he stirred slightly as she transferred him to his cot. Joy loved the smell of him after his bath and nappy change, and she knew that he would now sleep until the early dawn. She felt a sense of peace, knowing that each day was a step forward in building a life for herself and her son, a life where they could both thrive and find happiness in the simplest of moments.

Joy put on a Tom Paxton CD and turned the sound down so as not to disturb her precious boy. Picking up her hardbacked green notebook, she turned to a fresh page and began to write a poem for Chang. She knew that it would take time, much revision and alterations before being pronounced satisfactory. The next stage was to put the poem to music, accompanying herself on guitar. Her dream was to be a poet and songwriter, and she loved folk music, whether from Ireland, England, or the United States, but rarely from her birthplace, Hong Kong. She had seen the American Tom Paxton in concert twice and loved the way the words of his songs were the main element, backed by catchy guitar music.

As Joy began to write, the words flowed effortlessly, a testament to the deep love she felt for her son. Her thoughts wandered to the future, imagining the day when she and Chang would listen to her music together, sharing the bond that transcends time and place. She envisioned performing on stage, her heart swelling with pride as she sang songs inspired by their journey, each note resonating with the experiences that had shaped her. The quiet room, the tender moments, and the dreams that danced in her mind all merged into a tapestry of hope and resilience, painting a picture of a life where creativity and love intertwined seamlessly. Joy felt a surge of inspiration, and as she continued to write, she knew that her passion for music and poetry would one day lead them to a future where their dreams could flourish.

Joy's inspiration and serenity were suddenly disturbed by the shrill telephone call. Reluctantly picking up the mobile, she answered. Moments later, she ended the call and sighed. A glance at the diary confirmed her fears. The Bristol police had wanted her to translate for them on Thursday, and it was a day her mother was unavailable to babysit Chang. Joy could put Chang into childcare attached to the school, but didn't want to leave him all day. She knew they would miss each other, and Joy would feel safer having him with her. Apparently, a Chinese businessman had been accused of fraudulent dealings and had demanded an official translator. She would have to inform her school that she would be away for two days and take Chang with her to the police station in Bristol. The only positive aspect was that Chang enjoyed riding the bus.

She picked up her poetry notebook, but the moment of inspiration had passed. Damn, damn, damn, the best laid plans of mice and men, whatever that actually meant.

Joy took a deep breath, trying to dispel the frustration that the unexpected call had brought. She knew that life as a single mother was a delicate dance between fulfilling responsibilities and nurturing her own dreams. The translating work was intermittent but well paid, and the money was certainly helpful. Determined not to let the interruption mar her evening, she resolved to make the most of the time she had left with Chang before Thursday's daunting task. She would prepare for the translation work, ensuring she could be both a reliable professional and a devoted mother. Meanwhile, she would continue to pour her heart into her poetry and music, cherishing the quiet moments with her son.

Across Thornbury, Mel Chandoo closed the lid of her laptop. She had put the name of Jenny Clutterbuck into her search engine, yet could find only a reference to a Jenny celebrating her hundredth birthday in Tennessee and someone with the same name graduating in Fresno, California, two years ago. Neither was likely to be the Jenny Clutterbuck she was looking for. Very mysterious, most people left traces of their lives, either she did not exist, which was unlikely, or the Portal people at TRIPE had erased any reference to the interventionalist.

One of her housemates offered her a glass of white wine and asked if she was alright, as she had seemed so preoccupied recently.

'No, it's nothing, just heavy workload at the hospital,' but in reality, she had had several restless nights as her dreams became more vivid, dark and very disturbing. As she sipped her wine, very conscious that she could not share her burden of dreams and time travel with the two girls she shared the house with, she pondered on the easy way she used the acronym and the term interventionalist. Her dreams of carnage and the wreck of a double-decker had left her tired from lack of sleep.

But there was no denying the impact these nightmares had on her psyche, each night drawing her further into the enigmatic world of TRIPE and the elusive Jenny Clutterbuck. Mel knew she had to find answers, not just for her own peace of mind, but to understand the significance of these visions that haunted her. She resolved to dig deeper, to uncover the truth behind the interventions and the shadows that seemed to blur the line between reality and her dreams. As she prepared for another restless night, Mel hoped that the answers she looked for would soon come to light, providing clarity to the chaos that had seeped into her waking world.

A glimmer of an idea entered Mel's mind. The newspaper, which Jenny had shown her, dated in the aftermath of the bus crash, could of course have been part of an elaborate hoax, but to what purpose? Mel had read the front page several times but disregarded the usual local stories inside. Perhaps there was a clue somewhere that would prove the edition of the Thornbury Gazette to be really from the immediate future. Going to the paper recycling bin, she picked out last week's edition of the newspaper. Slowly going through page by page, she looked carefully for information which could be checked in Jenny's future edition. Mel felt a little bad at this seeking of verification, yet it seemed sensible. All her professional clinical training and instincts, not to mention her dreams, clearly led her to believe Jenny's extraordinary account of being an interventionalist, yet she had to suspend logical belief. Of course, a hundred years before, people would have scoffed at the concept of colour television, computers or the mighty internet, space travel would have been confined to science fiction, and yet science had progressed, why not time travel?

Chapter Twenty-Three: Days to Savour and Remember

The gearbox on the Ford Fiesta was definitely not right; the grinding noise as he changed gears convinced Will Hayes that taking the car to the garage in Thornbury and then travelling to his interview at Hurst Green by bus was essential, if not an ideal start to his big day. Yesterday, he had gone into his present school with a spring in his step, but today was doubly delightful. The unexpected expression of strong feelings which Abbie Thompson had for him had lifted his spirits beyond bounds. They had met for a Thai meal and agreed that the newly opened venue was just perfect. The conversation at the meal was initially dominated by Will's excitement about his potential successful interview.

Abbie's encouragement and the shared laughter had given him a renewed sense of confidence. While the car's issues were a minor setback, he was determined not to let them overshadow the potential of a new chapter in his career. The thought of discussing his passion for education and his innovative ideas at Hurst Green filled him with excitement, overshadowing any mechanical woes. Will's mind raced with possibilities as he envisioned a future where his professional aspirations and personal happiness intertwined seamlessly, much like the delicate gears of a well-tuned engine.

'But it will mean that we will see each other less often, and I will miss that,' Abbie said, bringing an unwelcome shadow to the evening. Will realised that his enthusiasm for Thursday's interview was selfish. He gazed at the younger girl with increasing feelings, unknown since the loss of his first love at Nottingham University, Emily Greenwood.

'But we won't be far apart, and we could always share a flat together.' The tentative ease with which Will made the suggestion shocked him, yet it seemed so right,

At the end of the meal, which Will had insisted on paying for, he was, after all, a traditionalist, and there was a moment of hesitation outside the restaurant. The evening was warm, and inside they had both enjoyed each other's company, but now there was a slight shyness.

They stood facing each other, and Will was uncertain how to conclude the best evening he had ever spent, at least since university.

Will hesitated, feeling the weight of the moment pressing upon him. Abbie's eyes reflected the warmth and uncertainty of the evening, and as they stood there, the ambient sounds of the town wrapping around them, he leaned in and gently kissed her. It was a promise, an unspoken vow, that despite the changes and challenges ahead, they would navigate them together. The kiss ended, leaving them both slightly breathless, yet filled with a newfound resolve. The night air seemed to hum with the possibilities of the future, both daunting and exhilarating. Will knew that the next few days would be pivotal, not just for his career, but for the burgeoning relationship with Abbie. With a final smile, they parted ways, each carrying the knowledge that their paths would converge again, stronger and more intertwined than before.

Abbie turned to find Will still standing there,

'Or we could share a bottle of wine in my fridge, I have a spare toothbrush, if you like, that is.' Abbie said, wondering if she had crossed an unwritten line and spoiled what had been a wonderful evening.

Will did like the idea, reluctant as he was to let Abbie go off alone into the night. The ridiculous thought that he had no pyjamas with him crossed his mind, but this was no time for sensible planning.

With a smile and a nod, Will agreed, and they walked side by side to Abbie's place, holding hands, the night air filled with a sense of promise. Inside, the cosy apartment felt like a sanctuary, a respite from the uncertainties outside. They shared the bottle of wine, their conversation flowing effortlessly from one topic to another, deepening their connection. The evening stretched into the early hours, and eventually, with toothbrushes in hand, they laughed at the spontaneity of it all. As they settled in for the night, the comfort of being together offered them both a sense of security and hope. Will knew that whatever the future held, the bond they were forging tonight would weather it all, and as he drifted off to sleep, he felt an overwhelming sense of gratitude for the unexpected turns that had brought them here.

In Alveston, at John and Amanda's house, Olena Marchenko sat nursing a cup of coffee, also with a feeling of deep gratitude. She and her husband, Taras, watched the daily news from their homeland in Ukraine and were glad to be away with their daughters, safe from rocket attacks and the deadly, frightening drones which brought indiscriminate death. They tried to shield the terrible pictures on the news from Sofia and Mila, and she was grateful to John for taking the time and effort to distract and play with the girls. Sofia in particular enjoyed his impromptu English lessons, although cricket terms eluded Olena.

As the warmth of the coffee in her hands offered a small comfort, Olena couldn't help but reflect on the resilience her family had shown in the face of such adversity. John and Amanda's kindness had been a beacon of hope in these turbulent times, providing not just shelter but a semblance of normality. Despite the heartache of leaving their home behind, the bonds they were forming in this new environment gave Olena a flicker of hope for the future. She often looked at Taras, whose eyes mirrored her own mix of relief and sorrow, and she knew that together, they would rebuild their lives, step by step. The laughter of Sofia and Mila, mingling with John's enthusiastic explanations of cricket, brought a smile to her face, momentarily lifting the shadow of their past. This newfound community, their sanctuary, held the promise of healing and new beginnings.

Olena had loved the way John had bought Sofia a small cricket bat and several tennis balls to let her try her skills with the strange game. Sofia and John were developing a real bond, whilst Mila was happy to be near her mother. Olena pondered the somewhat odd relationship between the older married couple. They had been married for many years but had separate bedrooms. John was open, friendly and warm; his kindness was obvious, but Amanda was a different case. Outwardly, she smiled, but it was clear that she was more interested in Taras than the rest of the family, not that the two husbands were aware of this, being men, but Olena could see the tell-tale signs. She tried hard to help with housework and to be useful where she could; it was not in her nature to be a burden, but she felt an underlying resentment towards her host. It's a little unfair, as the older couple had volunteered their home as hosts for six months.

She wondered if Amanda's subtle discontent stemmed from the disruption of their routine or perhaps something deeper and unspoken. The older woman seemed to take pleasure from belittling her husband, often finding fault with him. The tension hovered like a faint shadow, never fully acknowledged but always felt. Despite this,

Olena focused on fostering a sense of harmony, grateful for the sanctuary they had been offered. The children's laughter continued to be a balm, mingling with the hum of bees and the rustle of leaves in the gentle breeze. Taras, ever the optimist, spoke of finding work and creating a new home for them, his determination a pillar of strength for Olena. In these moments, amidst the uncertainties and the silent worries, there was a glimmer of hope that perhaps, just perhaps, they could find peace and happiness once more.

That night, Olena spoke quietly to Taras about Amanda, wondering if he had picked up any misgivings about their host.

'She is trying to be young, refusing to be seen as old and, I think, resents John, who is older and has cancer. He tries to keep her happy, but I think it just exhausts him more,' Taras replied thoughtfully. Olena nodded, appreciating Taras' perspective and sensing the deeper currents of their hosts' relationship dynamics. She resolved to tread carefully, offering gratitude and help wherever possible, while focusing on the future she and Taras were building for their daughters. The days ahead would be challenging, but as long as they faced them together, with the same resilience and hope that brought them this far, there was a promise of better times. The soothing rhythm of their whispered conversation became a lullaby, wrapping them in a cocoon of shared strength and quiet determination, ready to face whatever dawn might bring.

For Mel Chandoo, dawn brought a disappointing drizzle across the Severn valley and increasing uncertainty. When she was with the mysterious Jenny Clutterbuck, she was almost certain that she was indeed from the future, and it was, of course, possible that science in the future would develop such a fantastic facility. As she brushed her teeth, Mel slowly realised that it was the lack of hard proof which unsettled her logical, clear-thinking mind.

The drizzle outside mirrored the murky thoughts in Mel's mind, a haze of uncertainty clouding her usually clear and logical perspective. The enigma of Jenny Clutterbuck's origins gnawed at her, challenging her scientific principles and pushing the boundaries of her understanding. She had always prided herself on her ability to dissect and rationalise, but Jenny's presence defied simple explanations. As the early morning light began to filter through the clouds, Mel resolved to seek clarity, to dig deeper into the mysteries that now surrounded her. Her curiosity was piqued, and despite the drizzle, a spark of determination ignited within her. She would find the answers, no matter how elusive they seemed, because that was who she was—a seeker of truth in a world often shrouded in ambiguity.

On her bed was a notebook with attempts to rationalise the crashing of a huge double-decker and try to find reasons for this unlikely scenario. Jenny seemed to believe that the crash was inevitable and that three would die and others would be badly injured, including possibly Mel herself. Would this indeed be her own last few days on earth? Swilling her mouth out, she looked in the mirror and saw a sense of fear in her own eyes, yet she trusted Jenny. If the older woman was willing to risk her life to save one person, then she would stand by her. This would take some planning, yet both women were unsure how to proceed.

Mel tried hard to remember items from the newspaper which Jenny had shared with her. Apart from the obvious front page, Mel remembered an item about a church hall fire. She checked last week's Gazette and, looking through, found a small item inviting crafters to get a stall in the upcoming Craft Fair in the church hall. There was a number to ring to reserve a place.

Picking up her mobile, she rang the number.

'Hello, I wonder if you have any spaces left for a stall at the craft fair,' Mel enquired.

An apologetic voice replied. 'I'm very sorry but we have had to cancel the fair, there was a fire in the church hall kitchen last night, an electrical fault apparently, but we hope to be able to hold the fair next month, all being well. Should I put your name down for a stall?'

Mel was stunned and mumbled a vague reply before switching off the mobile. So, Jenny was right; she could not possibly have known about the fire and had a hoax newspaper printed. The only answer lay in the fact that Mel now had proof, solid concrete proof that Jenny was indeed a traveller in time. This confirmation was welcome but also frightening, and Mel felt a little sick as she realised the enormity of what Jenny had claimed and had been proven right.

Later that day, Mel had arranged to meet Jenny at the motel overlooking the cricket ground, and she determined to ask for more details about everyday life in 2056. She would be 62 and would love to have the reassurance that life would be good, safe and secure for older people as she would be, if she survived the dreaded bus journey on Thursday.

As she prepared to meet Jenny, Mel's mind raced with a mix of fear and fascination about the future that lay both ahead and within the grasp of the enigmatic woman she was about to see. She couldn't shake the unease that came with the knowledge she now possessed, yet the allure of understanding what lay beyond her current reality was too compelling to ignore. She hoped that their conversation would shed light on the mysteries still clouding her thoughts, offering insights into a world that seemed both distant and imminent. The motel's unassuming façade belied the gravity of their impending discussion, and as she approached, Mel felt a renewed sense of determination. Perhaps, by unravelling these secrets, she could find a way to alter the course of events, ensuring that she, and perhaps others, would not fall prey to the ominous predictions that had cast a shadow over her present.

As she entered the dimly lit motel lobby, the weight of her newfound knowledge pressed heavily on her shoulders. The air was thick with anticipation, and every step towards Jenny's room seemed to echo the gravity of the revelations that awaited her. Mel's heart pounded in her chest as she knocked on the door with its slightly crooked number seventeen, her mind a whirlwind of questions and apprehensions. When Jenny opened the door, her calm demeanour did little to ease Mel's anxiety, but the warmth in her eyes held a promise of answers. They sat down, the room's familiarity contrasting sharply with the extraordinary conversation that was about to unfold. Mel took a deep breath, ready to plunge into the depths of future realities and the secrets that had the power to change everything. The silence between them was thick, laden with the weight of unspoken truths, and as Mel began to voice her questions, she felt a surge of courage fuelled by the determination to understand and perhaps, alter the fate that lay before her.

Jenny noticed that Mel appeared troubled and suggested coffee across the courtyard in the pub.

'It should be quiet at this time, and we can talk without being overheard'

As usual, Mel felt more relaxed in Jenny's presence and agreed on coffee.

'Do you think that you can bring along your future copy of the Thornbury Gazette? I need to check something.'

'Of course, I'll just get my bag, will I need a coat?'

'No, it's just a little drizzle in the air and it's only across the courtyard.'

As they strolled across the courtyard through the soft drizzle, Mel's mind raced with questions about the future, the crash, and the eerie accuracy of Jenny's prophecies. Inside the cosy warmth of the pub, the quiet ambience seemed to cocoon them from the outside world. Jenny's presence, as always, brought a strange comfort, grounding Mel's swirling thoughts. Over steaming mugs of coffee, Mel felt her resolve harden, ready to delve into the mysteries that Jenny held. She needed answers, not just for her peace of mind, but to avert the looming disaster, possibly. Jenny, perceptive as ever, sensed the urgency in Mel's eyes and prepared herself to share more than she ever had before. The bond between them, forged in the crucible of shared secrets and impending danger, strengthened as they faced the unknown together, but there were questions to be asked, and plans made.

The clinking of cups punctuated their conversation as Mel, driven by a mixture of dread and urgency, began to articulate her questions about the looming bus crash, the nature of time travel, and the implications of knowing the future. Jenny listened intently, her expression gravely serious yet reassuring, as she began to unravel the intricate web of time, fate, and their roles within it. She explained how each action in the present could ripple through the timeline, altering future events in ways both minor and monumental. With every word, Mel felt the fog of uncertainty lift slightly, replaced by a clearer understanding of the stakes and the power she held to influence outcomes. They discussed potential strategies, weighing the risks and benefits of each possible move, their minds working in tandem to outwit the seemingly inevitable calamity. The quiet pub, with its cozy ambience, became a war room where plans were forged and destinies contemplated, and as they plotted their next steps, a steely resolve settled over Mel. She knew that the path ahead would be fraught with peril, but with Jenny by her side, the future felt just a bit less daunting.

Chapter Twenty-Four: Stage Whispers and Bittersweet Memories

Taras Marchenko always woke early, and as usual, his thoughts went to his native Kiev, war-torn and shattered by invading Russians. He wondered about their apartment, the home he and Olena had worked hard to buy and furnish. It was a home fit to bring up children, his children, and it may now be a pile of rubble punctuated by their belongings, those they could not pack to bring to England with them.

His thoughts turned to his beloved wife, Olena, sleeping peacefully at his side. Taras felt blessed to have won her love, and when they had their two girls, he could not imagine that life could get any better. Perhaps a son to grow strong and play for his team, Dynamo Kiev, but perhaps that was being greedy. The children Sofia and Mila were perfect in his eyes, and he loved listening to Olena reading to them as they prepared for the sleep of the innocent.

His thoughts of Olena made him wonder whether she would appreciate being awoken with a gentle kiss by an amorous husband. These pleasant thoughts were disturbed by voices from down the corridor, an angry, loud whispering female voice and her defensive, reasonable husband.

Taras liked John but was wary of the strident Amanda. Olena stirred and smiled up at Taras, reaching for her morning kiss. He loved the natural motherly smell of her in the morning, and his thoughts returned fully to his gorgeous wife, voices ignored.

At that moment, the door opened, and a sleepy Sofia entered and began to climb onto her parents' bed, determined to get in between and claim her share of the warmth.

'Why is Amanda cross with John? They woke me up.'

Taras gently ruffled Sofia's hair, his heart swelling with love and a tinge of concern.

'Amanda and John are working through something, sweetheart. Don't worry about it,' he whispered, trying to shield his daughter from the adult complexities that often disrupted their peace. Olena, ever the comforting presence, wrapped her arms around Sofia, pulling her into their warm embrace. Taras cherished these tender moments, fleeting reminders of the family harmony they had fought to preserve despite the chaos that loomed outside their sanctuary. He glanced at Olena, her eyes a well of understanding as she realised that his early morning plan for her had been thwarted. She was just contemplating returning Sofia to her own bed when a sleepy-eyed four-year-old Mila entered holding her teddy protectively to herself.

'I think someone has wet my bed, it may have been Teddy, I think?

Down the corridor, John tried to quieten his wife, but she was in full angry flow and difficult to appease when in this mood.

'Are you kidding me? We've both got to go to this review in Bristol? I have a hairdresser's appointment, why does it need both of us to go?'

Olena sat up, her eyes now holding a mixture of concern and curiosity. Down the hall, Amanda's voice grew louder, the tension palpable even through the closed door. Taras exchanged a knowing look with Olena and sighed, feeling the weight of their tumultuous reality pressing down on him. He kissed her forehead softly, his silent vow to protect their fragile haven from the encroaching turmoil. Meanwhile, John's attempts to calm Amanda seemed futile, the argument escalating over the importance of their review trip to Bristol, her words sharp and unyielding.

Olena left the warmth of an increasingly crowded bed and took Mila to find fresh pyjamas for her. A suspiciously wet teddy was placed on the nearby radiator.

Taras, now alone with Sofia, tried to divert her attention with stories of brave knights and enchanted forests, their laughter mingling with the morning light that filtered through the curtains. He glanced at the clock, aware that the day held its own set of challenges and duties. The argument between Amanda and John continued to echo through the hallway, a stark reminder of the fragility of their current peace. Yet, in that moment, surrounded by the warmth and love of his family, Taras allowed himself a brief reprieve, determined to face whatever came next with the resilience and hope that had brought them this far.

Amanda was now in full flow and did not care that their Ukrainian guests would certainly hear her raised voice. The full frustration of the last few years with their constant cancer-driven hospital appointments and John's spectacular loss of sexual desire was unleashed.

'Please, Amanda, you'll be frightening the girls.' John pleaded, despising Amanda's lack of dignity and control.

'That's all you ever seem to think about, those little girls, it's not healthy, not when you ignore me. When was the last time you held me? And another thing I have seen you glancing at their mother, why are you interested in her and not me? I'm your wife for God's sake, or is it because she is young and pretty with a slightly firmer body than mine?'

John was genuinely shocked and sat down heavily on the bed. The last three years had been filled with tablets, pain and injections, yet through it all, he had understood Amanda's undeniable frustrations, or thought he had. The level of venom was frightening. he had loved having children in the house, and he liked both Taras and Olena, but he had no sexual interest in the young Ukrainian woman any more than he had for any woman. The cost of his battle against cancer was the severe reduction in testosterone, which fed the cancer. This was so unfair.

Amanda sat at her dressing table and began to brush her hair angrily.

'I will go with you on the bus on Thursday, but I bloody well won't go to your precious review, I will be going shopping'

John tried to muster the strength to respond but found himself overwhelmed by the weight of their shared burdens and the intensity of Amanda's outburst. The atmosphere in the house grew even more strained as the echoes of their argument seemed to seep into every corner, threatening to disturb the fragile peace that Taras and Olena cherished. As Amanda stormed out of the room, John was left alone to grapple with his thoughts, his heart heavy with the realisation that the road ahead would be fraught with emotional and physical difficulties, not just for him and Amanda, but for everyone.

In Thornbury, Rosangel Chlebek went through her well-worn routine of preparing the children for school and herself for her shift in the A&E department at the hospital. Billy and Evie were lively and eager for school, where they had a large group of friends. Billy was hoping to play cricket for the school, and his Indian father, Sachin, was keen for him to learn the dark art of spinning the ball to bamboozle batsmen. Evie loved art and creativity and was looking forward to her art lesson later that day.

As Rosangel prepared the children's packed lunch, watching her husband, Sachin, playing cricket for Thornbury brought back memories of her own last cricket match at school in Newhill in Derbyshire. It was the Mullins cup final and a glorious, unexpected victory. She recalled with a deep sigh her special friends in the team that day. A team which included her two brothers, Sam and Mikolaj, her best friend Grace, and the captain, her first love, Billy Shakespeare, the diminutive West Indian Brummie. Her memory of that day was clear, and she remembered each run, each catch and every wicket, but foremost she remembered Billy's whispered declaration of love in the middle of the pitch. Those magical words were stored in her mind in a section never to be shared. She wondered how Little Billy, as he was often called, would get on with her husband, Sachin. Their shared love of cricket and Rosie herself meant that they would have a lot in common, but they were destined never to meet. A fatal car crash for Billy and his wife had ended any possibility of that unlikely meeting.

As Rosangel finished preparing the lunches, she reflected on the intertwining lives and destinies shaped by love, loss, and unspoken dreams, her heart heavy with memories yet hopeful for the future. She kissed Billy and Evie goodbye, their laughter echoing through the house, a beacon of light amidst the shadows of past sorrows. Perhaps with the unlikely possession of H.G. Wells' time machine, she could go back and save Billy Shakespeare, but this was sadly impossible. The world needed funny, lively and loyal characters such as the Ason Villa supporting cricket lovers. He was her first love and would always retain that magical place in her heart.

Sachin had gone to work earlier, and Rosie remembered with love her first meeting with the tall, handsome doctor from Mumbai. Rosangel considered a late cup of tea but, glancing at her watch, decided that it was time for her to go to work. Memories, she decided, were bittersweet sometimes to be relished at other times to be deeply hidden, but Rosangel was a pragmatist, and she pondered on her blessings. Her family, including Sachin and their two children, was special to her, while her family in Derbyshire was always in her heart. Her job working at what she considered the sharp end of the NHS suited her perfectly. She would often return home with stories of minor triumphs where she had made a difference, but sometimes her very capable expertise was too late, and emergency patients were lost. Then came the horrifyingly difficult job of informing family of the loss of a loved one, often in sudden, tragic circumstances, but Rosangel had done this too many times. Her calm, patient, professional manner was appreciated by the grieving, tearful families, later if not at the time. Staff at the department were always glad of Rosangel's leadership when on duty and were relieved that she took the dreadful burden on herself.

As the young doctor drove through Thornbury away from the historic castle where Henry V111 had famously sheltered from the London plagues with his wife, Ann Boleyn, the sun shone, promising a fine summer's day. Rosangel passed the bus stop and glanced at the varied group waiting for the bus. She recognised Madison, the would-be writer whom she had met at the cricket match. She waved but realised that Madison was not looking, not recognising the car. Having seen the schoolgirl and the way in which her delightful dog had charmed her children, she wondered if a puppy would be a sensible choice at the moment. Work and school left the house empty all day, so the answer was probably not at this time, but a puppy was very tempting.

Madison Marsden had been deep in thought at the bus stop and was unaware of cars, with or without waving drivers. The transfer to a secondary school in Bradley Stoke had been largely successful, yet it meant a daily bus journey twice a day. It was often a good time to get out her notebook and study fellow passengers, some of whom she recognised as regulars on the T1 to Bristol. But this particular morning, she was deep in thought; the end of term was approaching fast, and the question of what to do in the summer filled her mind.

As the bus drew nearer, Madison's thoughts wandered to her burgeoning passion for writing, a craft she nurtured quietly, often finding inspiration in the mundane moments of her daily commute. Each passenger had a story, a hidden fragment of humanity that she longed to capture with the stroke of her pen. The anticipation of the summer break brought with it a whirlwind of possibilities and the promise of uninterrupted time to delve deeper into her characters' lives. She could almost feel the weight of the notebook in her bag, beckoning her to jot down the next idea, the next scene, the next piece of the puzzle. A visit to

Bromley to visit friends would be welcome, but painful after the death of her grandfather, who had so encouraged her writing. A few days meeting her Polish friends there was on her definite list, and she would have liked to travel to Europe, possibly on a rail pass, but was wary of doing this alone. Although she had no special friend since Poppy had been whisked away to another school to be away from Madison's unwelcome influence, there were a few loose friendships, both male and female, but not strong enough bonds to travel abroad with.

As the bus arrived, Madison stepped aboard and smiled at the bus driver whilst putting her bus pass on the electronic reader. Frank Nelson exchanged morning greetings with the tall schoolgirl with a mass of tangled curly hair, recognising her as a morning regular. Both Maddie and Frank would have been surprised to learn that the other was planning a career in writing. One of the many coincidences of life is never to be discovered. Maddie took her usual seat upstairs but didn't get out her notebook; instead, she used her time to plan her summer activities. She yearned for a special friend to share her thoughts and travels with, preferably female, but this was highly unlikely considering how near the end of the term was.

Chapter Twenty-Five: Que Sera, Sera

The words of the old Doris Day song from 1956, followed by the translation, whatever will be will be, the future's not ours to see came unexpectedly into Mel Chandoo's mind as she sat with what she now believed to be an actual time traveller. Perhaps she now had access to the future in a way that Doris Day could never envisage.

The two women now looked at each other in a new light after their coffee arrived at The Ship Inn.

'You look tired, have you had dreams that kept you awake?' Jenny asked, concerned yet intrigued by the idea of someone being able to dream about the future in an accurate way. There were dark shadows under Mel's eyes, and it was obvious that she had not enjoyed a long night's sleep.

'After Thursday, I may not need sleep; it may be the ultimate long sleep for me.'

This devastatingly simple but harsh statement threw a dark and unwelcome shadow over their meeting.

'You don't have to catch the bus on Thursday, there is an eight to one chance that you are not the one I have to save, and if it is you, then my mission is accomplished, and I can go home,' Jenny replied.

'But an almost fifty per cent chance of being killed. Anyway, how could I sit at work all day wondering and waiting for news? I am 100% convinced that you are truly from 2056, and I will take my chances. Anyway, I feel privileged to have you share your information about being an interventionalist and want to do as much as possible to help. There is one condition, though, well two really.'

Jenny felt the burden of her task lighten with the support of this remarkable woman.

'And what are they, I hope it's not a request for Saturday's national Lottery tickets.' Both smiled, and the shadow eased but remained.

Mel looked down almost sheepishly, 'Can I call you a time traveller, it seems so much more Jules Verne or HG Wells than a clinically sounding interventionalist, although I can never tell anyone about all this even if I survive.'

Jenny laughed and took another sip of coffee. This was a woman she would like as a friend; perhaps she could seek her out in 2056 if circumstances allowed. Jenny was actually two years younger than Mel, although she had returned to 2024 as a sixty-year-old.

'And what is the other condition, if I say yes to being a Doctor Who character?'

'I have written a long letter to my parents if I am one of the three victims on Thursday, don't worry, I haven't mentioned time travel, they would think me insane. I just wanted them to know how much I love them. Could you deliver it for me?' Mel's voice trailed away, and she reached for a tissue to dab away the inevitable misty eyes.

Jenny put her hand on Mel's arm and looked her directly in the face. 'You are being incredibly brave, and I really appreciate your support. Being a time traveller can be lonely.'

'How can you stand this power of overwhelming knowledge? Mel asked.'

Jenny thought for a moment before replying. 'It is incredibly hard, but at the end of each intervention, I have the knowledge that I have changed the world, the future world, for the better, even if in a small way. This is probably my last time travelling adventure, and I will admit that I will enjoy the quiet life with my dogs and my knitting for my grandchildren. I am currently making a quilt for each of them, and it's bloody hard, I can tell you. it makes Thursday's task seem easy. But you haven't told me about your other condition for continuing.'

Mel laughed at the thought of a time traveller wrestling with the construction of three quilts

'I realise that you cannot let me know anything about the future, or at least anything which would mean that I could make a fortune, the results of the Grand National or football results, for instance. But how is life different in 2056?'

Jenny quickly ordered her thoughts, filtering information which could be dangerous to Mel or overpowering with too much knowledge.

'Well, I suppose looking back, the main item would have to be the rapid spread of artificial intelligence, which influenced all aspects of life and meant major changes in the way we perceived work. It streamlined so much in the same way as the everyday use of the internet and household computers, we couldn't imagine how much we would rely on the computer for information, thirty years ago. Of course, there were downsides to social media, but it has allowed families living apart to easily keep in touch.'

Jenny went on, 'Devastating climate change had an incredible impact, although some continued to deny its existence, but then some believe in a flat earth or in Millwall winning the FA Cup. The melting of the polar icecaps accelerated, and flooding around the world meant major shifts in population. Rise in temperatures brought about spectacular increases in intolerable heat to already hot arid countries, especially in sub-Saharan Africa, but then these changes could probably be predicted in 2024. Sea defences had to be massively reinforced at a huge cost, and the East coast of England is under constant threat. But these are predictable, you could probably work these out for yourself, but I will give you a small piece of information as a symbol of the trust I am placing in your hands.'

Mel felt a slight tremor in her stomach and wondered what she was about to be told. She was, however, determined to keep it secret and ignore any possibility of making a fortune from her knowledge.

Jenny paused and took a last sip of coffee to order her thoughts. Was this a wise thing to do? She was handing Mel information which could affect the present and possibly even cause a butterfly effect. Her remit was to remain anonymous and change things as little as possible. Anything she altered could ripple outwards and cause incredible change in the future.

'Do you know that in 1945 the Americans had planned to drop their second atomic bomb on Kokura?' Jenny said quietly. 'But unexpected cloud cover sent the American bomber to an alternative, Nagasaki, at the last minute, the butterfly effect as tens of thousands died, and the doomed in the original target were saved was unrecorded but immense.'

'I didn't know that, of course, I knew that Hiroshima and then Nagasaki were devastated by the only two atomic bombs used in war. So that simple change of the second target due to cloud cover changed the lives and future generations of so many in both poor, sad cities.'

'Of course, we will never know the real impact of that one butterfly effect. Who knows how many engineers, inventors, writers, teachers and world leaders were saved that day? That change had an impact beyond thought. By comparison, my interventions are probably very minor but still capable of world change. Imagine if I had been able to prevent Abraham Lincoln from going to the Ford theatre that night when he was assassinated, or if Genghis Khan had been killed by his enemies as a young man. Millions of men can allegedly trace their DNA back to the Mongol warlord, mainly in Mongolia and Asia, of course. Not that we are capable of going back so far, but it isn't too much of a stretch from a limit of around 30 years to about 160 years in Lincoln's case.

'Wow, this is almost too big to take in, it's like wondering about the edge of the universe, human minds are not capable of such thoughts on such a scale.' Mel pondered.

Jenny knew of the tactical nuclear strike on Kiev in the Ukrainian war in the near future but wisely kept that awful information to herself.

'So, you see, I cannot divulge much direct information about the future, at least up to 2056 except to say that science works hard to counter the impact of diseases, cancer for instance is finally defeated, AI has meant that food production has become refined, seaweed is a vital source as the basis of food production

Mel exhaled and said that she was so impressed by the knowledge which Jenny held in her head, but she looked back thirty years and noted the leaps which humanity had made with technology and science. When the Wright brothers first flew a short distance at Kittiwake in 1903, less than seventy years went by before the first flight of the supersonic Concorde.

Jenny went on, 'Most homes are smart with interconnective devices and appliances, all designed to make life easier. The house monitors temperature, air quality, our health and light and automatically adjusts. People have access to smart glasses, and many have chips implanted under the skin on their hands to pay for goods with a simple swipe. Electric driverless cars are becoming common despite the collapse of Tesla in the late thirties.

Jenny was in full flow but had to rein in her enthusiasm as she shared knowledge with her new friend.

'I will give you a clue as to the next American president after Donald Trump. He wanted a third term, but ill health ended that particular dream. I won't say any names, but a Democrat from Oregon came from nowhere, an unknown in 2024, but his rise was spectacular. He chose a very familiar name as running mate, the daughter of a past president. Their youth and zest were seen as a breath of fresh air following the earlier dark hints of federal corruption and aged leaders.

'How do you sleep at night knowing all this?'

Jenny laughed, 'I have to switch off and remember that all the changes to come are relatively gradual, and I probably sleep better than you with your future predicting dreams, speaking of which, have you had any useful dreams about crashed double deckers recently?'

Mel drank the small amount of coffee remaining in her cup before replying,' No, not about buses, but I have had dreams about babies, but I put that down to wanting to settle down with a family of my own. I am thirty and my biological clock is ticking as they say, quite cruelly to my mind.'

Jenny sighed and thought of her own lovely family, whom she loved so deeply, so near and yet so impossibly far.

'I suppose,' Jenny said, shifting in her seat to get more comfortable, 'I suppose that a simple dream that gave us the answer to our Thursday problem would have been too much to ask for.'

'True, but then I can't order my dreams; they just happen in a random manner, and I have no power to dictate their direction. Until recently, I have kept my dreams to myself. In the seventeenth century, I would probably be put on trial as a witch. I did have one thought which may be useful. You mentioned that I have the option to miss the doomed bus, but I was thinking what would happen if we prevented the other seven passengers from boarding the bus on Thursday, that would eliminate the one whom you were sent to save.'

'We cannot prevent the crash, too many implications for the future generations, not on the scale of Genghis Khan, but nevertheless significant. The three killed may not all be on our list, although at least one is.'

Mel was grim-faced. 'I didn't say that it was a good idea, but we don't seem to be getting anywhere fast, let's go through our eight and place them in order of probability.

The ones with a real chance of making significant change in the future.'

Jenny reached for her trusty sashiko bag and took out a notepad and pen, thinking how old-fashioned they now seemed. Turning to a new page, she wrote 1–8 down the side. 'Let's try it. It can't do any harm.'

Mel was pleased that her idea was not dismissed outright as unhelpful. 'Well, you can certainly put me as number eight. I can't even find a life partner, let alone change the lives of others significantly.'

'It may not be you, but one of your clients, someone you alter their lives and then the butterfly effect kicks in.'

'Unlikely, knowing my current list of patients, but certainly an interesting and thought-provoking idea, there was a chance of me being important for a moment. Just my luck that it may be one of my clients instead.'

Jenny went into businesslike mode and ordered another coffee and two toasted teacakes. 'So, who can we discount, although it may be dangerous, our target may not be obvious, that would be too easy.'

Mel thought for a moment, 'Perhaps the bus driver, Frank Nelson. It is difficult to imagine that he will undergo a career change which could alter the world.'

'OK, I will agree for the moment.' She wrote Frank's name as number seven on the list.

Jenny declared, 'There we have reduced the list by a quarter already. Two more and we will deserve our coffee and teacake, which, I see, is on the way.'

'Well, my name is on the list but only as a ninth person. I can guarantee that TRIPE has not sent me back at a huge cost to save myself.'

Mel smiled, revealing her white teeth, which contrasted beautifully with her light brown skin. 'I had forgotten that you were on the list, so we still have to concentrate on our six left. Who actually came up with the acronym TRIPE?' Bloody awful food by the way'

'It's far easier than saying Time Research Interventions Research (Environmental) every time. I agree that it is a very disagreeable food, but in my future time, it is virtually impossible to get, not that I have tried. But we are straying from our straight and narrow.'

The two women had talked for some time, and the freshly hot coffee was most welcome, and they took a little time to spread the small packets of butter, which never seemed enough to cover the size of the teacake. Jenny resolved not to get on any weighing scales anytime soon.

'I think we should add John and Amanda Buckley to our unlikely list. He is ten years older and a delightful man. I met him watching cricket on the ground nearby. I may be guilty of agism, but I cannot imagine that a pair of pensioners will be the subject of a multi-million-pound intervention. Amanda is only about my age, and I don't think that I have met her, so I'll put John Buckley on the list, but Amanda just above him.

Jenny wrote and was annoyed that her neat list was now adorned with buttery grease marks. She wiped her hands on a napkin and went on. 'Well, that leaves four, and the choices now become more difficult.'

Mel thought that everyone seemed to believe that old age is fifteen years older than themselves, but wisely kept this to herself. Jenny may be in her early sixties, but she certainly seemed younger with her fresh complexion and healthy-looking figure.

'So, who is left? Who can we now discount?' Mel asked.

'Well, we have William Hayes, Madison Marsden, Joy Chen and Rosangel Chlebek.' Joy is a teaching assistant, originally from Hong Kong and a part-time translator for the police when they need a Mandarin speaker.

'So, you have spoken to her, on the T1 bus as I remember, what are your thoughts?' Mel asked, 'We have to be careful not to fall into the trap of being guilty of a stereotypical bias in our approach.' Mel replied, conscious of her clinical and careful training.

'Well, with that warning in mind, I would say that she is a single mum with a delightful toddler, struggling to make ends meet. Of the remaining ones, she would not seem the most obvious, even allowing for non-political correctness, I would put her at number four,' Jenny said, remembering with warmth the delightful toddler revelling in being on the bus with his mother.

'I would agree,' Mel said, and Jenny wrote on the now greasy notepad. 'What about Rosangel Chlebek?'

'Mmm, she is the odd one out as I know that she is a doctor at the Bristol hospital, but she travels to work by car and is not on the bus,' Jenny spoke her thoughts out aloud, trying to make sense of their list.

'As you said, the target person may be one of my clients whom I help, hopefully help, it may be that Rosangel saves your vital person in Accident and Emergency, perhaps after the crash.'

'That leaves William Hayes, who is going for an interview for deputy head at a local primary school on Thursday, and young Madison Marsden. She is young and therefore has the full potential to be almost anything she wants. At the moment her ambition is to be a writer, and it may be that she writes an epic which changes people's lives, but at her age she could change the path she takes.' The two women looked at each other and nodded slightly.

Jenny closed her notebook, 'On the law of probability, Madison is certainly the favourite according to our calculations, but we could be very wrong and I amn't risking putting our efforts into protecting her and finding that we have misjudged.'

'Quite a responsibility being a time traveller with a specific mission. I don't envy you one jot, Jenny,' Mel said in admiration.

'I don't envy myself either, this is definitely my last intervention, the stress is too much, I need a rest.'

Chapter Twenty-Six: Chinese Food and Unexpected Danger

Police Constable Georgina Bratton was not a feminist. More of a pragmatist, really. When she joined the Avon and Somerset Constabulary, her parents were relieved that she was embarking on a career and one that suited her. At school, she was somewhat below average but certainly not in the special needs category. University held no serious attraction for her, and she hated the idea of a safe, secure and probably boring job in an office.

At her passing out parade, her mother had cried with pride but also worry about her little girl doing a hard, dangerous job, sometimes at night when the dregs of criminal society seemed to come to life. Her father had the same worries but didn't cry, well, just a little, but recognised that they would suffer sleepless nights wondering if she was safe at the sharp end of human existence. He had watched his girl grow and could easily see her sense of fairness and justice; she refused to back down if she thought she was right. Her determination, coupled with a body honed by work at the gym, field hockey and occasional half marathons, meant that she could not be seen in any way as a weak and feeble woman. As Shakespeare famously said, 'Though she be little, she be fierce,' not that Georgie Bratton was little, being above average height.

Mr and Mrs Bratton were pleased when Georgie got engaged and began to look forward to the pleasures of grandchildren. Her choice of Gary Wilkinson was certainly approved of; he was well-liked in their household. Unfortunately, he was also in the police force and, therefore, unlikely to persuade their daughter that an office job was an attractive proposition. Gary played rugby, and Georgie contemplated joining the women's team but reckoned that it would be enough for one of them to be battered and bruised each Saturday.

Georgie Bratton was not a feminist but did enjoy the occasional days when the police station played host to any Chinese-speaking suspects. These were the good days, the days to look forward to, not that she would be any use in interviewing Chinese potential criminals; her knowledge was based almost entirely on the menu in her local Chinese takeaway, the Yang Ten in Bedminster.

On those lovely days, Sergeant Ralph Broadhurst would call her to the front desk and declare that there were Chinese suspects to interview, and she was to undertake special duties. Georgie was thrilled but kept a passive face, as she knew that in all likelihood Joy Chen would be travelling by bus to Bristol to translate Chinese into English and vice versa, she knew that the desk sergeant chose her for the job as Joy would often bring her toddler, Chang, into the station if her mother could not fulfil baby-sitting services. Georgie, as a female, would have the task of caring for the young Chang, as Chang's translation skills were of no use in interviews.

Joy and Georgie had met on one of Joy's first excursions into the world of the translator and had quickly formed a friendship. Georgie was often disappointed when Joy's mother provided the babysitting and Chang didn't come in as she and Gary had spoken of marriage and looked forward to being parents, an exciting but daunting thought.

On this particular midweek, Georgie was delighted to see that Chang was with Joy, which meant a couple of hours playing with Chang, hours she was both paid for and safe from potential harm out on the streets. For his part,

Chang was excited to see Georgie and held out his arms to go to her, his lovely oriental face a picture of excitement. This was a baby who loved company, and he knew that his visit to the police station was a positive, lively and playful experience.

'Hello Joy,' Georgie said, 'I see that you have brought me my little criminal to prevent me getting on with the real job of fighting crime.'

Joy grinned and, taking off her toy and snack-laden rucksack, she responded, knowing full well that her friend was teasing and really loved Chang as most people seemed to do.

'He was only sick on your nice uniform once, when you become a mum, yourself, you will learn the warning signs and wear an apron.'

Georgie laughed, completely at ease with Joy's company and friendly banter. She loved the idea of motherhood and felt it was a role she would enjoy. Having a partner made the prospect easier and recognised that life on a low income was hard for her friend, but Chang made up for this; he was a cuddly bundle of delight.

Joy turned down the offer of a cup of tea and went to see the desk sergeant, slightly disappointed that Chang seemed happy to play with Georgie and was not distressed by her departure. She thought that her friend and Gary would make wonderful parents. The other police officers often found an excuse to go to the spare interview room to see the familiar figure of the little boy from Hong Kong and, more latterly, South Gloucestershire. Joy was always welcomed as she herself was a popular visitor and efficient translator.

'What have we got today, Ralph? The usual drug smugglers through Avonmouth docks or illegal immigrants working in car wash establishments'

The burly sergeant with a full beard and a matching full broad Bristolian accent looked up and replied.

'Not this time, Joy. Our lads picked up a chap acting suspiciously near the railway station at Parkway. He hasn't committed any crime that we know of, but his only identification is his passport, which tells us he is Chinese. That's where you come in.'

'So why are you holding him?' Joy asked.

'Who carries their passport around with them, and he is refusing to speak in any language, and there is something about him that concerns me deeply. A disturbing man. You'll understand when I take you to meet him. I've been with the force for more years than I care to remember, but this is a new one on me. My instincts are good, and they are warning me that something is not right.'

'How old is he?' Joy asked, intrigued by Ralph's unease.

'His passport says thirty-two, but of course that may be a false one, seems about right though.'

'And his name is......?

'His passport says,' and here he consulted a red passport, 'Zhang Wei, sorry about the pronunciation, my Chinese is in need of WD40, very rusty.'

'That's interesting.' Joy said, looking at the passport.'

'The fact that my Chinese is not the best?' Ralph enquired with a grin.

'To be honest, your Chinese, Cantonese, or Mandarin doesn't extend beyond Chow Mein or wonton.

Your Bristol English is almost up to average, truth be told. No, his passport name is a very common one, like John Smith in England.'

'Almost a way of hiding a real name if his passport is indeed false. We would have to get the Foreign Office chaps to check it out, but as I say, he has not committed a crime except suspicious loitering and refusing to talk. Hopefully, that will change now that you are here. By the way, you can add sweet and sour pork to my extensive list of Chinese language skills, and furthermore, I speak perfect Brizzle, thank you very much.'

Joy liked the camaraderie and banter in the police station, and she knew the desk sergeant well enough to chat informally and often with humour.

'I know that you are an expert on China, Ralph, but did you know that the Chinese put the surname first and the given name last, so his name is really Wei Zhang, in the western format, if that is indeed his name.'

'So, you are really Chen Joy?'

Joy sighed in an exaggerated way, 'No, when my family moved from Hong Kong to England, my parents decided to become English to integrate fully, so Joy is sort of a nickname. Chen is our family name, so in China, I would be Chen Linjin. There are almost 100 million Wangs in China.'

'Bloody hell, Joy, when I was a lad, it was simple, Christian name then surname, but then I am a little old-fashioned. The Beijing telephone directory must be a sodding nightmare.'

'Only about thirty years out of date Ralph, at least you didn't use the old joke about winging the Wang number.'

The stocky desk sergeant indicated that Joy should follow him to the interview room. He liked the translator and enjoyed her company. Today, he felt he would be glad to have her in the room with the disturbing man from China. At least he had not used the old telephone directory joke, but he was relieved as he had just been about to do exactly that.

Down the Spartan corridor, Cai Yuanyun sat calmly in the interview room with eyes closed and hands clasped on the table. He allowed himself to drift into well-practised zen meditation, assessing his present situation. He concluded that there was no danger to himself or his mission. He still had time to achieve his set goal. The police holding him were merely local and unarmed; there were no charges or evidence against him. He would be released soon; this detainment was merely inconvenient. Nevertheless, he went over his cover story, deliberately in English. His passport forgery was of excellent quality, as was his student visa. The name Zhang Wei brought a slight smile to his lips. It made him virtually anonymous and untraceable. He went over the details which he had learned by heart. He was in England as a student at the University of London on a cultural exchange. His journey by train to Bristol was primarily to visit the sights such as the Clifton Suspension Bridge and the SS Great Britain. In his rucksack were leaflets about the city and the great engineer Isambard Kingdom Brunel. He was confident that his cover story was sound and certainly enough to satisfy very non-threatening local police.

Yuanyun regulated his breathing as he had been taught. It brought him welcome calm and peace.. His name actually meant deep and profound clouds and serenity, but also softness, although Cai Yuanyun was anything but soft. The desk sergeant had assessed him as being in his early thirties, confirmed by his passport. He was dressed in jeans, white trainers, and a green sweatshirt, with a casual jacket hanging on the chair behind him. Despite being of average height and build, he was not a man to argue with.

He looked back at his inauspicious start to life as the child of a Uyghur mother in the northwestern Xinjiang province. The state had decided to redistribute Uyghur babies, and Yuanyun was taken to the city of Wuhan in the Hubei province and granted to a childless family of government economists. These details of his early life were forgotten, only to be unearthed as a teenager. He felt loved by his adopted mother, but his father had reservations about having the child of a persecuted and hated Muslim Uygur in his house. Words were never spoken of his real parents, but Yuanyun felt a coldness which he took as normal, relying on the warmth of his adopted mother's love. All would have been well, but in her old age, his mother had accidentally revealed his background and life, and for Yuanyun, it became suddenly harsh.

At fifteen, he had learned all the xenophobic words of hatred as he was cornered by local youths, some he had known since childhood, and the bitter words were accompanied by blows. Beaten down, bloodied and badly bruised, he swore silently to himself never to be defeated in a fight again, whatever the odds. That day in a muddy alley in Wuhan, he grew hard and mentally strong.

From that day forward, he immersed himself in rigorous physical training and combative arts, embracing the resilience of his Uyghur heritage while mastering the disciplines his adoptive father revered. The years that followed were marked by a relentless pursuit of martial skills.

His father disliked the reflected hate which Yuanyun had inadvertently brought on his family. Despite his wife's tearful protests, the boy had been enrolled in the People's Liberation Army. His determination and quick mind had led to promotion, and he was marked for a good military career. In the skirmishes against India in 2020, by the Pangong Lake in Ladakh, there was agreement that no firearms were used. Fists, batons, iron rods and rocks were the order of the day. It was brutal, and scores were injured or killed. The cold of those days in the Galwan Valley, even in May, cut through to the bone, razor sharp and never to be forgotten.

Whenever his troop wavered, it was Sergeant Cai Yuanyun who rallied the men, standing firm as a rock surrounded by waves of enemy Indian troops. In those harsh, bitter, bruising days, the Western Theatre Command of the PLA saw the meteoric rise of a new leader of men.

A transfer to the elite Snow Leopard Commando counter terrorism unit was inevitable, and he learned of hostage rescue and high-risk arrests. Sniping, explosives and close-quarter combat became part of his trade, and he excelled.

A letter from his father informed him briefly of the death of his adopted mother, the only one who offered warmth and comfort in a harsh world. He had sighed deeply but didn't reply to the letter or go back to Wuhan again. Revenge against the bullies of his youth would have been gratifying and easy, but without real purpose, and he was task-driven. He was now an agent of the state, a well-trained arrow to be hurled without mercy against the enemies of China.

Beijing saw fit to send the newly promoted Shao Xiao, a major, to Hong Kong to infiltrate human rights protestors and anti-China rioters. He created riots, which led to the arrests of Hong Kong citizens, and his English quickly developed. In his mind, he saw his clandestine antiterrorist actions as bringing long-term peace and prosperity, the best response to the capitalist lies of the West.

Eight months in London and Southampton under the guise of a cultural student honed his linguistic skills, and the investment in his future was beginning to pay dividends.

Now, seated under the fluorescent glare of the interview room, Yuanyun's mind was a fortress of unyielding resolve, strengthened by a lifetime of adversities overcome. As the door creaked open, he opened his eyes, ready to face whatever lay ahead with unwavering composure and the hardened spirit of a man forged in the crucible of both early love and racial loathing.

Joy Chen entered the room and said, 'Good Morning, my name is Joy, I will be translating for you today, if you need it. I will be neutral and promise to translate your words accurately without bias. I am not a police officer but a civilian.' This well-used introductory phrase was intended to instil confidence and trust, and she sat down, allowing Ralph to sit opposite the detainee.

It quickly became apparent that Zhang Wei, as they had to call him, was not in need of calm or reassurance. Joy understood what Ralph had warned her of; here was a man who exuded power and strength. He was without fear, knowing full well that he could easily overcome everyone in the police station without breaking a sweat, especially the overweight one in front of him. but he waited patiently for the questions to come.

The interview proved brief as there was nothing more than instinctive suspicion against this man. Joy realised that he understood the English questions and replied in Mandarin in order to conceal his linguistic ability. She translated as she was paid to do, but felt uncomfortable in the small room, glad not to be alone with the stranger.

Later, Joy left with the desk sergeant, both happy to leave the room.

'Well, Joy, what do you think?'

As they walked back to the outer office, Joy gathered her thoughts.

'Well, I'm glad that you warned me. A photograph of him would show an unremarkable young man in his physical prime. Inscrutable and self-confident, but meeting him was totally different. I felt his power and silent threat, and without him saying anything, I wanted to leave his presence as soon as possible.'

''Do you believe his story? Is his passport false?'

'I don't know Ralph, and it's not my job to pass judgment.'

'But your instincts?'

'I would say that he understood your questions and didn't need me to translate, his passport may be real, not my area of expertise, I'm afraid, but I would say that his potential as a danger is immense.'

Ralph sighed, 'I would agree, but I can't arrest a man on potential alone or instincts for that matter. We will have to release him and return his passport. I'll be glad when he is off my patch. I will inform the powers that be about Zhang Wei or whatever his name is, they will no doubt want to keep an eye on him.'

They went through to the interview room where Chang Chen played happily with his friend Georgie and two male police constables who found time from their duties to play with the toddler.

'Have you lot got no work to do, if not I can always find something,' Ralph said gruffly, although he understood the attraction of the smiling, chuckling boy. He wondered at the comparison between the young, delightful Chinese boy and the man sitting down the corridor, waiting to be released.

Later that morning, Cai Yuanyun easily evaded the very amateur policeman in plain clothes sent to follow him. He returned to where he had carefully hidden a small package and, looking around to ensure complete privacy, he took out his beloved QSZ-92 pistol and spare ammunition. Tucking the pistol in the waistband of his jeans behind his back, he pocketed the ammunition, aware that they would not be needed. He smiled as he thought that any potential difficulty in bringing the deadly weapon through British customs had been overcome. Entry into the country had been remarkably easy and most unusual.

Cai Yuanyun was a seasoned time traveller, not here to indulge in a gun battle but to kill quietly and efficiently, as ordered by the Chinese State. Someone on the T1 double-decker to Bristol had to be eliminated, and Yuanyun fully intended to do without mercy.

Chapter Twenty-Seven: Life is a Fast-Closing Oyster

Amanda Buckley seemed to be in a perpetual state of irritation, mainly with her husband John, but more recently with the Ukrainian family staying with them to avoid the ravages of war. She had tried to calm herself by listening to her favourite, most relaxing violin piece, Air on a G string by J.S.Bach. For years, as a teacher of music, she had had to endure the screeching strings of schoolchildren trying to play this prince of instruments. At home, she often played Bach to clear her mind of the desperate efforts of obviously non-musical pupils. Now retired, her calm had been broken by the voices of the two Ukrainian girls, Sofia and the younger Mila.

Going into the lounge, she had found that they had taken her collection of thimbles from the frame display on the wall and were examining them carefully. As Amanda was to say later, they had not caused damage and were certainly not noisy; it was just that it felt like an intrusion on her private life. Their mother, Olena Marchenko, had apologised profusely and helped her daughters restore the well-crafted display unit.

With a thin smile, Amanda had accepted the pretty mother's apology and had said that no damage had been done; the children were careful and considerate. It was just that Olena had what she herself could not have. It wasn't the children; she had long ago decided that pregnancy would be super bad for her figure, which she cherished. Amanda felt the pangs of jealousy as she realised that Olena had what she hadn't had for years now, a handsome, loving and virile husband. Despite her determined, painful to watch, flirting, Taras has shown no interest in any woman other than his beloved Olena.

No, thought Amanda, it was all John's fault. Since the onset of his cancer, he had become old and perpetually exhausted almost overnight. He was, after all, ten years older than his wife, and she hated what he had become, a shambling old man with a stick and a voice like the whine of a lost dog. His lifelong habits were increasingly irritating, and she began to contemplate the freedom of divorce. She considered taking up cooking, the sexy, trendy sort seen on television, not the sausage and chips version which John seemed to prefer. His liberal use of tomato sauce and his putting the toilet roll on the holder the wrong way or wrong to Amanda's mind were just two of the ways he seemed to taunt her. He liked music well enough, but not enough to satisfy Amanda, not that he did anything these days to satisfy her in any way, shape or form.

For his part, John Buckley hid strategically behind the Daily Telegraph, trying not to listen. The online training videos giving copious advice about hosting a Ukrainian family had not mentioned the negative effect on his wife, and he recognised that no matter how hard he tried, she was in a constant state of irritation. A fast-closing emotional oyster refusing to open.

John had had a very pleasant time, reading his paper and looking up occasionally to smile at the two girls whom he had grown to adore as they played with the thimbles. He was planning what to him would probably be the best Christmas ever, with guests and children opening their presents by the Christmas tree. He had done some research and was beginning to order presents for them on a large scale. It would be his one and only opportunity to be part of a real family, and he was determined to enjoy it to the full.

The night before, Taras and Olena had sat up in bed very quietly discussing the open wound tensions between their two hosts. Not that they weren't grateful, it was just that the girls were beginning to notice and were visibly siding with John, their adopted grandfather figure.

'It's too late to change hosts, and that would seem ungrateful. The children are settling well into school, and I am getting more and more work. Perhaps we need a break, and maybe Amanda and John need one too,' Taras said quietly.

'I think it is too late for Amanda, I think she really dislikes John,' Olena said wisely. 'It's so sad really, such a bitter lady, she doesn't know how much she has.'

They tried to speak English even when alone together in order to improve their skills and become more fluent in English. But Olena reverted to her native language when she suggested a visit to their parents in their home city of Kiev. The children would love to see their grandparents, and they could check on the state of their flat. Taras thought this a good idea, and a visit to the doomed city was planned in outline. They were, of course, not aware of the impending catastrophe awaiting the capital city, already bombed and in shock.

At lunch in the driver's room at Bristol bus station, Frank Nelson contemplated his small lunch of a soft pitta bread with corned beef and crisp raw onion, his particular favourite, accompanied by a mug of steaming hot tea, strong enough to stand the spoon up in. The small size of his packed lunch helped his attempt at losing weight and increased his appetite. Lillian had informed him before he left for work that the evening meal would be a steak and kidney pie, chips and peas with a large helping of her special dark, rich gravy. Normally, Frank would have said that life was very good; he was making surprising progress with his attempts at writing and enjoying his new role as a writer, certainly more respectable than his earlier embarrassingly secret desire to perform as a reality television drag queen. This felt somehow cleaner and more respectable. No, life was good for him, and he had contemplated doing the 10k charity walk next week, but that would now be impossible. Frank's new cowboy-style boots, which he loved, were pinching him, and he had a large, painful blister on his left foot. Charity walks were definitely out for the time being.

Across the city, that afternoon, the weather was disappointing; the fine summer had given way to almost autumnal grey skies and drizzle. Mel Chandoo tried to catch up with a backlog of work in her office at the hospital, but she had a large, thumping migraine-like headache, which made her meeting with one of her clients difficult. Two paracetamol and a glass of water did not seem to help. A half-eaten tangerine and a strawberry yoghurt lay on the desk, not very professional, she thought. Tomorrow was the day of days, and she knew that she would be involved in a bus crash, in what might well be a fatality for her. If it was meant to be, it would be, she pondered. It had not been one of her predicting dreams, which told her of this crash, but a lady time traveller from the future. As she thought this, it seemed too ridiculous to be possible, but she trusted Jenny Clutterbuck and was determined to support her and help if she could. Her client asked if she was truly listening to him and threatened to inform her line manager. Mel smiled, impending possible death made legal action threats seem pale and insignificant. Nevertheless, she apologised and tried hard to concentrate on the man's problems. One day, it will be my day, one day, she thought. Perhaps this was to be her last day, and she shivered slightly.

As the clock ticked relentlessly through the afternoon, Mel's headache only seemed to worsen, each throb echoing the relentless stress of her responsibilities and fears.

Meanwhile, Frank, having finished his modest lunch, daydreamed about the comforting dinner Lillian had promised, hoping it would soothe the ache in his foot and the sting of his thwarted old ambitions. After eating, he would take up his notebook and write the character sketches which would become the principal protagonists in his book, 'Murder in the Blitz.'

The city buzzed on, indifferent to residents' struggles, as life moved inexorably forward. Mel, despite the premonition of doom, resolved to face whatever came with a steely determination, though the weight of the impending bus crash lingered ominously in her thoughts. In a different part of the city, Frank sighed, adjusted his boots, and wondered if he could somehow salvage his pride and enter that charity walk, despite the odds. Both, in their separate worlds, braced themselves for the unknown challenges that tomorrow would surely bring.

In Thornbury, at the end of the school day, the roaring noise of pupils happy to be released into the community echoed slowly away. Joy Chen, teaching assistant and part-time translator, completed the task of tidying away the recently used science equipment whilst the teacher marked the resultant experiment results.

'Phone call for you, Joy, in the office,' Alice, the school secretary, called, popping her head into the classroom.

'Did they say who it is?' Joy asked, looking up.

'I think he said Ralph, but he had the broadest Bristol accent that I have ever heard.'

Joy laughed, 'That'll be Ralph Broadhurst, I would imagine, desk sergeant at Bristol police station. Probably another translating job.' As she left to go quickly to the phone in the office, Alice and the class teacher exchanged wry glances. Another day at the police station meant that Joy would again be unavailable for work the next day, and she was a valued staff member who was not easily replaced.

Walking briskly along the fast-cooling corridor, Joy's mind was full. A day in Bristol assisting the police interview Chinese suspects meant a day without school pay. This was offset by payment for her translation duties, but being away from school too often did little to enhance her credit. She would have to see the head immediately, so a cover for her could be arranged at short notice.

Of course, it may not be a request for her translating skills; it may be an update on the disturbing man she had helped interview recently. The thought of him being free to roam at will in the area was very worrying. He had not said or done anything remotely threatening, but nevertheless, she felt very uneasy. Joy hoped that she would not be called upon to be with him again in that room, empty of all but a table and four chairs. There was something about him which Joy could not easily define. It was certainly powerful, like a relaxed, coiled spring with dangerous capabilities.

Looking back, she thought that she had given him her name as simply Joy; if so, she was untraceable, he could not possibly find her, but this was ludicrous. Why on earth should this man seek her out? All she had done was provide an honest translation. But the glance at her when they first met would remain with her for a long time, or so she thought.

A more immediate problem would be her son, Chang. Her mother usually looked after the boy whilst she was at school, but Mum had shown signs of a heavy cold. No good for her and certainly not for Chang. Joy would have to make short-term arrangements for Chang tomorrow, and another bus journey to Bristol would be necessary. Even if Joy was not called in to translate, hopefully for more ordinary criminals, she may well have to arrange for

Chang to be looked after anyway. Life was so complicated, especially for single mothers. It may be better to turn down the work at the police station.

'Hello, Ralph, this is Joy. What can I do for you?'

'How did you know it was me?' Ralph said in a thick Brizzle accent which you could cut with a blunt knife.

'Put it down to my developing detective skills, is it another job for me?'

'Yes, it's tomorrow, I'm afraid, a couple of potential drug smugglers need a fair translator. And you are the best we have.'

Joy wavered, deliberately ignoring the obvious over-the-top compliment. This was the moment to say no, at least it wasn't the previous interviewee. She decided, a small decision which was to alter everything, not that she knew it at the time.

'I'll be in tomorrow first thing, Ralph, but I'll have to bring Chang with me, my mother is ill.'

'Georgie and the lads will be gutted, that boy slows work rate down dramatically.' He knew that Georgie loved playing with the small Chinese boy, but it did take her off the roster for a time. He supposed that she and her husband would soon be producing a baby of their own; it was obvious what she wanted and deserved.

'That will be fine, Joy, we can always lock him in a cell for the morning. Hope your mother isn't too bad.'

'Just a heavy summer cold, this rain hasn't helped. I'll see you in the morning, put the kettle on.'

The desk sergeant laughed, 'It's never off Joy, we run on tea and custard creams of course.'

Putting down the phone, Joy went to see the head to explain her latest absence. She sighed, not looking forward to this. Perhaps the time had come to start saying no to the increasing police requests. She yearned to be accepted for herself and not as a diversity symbol or mouthpiece of Chinese criminals.

Joy tried hard to integrate, but she had faced racial dislike, not to mention hatred. Not often, but enough. Every rejection was a building block of hatred to be smashed through. She worried that Chang, too, would have to face unwarranted discrimination in his life because he was obviously different. Yet everyone he met loved the happy, chuckling boy.

Chapter Twenty-Eight: 'A Beauteous Evening, Calm and Free'

Will Hayes was busy in the kitchen preparing an evening meal for his new girlfriend. The phrase seemed somehow old-fashioned, but he liked the sound of it. He made liberal use of the microwave, skills from his lonely pre-Abbie days. He warmed the plates and took a bottle of white wine from the fridge, and placed two glasses on the table.

'Anything I can do?' Abbie Thompson asked, looking round the flat. It was a man's flat and would need a woman's touch. Not too quickly, but change had to come about.

'Dinner will be ready in two minutes or an hour if it's not successful and we have to bring in a pizza.'

'I'm sure it will be fine, what are the wooden figures by the way, they look oriental, Chinese?'

'No, I have a small collection of netsuke, Japanese,' he replied.

'They are beautiful, so smooth and wonderfully carved; do they have a purpose?'

'Once they were part of a Japanese traditional costume, today they are more valued as sculptures. The authentic ones cost hundreds of pounds. Mine are mainly reproductions, but I do like them.'

'So do I, they are so tactile, everything the Japanese do seems to be aimed at perfection.'

'Come and sit up, I hope this is OK for you, I've done peaches and ice cream for afters.'

Abbie smiled to herself, sometimes Will's Sheffield background came out in his use of certain words. Dessert was not part of his South Yorkshire vocabulary. As Abbie sat, she deemed herself lucky to be here with the man she had grown to love, and discovering all about him was part of their developing relationship. She took a forkful of carefully wound spaghetti and declared it to be wonderful.

'What are those framed programmes on the wall?'

'Sadly, I collect football programmes or rather did. The one on the left is the famous 1953 cup final, the Matthews final. Blackpool were 3-1 down to Bolton

Wanderers and came back to win 4-3. It was forever known as the Matthews final, but his teammate, who actually scored three goals, and the full-back marking Stan Matthews were limping. Ironic really. It's the most valuable programme I have.'

'Fascinating,' Abbie smiled as she lied. 'What about the other one, it looks quite crumpled.'

'My dad gave that to me before he died; it's a family heirloom. The cup final of 1966, at half time our team, Sheffield Wednesday, were winning 2-0 and Dad said he wished time could have stopped right then and he would have gone to heaven quite happy.'

'And in the second half?'

'Dad said Everton got three very lucky goals, and we lost. Of course, if time had stood still that May day, we would never have seen England win the World Cup two months later, and I wouldn't have been born.'

'So, you got on well with your parents?'

Will thought for a moment, 'Yes, I suppose I did. Dad was a miner and Mum a dentist's receptionist, but both have sadly passed away now. I still miss them and think that I let them down in so many ways, I was never a winner, I felt eternally average, never achieving much special. Dad would have loved me to play for Sheffield Wednesday, but I was always mediocre at best. I always joked that I was so bad at football that I was qualified to play for them.'

'Well, tomorrow will change all that, you're going to become a deputy head and a fine one at that, and after that, who knows?'

At that moment, Will decided that he loved this girl and wanted to walk through life with her by his side. His long and lonely days collecting football programmes and netsuke were over, and his heart soared. He was confident that the interview at Hust Green with the head, Curtis Warren and governors would go well, but his track record was not good; anything could go wrong and usually did.

Will would have preferred some time to prepare for his interview in the morning, but having Abbie here relaxed his mind. The worry about his car's gearbox was moved to the back of his mind.

They finished their main course and decided to eat their peaches and cream in the comfort of the lounge. When they had finished, Abbie went to take the dishes into the kitchen, but Will stopped her.

'Leave those, Abbie, we can wash up later, I need to talk to you, seriously.'

They sat close together on the sofa, and a shadow of worry passed over Abbie's mind. Was he ending their new relationship and sweetening it with peaches and ice cream?

They snuggled close. Surely, this was not the action of a man trying to get rid of her.

'Abbie, have you done much travelling abroad, I mean?'

'I've been to France and on a school trip to Holland, but I've never really had enough money to contemplate much travelling, why do you ask?'

'Well, I was thinking, hopefully tomorrow will go well, and I will move onto a higher pay grade, and I have some savings set aside. It's too late for this summer, but I was thinking that we could go to Japan together,' Will said tentatively.

He went on about brochures and tours he had researched, but she didn't hear him; her heart was full. This was far from a rejection.

'Perhaps this summer we could go to Italy; we could arrange that quite last minute. I've always fancied Pompeii and Herculaneum. That would leave plenty of time to arrange a trip to Japan. Sometimes the best bit of a holiday is doing the research beforehand. I've looked it up and we can organise a rail pass on their incredible trains and stay at traditional Japanese inns. We would be travelling alone, but it would be an adventure. We can even wear kimonos and everything, if you don't mind that, is.'

'My answer is a resounding yes to both trips, this is so exciting.'

'There is a third question, best of three, so to speak.'

'What is it, Will?'

'Would you marry me if I asked. I don't want to ask if you would say no, we could still go to Italy and Japan, even if you say no, it's not blackmail or anything.'

'You don't have to ask, I would say yes and yes and yes,' Abbie leaned into Will and kissed him hard and fiercely before standing.

Will was slightly puzzled at her unexpected move. Was she intending to wash up now, at this special moment?

'Time for bed, Mr Hayes, deputy head in waiting.'

'But it's only half past eight, and what about the dishes?'

'Bugger the dishes,' she said firmly leading him towards the bedroom by the hand.

'Oh, I see,' he said, feeling somewhat dim.

In Thornbury, Doctor Rosangel Chlebek handed her husband, Sachin, a glass of red wine. Both had had a good but full day at work. Sachin was working on cancer research and felt positive about the latest test results. Rosie had had a successful day stitching wounds and setting broken limbs, routine but satisfying, especially where children were involved. Her motto was to be bold, decisive and brave in her decision-making. Always take action today.

They settled down with their wine, listening to gentle, calming orchestral music; 'Lark Ascending' was a particular favourite.

Rosangel began. 'I was thinking...'

'Always a dangerous sign, my darling, but do go on,' he grinned, adoring his wonderful Polish wife. He felt blessed to have met and married her.

'To continue,' she said firmly, 'I was thinking of a trip to Newhill to see my parents. I haven't actually seen Dad since he was elected MP in the landslide by-election. When he goes to the House of Commons, I will go to the visitors' gallery and hold up my Polish flag. I know he will like that. I gave him one before, after we had won the cricket cup final at school.'

'We must make a family trip of it, the kids will love seeing grandparents again, it's been too long,' Sachin agreed.

Rosangel sighed. The cemetery in the old churchyard in the small Derbyshire town held so many memories for her, and she knew that she would need several bunches of flowers to lay on graves, not least Little Billy Shakespeare, her first and abiding love.

Sachin saw how much it would mean to his wife, 'Of course we must go, to Newhill and the House of Commons, I'll hold up a Polish flag myself, but there is one condition.'

'Does it mean a reprieve from washing up for a year?'

'No, nothing like that, although now you mention it, that does seem an excellent idea. No, I was thinking of a trip to Mumbai and a visit to the Taj Mahal. Would you like that?'

'That sounds wonderful,' Rosangel had visited his parents before on a never-to-be-forgotten trip to that magical country.

'We would have to coordinate school holidays with our work schedules, but it should work. I might even let you off washing up for a week.' Rosangel continued.

The handsome doctor was going grey, and this made him seem even more distinguished.

'Sachin Agarwal, you are definitely my favourite husband so far.'

'I'll settle for that as long as we make it two weeks without washing up.'

'Sachin, you do know we have a dishwasher, don't you?'

'Yes, of course, I think it is one of the white ones in the kitchen, but I'm not sure which.'

Rosangel laughed in easy companionship and began to look forward to seeing her three brothers and parents. She knew Sam and his wife Belle and Mikolaj and the baby of the family, Jacob, would not miss seeing their father in the House of Commons, something he had worked so hard for.

Perhaps the wine and euphoria of planned visits were kicking in, but she asked, 'What do you think of a puppy, Sachin?'

'As a pet or a meal, I personally would prefer a puppy less curry.'

'Don't let the kids hear you for heaven's sake, they would never forgive you.'

'Seriously Rosie, you know that a puppy would be alone most of the day, not good for the animal or furniture for that matter.'

'And what if I were to stay at home with the puppy?'

'What about work, or have you won the National Lottery?'

'I may have to stay at home before too long, maternity leave and all.'

Rosangel laughed as her husband choked on his red wine as he suddenly understood.

'Rosangel, that's wonderful news, the best ever. Can I go and tell the kids about the puppy?

'Don't mention having a baby brother or sister, it's too soon,' she called out, but he was gone, running upstairs full of excitement.

In nearby Church Road, Madison Marsden lay on her bed thinking deeply of the plot lines for her book. Now was the time to make a significant start. Her characters were ready, and the plot was set out. The school holidays would give her time to do several chapters, hopefully more, but she felt that a break was called for, and she began to plan a trip to Bromley to see newly found friends and visit the grave of her recently deceased grandfather, the writer, Daniel Finney. She had only met him recently and quickly formed a wonderful partnership. When his will was announced, he had left a substantial amount to Madison, together with his special fountain pen. He had told her not to be afraid to speak out, be critical where necessary, but praise often. Do at least one good deed a day. That advice was both good and profound, and Madison intended to live by it. She opened her laptop and began to research universities, searching for ones that read English Literature. Her inheritance meant that she would not have to worry about tuition fees and the rest. She could plan her next adventure with confidence. There was, of course, the issue of Rosie, her dog, gifted to her by her grandfather's friend.

University was two years away, but it's best to plan now. Life was beginning to look up after her difficult year.

Lying on her bed in the motel room, Jenny Clutterbuck felt abject, sick to the stomach. She had failed, for the first real time, and she would return to her own time, 2056, not having achieved her goal. This was her last intervention, and Jenny was glad. A cosy life with her grandchildren and dogs seemed appealing, but there was the overall feeling of having failed. On the other hand, how could this intervention have been unsuccessful when she had had those magical few moments of seeing her deceased husband, alive and well, in a Bristol cafe? With every fibre of her body, she had wanted to go to him to hold him and warn him not to go fishing on that fateful day when the treacherous North Sea had claimed him. Her self-discipline and training had prevailed; she could not alter events at her own personal whim, and there was the question of the mysterious, attractive girl sharing his conversation and table.

It had, of course, transpired that they were remote cousins, and both were doing research into family history. Steve had looked across at her without recognition, and this had jolted her emotions. He had not been expecting a much older version of his wife, especially so far from home, and had turned back to his companion. Looking back, Jenny felt so foolish when she had fainted, like a character in a Jane Austen novel, and when she came round, Steve had gone from her forever.

Perhaps just for once, her bosses at TRIPE would have allowed her a brief moment with her husband, but it was not to be.

Jenny touched her watch, checking it for the hundredth time as it was her only link to the future. Without it, she was trapped in the present day. She felt sick and queasy knowing that she had identified most of the people on her prescribed list but failed to identify the one she had been sent to save. The meeting with Mel Chandoo had proved very successful, and Jenny had offered her the chance not to board the doomed double-decker tomorrow, but Mel had refused, wanting to help despite the dangers.

Jenny's parents had run a small B&B on the seafront on the North Bay at Scarborough, untroubled by world events. Perhaps Jenny thought it would be good to retire from time travel and run such a small hotel. But she herself was extremely anxious about world events.

There had been whispers that the Saudis or the Chinese had actually developed a way of sending interventionalists into the future. The implications of this were awesome and in deep need of careful regulation. It may just be rumour, but such Chinese whispers had to begin somewhere. Jenny decided that she could do no more and hoped that she would be overwhelmed by welcome sleep, but knew it was unlikely; her mind was too full of disturbing thoughts.

Tomorrow was the day when all the jigsaw pieces would fall into place, and some would die, perhaps including the one she was sent to save. Failure was awful to contemplate.

Cai Yuanyun had no such reservations; for him, failure was not an option. He had checked into a Holiday Inn Express and stayed there all day with his thoughts, hidden away, ready to be a highly trained missile of the state about to be hurled against the enemies of the Chinese people.

He was a leading member of the Xin Dong Cangku Shijian Tiaozhehg, chosen for his past meteoric rise in the PLA. The New Eastern Depot Time Adjustment was dedicated to ensuring the safety and security of the Chinese people and state. It took its name from the Eastern depot in Beijing, a security arm of the empire run by eunuchs from 1420 to 1644. In those days, spying and espionage were its weapons. The Xin Dong, or New Eastern, as it was called by those few in the know, had the advantage of the newly developed scientific ability to send interventionalists into the future. Chinese know-how and Saudi money, a formidable combination.

As Yuanyun checked his QSZ-92 pistol and all-important watch, he reckoned on an easy kill tomorrow and a return in triumph, having achieved his primary goal.

Time moved slowly, and the Chinese time traveller prepared to sleep, totally unaware of another interventionalist a few miles away suffering the pangs of potential failure. Yuanyun, on the other hand, was confident and resolved to kill as he was ordered to do, without hesitation, question, or mercy, ready for action tomorrow.

Without realising it, he went through the same thought process every night. When he was warm, he remembered the bitter cold of the Galwan valley fighting against India and relished the warmth he now enjoyed. The second thought concerned his second love, his adopted mother, who was the only one who showed him any affection, but he had recently met a young girl, a lecturer at the university, and he responded to her love. Just before sleep took him, he remembered that last sweet kiss before she turned and stepped in front of the tram in Shanghai. It was no one's fault and thankfully instantaneous, but in his deepest grief, Yuanyun swore never to love again.

Tomorrow was a day to kill, not love. And Cai Yanyun of the Xin Dong knew exactly who his target was.

Chapter Twenty-Nine: Footprints on the Sands of Time

Dawn inched its way over the eastern horizon, almost apologetically, bringing rain clouds and a dark streaked sunrise. It was a July Thursday morning, and it should have brought hope, sunshine, and a fast-approaching weekend.

Jenny Clutterbuck had always regarded herself as a morning person; she woke up quickly and, as usual, thought first of her lost husband and her children and grandchildren. But today was different, it certainly felt different as she pondered the myriad of possibilities, all out of her control. She got out of bed and opened the beige curtains to see the rain clouds obscuring what should have been a fine summer's morning.

She put on her precious watch; it was early, far too early for the world to be stirring and certainly for a full English breakfast. Not that she seriously contemplated such a meal, Jenny was nervous, more so than at any time on any of her time-travelling adventures. Today was a day destined for failure, not fried bread, sausage, and scrambled eggs.

She began to prepare a cup of hot, strong coffee in her room, smiling to herself as she remembered one of her young grandsons wanting scrambled eggs for breakfast.

Sitting up in bed with the welcome warming bite of coffee, Jenny's mind went back, a long, long way to her childhood days in Scarborough. Jack Clutterbuck, owner of the small Sea Breeze hotel, was always up early, and he would walk to the harbour to collect cod and Dover sole from the early returning trawlers. His wife Angela would be busy preparing generous breakfasts, and the answer was always in the timing, she would declare. Since she was old enough, Jenny would delight in accompanying her father as he walked past the old castle walls and down the steep, history-laden streets to the harbourside. Jenny loved those special times with her father, and they would hold hands as they talked of all and nothing. Jenny had been pleased that her older brother, Colin, was a night person and had no interest in walking anywhere at such an early hour. This was her special time with her father, and she listened in awe as Jack regaled his daughter with tales of the mighty Yorkshire cricket teams and famous matches of the past in Scarborough. As they passed St Mary's church, he would tell her of the grave of Anne Brontë, the quietest of the three famous Yorkshire writing sisters. Anne had loved Scarborough and moved there believing that the sea air would help her disease-ridden body. Jack told her that Anne had died three days after arriving and had been buried in the churchyard, overlooking the sea, the only one from her family not to be buried in Haworth.

Jenny had thought of the sadness of this death in 1849 and resolved to read one of her books when older, and she did, in remembrance of her father and their early morning walks. The harbour side had always assailed her senses with rain-washed pavements, harsh cries of insistent swirling seagulls and the fresh smell of the sea, seaweed and fish. Wonderful days, yet strangely, she didn't really remember the return walk uphill in the early morning. When you are a child, all walks seemed easy, and you were always skipping downhill.

Jenny finished her coffee and sighed at the memory of her long-gone parents. They had given her so much but would never have understood modern technology, let alone time travel. Flash Gordon on television was the nearest they would come to comprehending being able to travel through time, defeating the old enemy.

Jenny had no plan, but the walk to the nearby bus stop to board the ill-fated double-decker would only take a minute. She decided on a whim to take the long walk down the steep and winding hill again through the early morning wet streets, alone with her thoughts, but in her mind walking hand in hand with her father to the harbour to collect fish.

Later, she arrived at the Thornbury Health Centre where the T1 double-decker stood silent, ready for its first passenger-filled run of the fateful day. It had been a mistake, walking so far, and Jenny was tired, breathless and with aching calves. She had forgotten that she had been nine when she skipped along with her father all those years ago to the harbour.

Jenny paused a moment to take a deep breath and stepped onto the bus to present her bus pass. Surprisingly, the driver was engrossed in writing on a small pad resting lightly on his steering wheel. They exchanged morning greetings and Frank remarked, 'None of us are getting any younger, are we?'

It was meant in a kindly way, but Jenny thought that for some of his passengers, today would get no older. A sombre thought. Frank was in full flow but took a moment to write CHECK BRAKES in bold capitals. He had noticed a spongy feel to them and would insist on having the pads replaced sooner rather than later, a false economy, he thought.

Jenny looked down the almost empty bus. Joy Chen was already seated with Chang Chen, looking mournful on her knee. Jenny and Mel had decided to take half the bus each, Mel upstairs, Jenny downstairs, and the older woman was glad of this plan as her legs ached and the stairs seemed daunting.

Sitting on the left-hand side opposite Joy Chen, she smiled and noted that the usually happy little boy seemed grumpy.

'He has a tooth coming through, I think,' Joy explained.

'Poor little soul, I don't envy him. Do you have Calpol?'

'In my bag, along with all the usual paraphernalia,'

'Another day translating for the police, I suppose, must be interesting.'

Their conversation was interrupted by the roar of the huge engine as Frank pressed the ignition; Jenny automatically checked her watch. It noted her unusually high blood pressure, not surprisingly, really, considering her long, ill-thought-out walk and the journey ahead.

Frank skilfully manoeuvred his vehicle towards Rock Street, where several passengers were waiting, sheltering from the rain as best they could. Mel Chandoo stepped onto the bus and looked down at the passengers. She smiled seeing Jenny, and the older woman felt her heart lift with relief to see her newly found friend bravely stepping forward, but to her surprise, she came and sat by Jenny.

'Hi, did you manage any breakfast this morning? I couldn't manage a thing.'

'Me neither,' Jenny replied,' It is most courageous of you to come, many would have opted out.'

'I'll go upstairs as arranged at the next stop; I thought that I would check in with you first.'

'Can you check out the emergency exits upstairs?' she whispered, 'The bus goes down on the left, so there should be a roof and back window exit. Same down here, but the side window means getting out on what will become the top of the bus. A difficult climb down, I think, for the elderly or handicapped.'

They both looked up to see a smartly dressed Will Hayes with a briefcase. Abbie had given him a yellow tie, saying that it was well known that this would project a professional manner. They had kissed at the door, and Will had readied himself to travel north to the garage, praying that the gearbox would not fail him on his special day.

'Tell me all about it tonight, I've booked us into an Italian restaurant to celebrate and we can plan our trip to Italy.'

'And our wedding,' Will added with a smile, 'although we mustn't count our chickens before the interview. Anything could go wrong.'

'It won't my love, I just know that it won't'

On the bus, Jenny frowned. Madison Marsden was nowhere to be seen among the embarking passengers. Good, that meant she would be safe and one less thing to worry about. She and Mel had worked out that the young and talented girl was a very possible candidate for the to save list.

Glancing back, Jenny saw to her horror a sprinting Madison desperately trying to catch her bus. Madison was already late and could not afford another confrontation with the Year group head about tardiness.

Jenny willed the bus to move away faster and not allow Maddie to catch up, but Frank went through his routine for safely setting out. Glancing at his side mirror, he saw the schoolgirl trying her best to run, although she would admit that she was no athlete. He smiled and stopped the bus, allowing a breathless Maddie to give her thanks and proceed upstairs to take a seat at the back of the bus.

Moving smoothly past the leisure centre and up the winding hill, Jenny settled down and wondered how she could have been so stupid as to walk all the way down the hill and through the town to the Health Centre, which marked the start of the journey. She could have simply waited outside the cricket ground, but that meant a longer, stomach-churning wait. Better to be active, she thought.

Frank saw the Buckleys standing at the Alveston bus stop opposite the church. He groaned inwardly, hoping that the woman would not be confrontational again.

As the bus slowed, Mel took the opportunity to move upstairs after wishing Jenny, 'Good luck.'

She went to the middle of the seats, the safe seats and began to look carefully at the clearly marked emergency exits.

Amanda Buckley followed, briefly displaying her bus pass and ignoring the driver, whom she felt was not worthy of her attention. To Jenny's surprise, John Buckley stayed downstairs, not being able to follow his wife, and shuffled with his stick for aid to a seat near the front on the right.

The double-decker set out into the busy traffic, and Frank started the windscreen wipers. The rain showed no sign of abating anytime soon.

Upstairs, Madison Marsden made a quick calculation. By the time the bus reached her destination near her new school, she would be very late. Her timetable said P.E. followed by religious studies, to Maddie's mind, both a waste of her time. She made a decisive decision. She would stay on the bus and go into Bristol to the fine library and work on her book, much more useful than netball or learning the parables of the man from Galilee.

Downstairs, Will Hayes closed his eyes, not that he wanted to, but he was tired. Yesterday had lasted long into the night, and plans for an interview, trips to Rome and Pompeii and a possible long trip with his girl, Abbie, to Japan had filled their hours intermingled with gentle lovemaking. They had sat up in bed planning a summer wedding, and now Will was dog tired. He could not keep his eyes open.

Will woke with a startled jolt and, to his horror, saw that he had missed his stop. Anxiety fuelled his actions, and he rang the bell for the bus to stop. he would have to walk back to Hurst Green Primary and arrive dishevelled and wet for his interview. Another disaster, one of many, as usual.

Frank heard the bell ring for the bus to stop and was distracted. As he approached the roundabout, his new boots caught in the controls, and he pressed the accelerator in error. The throbbing pain from his blister had to be ignored; he had to wrestle back control of the bus as it skidded on the wet road at full speed towards the ramped wall of the landscaped roundabout. Frank glanced right and was relieved that no vehicle was coming from that side, but he heard three distinct thuds as a pistol was fired quickly and with deadly accuracy.

Cai Yuanyun had bided his time, and as the bus approached the roundabout, he shot away the front tyres, taking away any chance of the driver controlling the huge vehicle. There was a frightening bang as the bus went onto the roundabout and began to tilt dangerously, and almost in slow motion. Finally, it had no option but to fall slowly on its left-hand side.

Survivors were to speak later of the horror of the screaming cauldron of bodies and blood-stained windows. For them, there was suddenly no sense of direction, indeed no sense of what had happened.

Accounts conflicted, but all agreed that Will Hayes was a hero. Bodies were thrown involuntarily sideways against unforgiving windows. Chang Chen was hurled left and landed against Jenny's soft body, and she instinctively hung on to the small child. Flung backwards, Will had hit his shoulder badly but managed to stay clear, thinking. He had been on enough school journeys to have glanced at emergency exits almost automatically, and as a teacher, he knew that the situation needed calm and orderly leadership.

He managed to crawl over seats now on their sides and get to the rear window, which he opened, allowing passengers to crawl through, at least those able to move. Despite his damaged shoulder, he assisted many to get out, including Jenny Clutterbuck with a cut on her forehead and a rapidly developing bruised face. He vaguely recognised her, but this was not the time for socialising. Will took charge, and when handed a baby screaming in terror, he passed the child back to Jenny as she crawled out and shakily stood. Upstairs, Mel had been prepared and opened the emergency roof exit, now at the side of the fallen bus. Amanda Buckley had managed to crawl over the seats and out where Mel was helping passengers to stand or sit dazed on the wet road.

Many survivors spoke of the screams and confusion.

Maddie Marsden was shocked and wished that she had got off earlier and gone to school; her arm was obviously broken, the large clue being a white bone sticking through the skin. Not good, she thought, but at least there was no chance of P.E. for a while.

Will wondered if the gas-powered bus would catch fire and went back in painfully to check on survivors.

Frank Nelson was still in his cab, shocked and with a leg dangerously twisted, providing him with his own personal agony.

Will ushered the bewildered passengers away to safety as emergency services sirens began to wail as they rushed to the scene, but Rosangel Chlebek was quicker. She had been driving to work and witnessed the seemingly slow-motion horror, pulling up to the side to allow fire engines and ambulances space, she took her bag and ran to help.

Cai Yuanyun checked his pistol and prepared to complete the task. Will Hayes looked up and saw the man with a pistol, and for a moment held his gaze whilst struggling to make sense of what he saw. Will knew he was no hero, but he acted quickly without weapon or plan; he moved towards the Chinese man, who looked dangerously calm. Will tried to reach him before he could lift the weapon, perhaps to knock him down.

Yuanyun smiled, his training said, cut out the leader, the head of the snake. He assessed the danger of the tall, fast-approaching Englishman and fired twice in quick succession, head shots. Always leave no witnesses. He turned and saw Jenny holding Chang Chen, trying to soothe the child. Here was his target, and he raised the pistol, but a searing pain hit him square in the back, and he writhed in agony, falling to the ground and dropping the weapon, where Jenny kicked it away.

PC Georgie Bratton had been tasked with surveillance of the seemingly innocent but worrying Chinese suspect. She had driven in her own car for discretion and parked outside the Holiday Inn Express to follow Yuanyun. She had been horrified to see his swift and brutal actions, but did not hesitate. She had only used a deadly taser in special training, but blessed its power and effectiveness. Quickly, she put handcuffs on the agonised body. Looking around, she was glad to see reinforcements arrive and began to shake as she realised what she had seen and done.

The remaining passengers were being taken from the bus by very efficient and calm fire crews. A fleet of ambulances took the injured, many with blankets around them, shocked but glad to be alive. John Buckley's crushed body was taken out and carefully laid on a stretcher. Rosangel checked his pulse, but he was obviously dead, and she moved quickly on to others more in need of her.

Mel Chandoo, now with a blanket around her, went to stand by Jenny, taking the comforting blanket from her shoulders, she placed it gently around Jenny and the frightened Chang Chen.

Jenny glanced at her friend as Mel asked simply, 'Joy Chen?'

'They brought her out, but after the doctor checked her, she was stretchered into an ambulance with a blanket over her to cover her face.'

Rosangel clambered into the bus after explaining that she was a doctor. Frank Nelson was trapped, confined in his cab with a twisted, shattered leg. With years of experience in accident and emergency, she knew instinctively that the leg would have to be amputated. There was no other way to get him out. This was going to be difficult, she thought as she gave him an injection of painkiller.

'Careful of the boots, they're my new pair, they pinch a little, but I don't suppose that matters now,' Frank joked to ease the tension, but he was afraid and thought of Lillian at home, not knowing what had happened.

Jenny shifted the wriggling baby in her arms and looked closely at Mel, 'Are you hurt?'

'I don't think so, but I feel that I've had an hour in the ring with Mohammed Ali and been put in a tumble dryer afterwards. But you are bleeding and it's going on the baby.'

They swapped the confused child, who wondered where his mother was, and his lip began to quiver. Jenny took out a tissue and held it to her head; it was, she decided, a superficial wound and not one to fuss about.

'You'd better get young Chang Chen here to the hospital to be checked out, and yourself, for that matter.'

'And what about you, time traveller, what happens to you?'

Jenny took a deep breath, glad of the damp of the drizzle which cooled her head and mind.

'Tomorrow I will be going back to my life and home in 2056. No more worries about buses and who should be saved. I might even have a long lie-in.'

Jenny knew that after tomorrow, there would be no more adventures in the past, trying to help shape the future. Her retirement was something to look forward to. Her garden seemed a wonderful, welcoming haven of peace in a tumultuous world.

'And did we make a difference? It doesn't feel that way just now,' Mel asked as an ambulance driver beckoned.

Jenny looked at the fallen, smoking bus surrounded by the emergency vehicles and smiled ruefully.

'It's too soon to make a judgement, but time will tell as it always does.'

'And will I ever see you again, Jenny Clutterbuck?'

Jenny smiled, 'I think that we may well meet again, my good friend, we just may.'

Chapter Thirty: Sometime Later

Amanda Buckley had taken a hot soothing bath filled with every shade of bath salts, and afterwards looked at her body, bruised black and purple in the mirror. She was desperately stiff, despite the bath, but none of this seemed to matter. John was gone and would never return home to her again. Wrapping herself up in a comforting, thick, warm dressing gown, she went to lie on her bed, realising that the void to her left would never be filled by the love of her life again. She cried gently and regretted deeply her bitter sniping at him for things out of his control. If she could only turn back time, she would do things differently. He was a fine man who deserved better than a self-centred, vain wife. Too late now to make amends.

The Marchenko family had cancelled any thoughts of returning to Kiev and decided that their host, Amanda, was in deep shock and needed their support. Mila had not understood but had crawled onto Amanda's knee to offer her the best cuddle. It was a poignant moment, and Amanda had hugged the delightful Ukrainian girl with her mass of blond curls, taking comfort from her warm little body. John had been right, she thought, children would have been good to make them a real family. He had been right about so much, but was now gone forever.

Madison Marsden's arm had been set successfully, if painfully, and she now possessed a pot on her arm full of adolescent names and attempts at humour. For a short time, she had achieved hero status at school and felt somehow accepted. Her broken bone would mend, she was young and the young healed quickly, and she reckoned that she would be able to travel to Bromley to visit friends in the summer, especially her Polish godchild and her family. Her father had refused to listen and insisted on driving her there. He realised that he had almost lost his precious, wonderful, talented daughter and wasn't about to let her travel alone to London. Besides, they could perhaps visit the marvellous gardens at HS Wisley on the way. Madison experimented and realised that typing with a broken arm was possible, and after the traumatic crash, she had a wealth of potential stories to write about. A road trip with her dad was something to look forward to; life was looking good.

Mel Chandoo had taken a few days off work; in fact, her line manager had insisted despite Mel's protests. She had reluctantly agreed and booked into a small hotel in the Devon town of Sidmouth. She would walk along the promenade with its ozone-rich sea air and try to make sense of her recent experiences. It was not easy, and her disturbing dreams did not help. The recurring image of the baby Chang Chen being thrown from his loving mother's arms against the soft cushion of Jenny Clutterbuck rather than the unforgiving hard window convinced Mel that she had the answer to their primary question. The time traveller had come to save the small Chinese boy, and by sitting where she did, Jenny was able to do just that, even inadvertently. Jenny had the strong instincts of a mother and held onto the boy, turning her body to protect him from the impact

Mel enjoyed those few days away and felt refreshed and revitalised. At breakfast, she had met a travel writer called Daniel from Bristol who was researching the qualities of the old Victorian resort in order to submit his work for a magazine. They had chatted and one day arranged a walk together along the beach. He was not what you could call handsome in a shallow Hollywood way, but interesting and humorous as he spoke of places in the world he had visited. One evening, they sat together in a pub, reputedly used by pirates and smugglers and sampled the local cider. Dan and Mel formed an instant liking for each other, and it was no surprise when he shyly put his hand on hers and asked if she would be interested in meeting up again in Bristol. Both were unmarried, and Mel looked forward to a new, fresh, and, if truth be told, a more honest relationship.

Lillian Nelson had received the news of the bus crash in sharp shock and asked if her husband, Frank, the driver, was responsible. Not that that mattered, but it was reassuring to hear that he had tried hard to save the passengers, and more importantly, he was alive.

She went to visit him in the hospital after the female police officer had broken the awful news to her and carefully informed her that part of his lower right leg had had to be amputated to get him out of the bus. With mounting trepidation and a trembling, fluttering stomach, she made her way to the ward where Frank lay with a tent over his legs. She feared that he would enter depression as he would no longer be able to drive. She breathed deeply before entering the four-bed ward, fearing the worst.

Frank sat up in bed with two young nurses fussing around him. He grinned on seeing his beloved wife and began to complain. 'Do you know what they've done?

They've only gone on and cut off my right leg. They could have helped me by cutting off the one with the bloody blister, just my luck.'

Lillian went over to him and hugged him tight, 'You daft bugger, I thought that I had lost you,' and she began to cry. The two nurses diplomatically left, drawing the curtain around the couple to give them some scant privacy.

'I expected to find you all miserable and depressed, but here you are joking and flirting with nurses. What are you going to do?' It was a question she had meant to hold back till later, but it sort of blurted out.

'I'm going to be on crutches for a while, but I'm told that I'll have a false leg fitted, which will be guaranteed blister-free. I'll be walking again in no time with a pretty young nurse on each arm.'

'Seriously Frank, I'm glad to see your sense of humour is intact, but what will the future hold for you, for us?'

Frank became serious for a moment, 'Well, driving will be off the agenda, but I reckon I can get on with writing, it's something I find I enjoy, and there is something else I have thought of.'

'Does it involve nurses?'

'I don't think so, more's the pity. England has a wheelchair rugby team. I won't be using a wheelchair regularly, but I reckon I could hold my own and would like to try for that. Besides, the insurance payout will cushion us for a long time. We'll be alright, you and I.'

Lillian marvelled at her husband's resilience and determination not to be a victim.

Curtis Warren, headteacher at Hurst Green Primary school, had been very worried; the non-appearance of Will Hayes for the interview was bewildering. He had been confident that Will would be appointed as deputy head and was convinced that this was what Will had wanted. A phone call to Will's current school and subsequent enquiries revealed Will had been killed in a bus crash, strangely beyond Hurst Green. Curtis mourned the loss of a promising partner in developing the school and was deeply upset.

At the hastily called staff meeting that afternoon, after school, the head of Will's current school had announced with all due solemnity the untimely death of their colleague. Some regretted calling him Silent Bill behind his back, and all tried to recall his fine virtues.

Abbie Thompson sat quietly in a corner, and large tear drops fell onto her lap. Pompeii, Japan and marriage to her love had been dashed cruelly from her, and she would never see him again. Later, the police had strongly advised her not to see the body as she had requested. Two assassins' bullets to the head did not make a pretty sight, and she reluctantly agreed. Abbie mourned deeply for a long time but was heartened to think of Will as a hero trying to save others. It was all she had to warm her memories. At home in her flat, she looked at his collection of netsuke and held them close; they were her only link with her adored Will.

Postscript

Tea for two in the garden

Jenny Clutterbuck had slept long and deep on her return to her home in 2056. The usual official thorough debriefs had been strenuous, and Jenny was glad when it was over. It was something she would thankfully never have to go through again. She felt too old and burnt out; time travel was for the younger interventionists. It was her time to tend roses and plant border flowers.

Sitting at the table outside in the warm July sunshine, she pondered the effectiveness of her last journey into the past. The events of thirty-two years ago were merely a week to Jenny, as she had been transported with the aid of her watch to the portal headquarters. She noted that the grass had grown as it always did and wondered if she would have time to cut it before her special visitor arrived, a visitor from that tumultuous time in 2024.

Jenny heard a car draw up, and her dogs warned her with friendly barks. She stood, still with a wound dressing on her head and prepared to greet Mel Chandoo.

Mel came through the gate and was amazed to see Jenny looking just as she had on the day of that tragic bus crash all those years ago, but then she had the advantage of time travel.

Mel herself was certainly older, and her tight black curls were grey, which somehow enhanced her distinguished look; she had put on several pounds, but could not be said to be portly. The twenty-four years had been kind to her, and she and Dan were planning on a celebratory silver wedding anniversary.

'Jenny Clutterbuck, I cannot believe how well you look, you've even got your wound dressing from the crash all those years ago'

'I'm a slow healer,' Jenny laughed, all nerves at meeting Mel again disappeared as she stepped forward and hugged her long, before offering tea and cake.

'We have much to talk about,' Jenny said, looking closely at her friend's increased laughter lines around her eyes. 'I forgot that you were actually two years older than me.'

It was Mel's turn to laugh as she sat down in front of the cake-laden table. 'Older but certainly no wiser.'

'So, you are now a time traveller in your own right, Mel. Is it true that travel to the future has actually been developed?'

'Officially, I'm not allowed to say, but I will say that the answer is the opposite of no,'

Mel delved into her bag and brought out a book, Jenny looked at the cover, 'Forever Now' by M.C. Marsden. Inside, it had been signed 'to Jenny Clutterbuck, my inspiration, Maddie.'

Jenny smiled as she placed the book carefully on the table.

Mel said, 'Maddie only wrote three books, but they were regarded as masterpieces in modern English Literature, taught in schools no less. Sadly, leukaemia took her far too early.'

Jenny was silent for a moment as she remembered the girl with the curly hair and determination to be a writer.

'And what of the others, from that horrible fateful day?' Jenny asked whilst pouring the first of several cups of tea.

'Well, Frank Nelson went on to write a series of paperbacks, not great literature, but with huge commercial success. He also played wheelchair rugby for England for a while.'

'What happened to Will Hàyes' girlfriend, Abbie?'

Mel sipped the hot tea. 'Abbie went on to have a fine career in education, two headships, but never married. She went to Japan several times, alone, sadly.'

'You seem well informed, Mel, as usual, your dreams?'

'No, I went to all three funerals and met Abbie there, a lovely girl, so very very sad.'

'And the famous Chang Chen. I know more about him, of course.'

'As you probably know, he went to a Chinese foster home and was later adopted. He learned all he could about his mother and the oppression of the Chinese state at the time. He led the Hong Kong democratic freedom movement, and when it spread to mainland China, the government there crumbled in the face of overwhelming popular opinion. He is known as the founder of true democracy in China.'

'So, you were very successful in your last intervention, Jenny. You helped change the future in a massive way, you must be delighted.'

Jenny cut the lemon drizzle cake and put slices on two plates. The two friends ate in silence, happy with each other's company.

Jenny thought of Will Hayes, who rescued her from a mugging, a quiet, unassuming man plucked from a potentially flourishing life with his girl by his side. She thought of grief and loss. The news that Maddie had died so cruelly was devastating, and Jenny recalled the cake she had shared with the young girl as they talked of her ambitions to be a writer. The lovely Joy Chen, whose eyes lit up with delight when she cuddled her laughing son. She would have been so proud of his achievements

Time moved forward so profoundly, inevitably, and terribly, bringing utter misery, laughter, triumph and tears. Jenny did not feel that her last mission had been successful; she had missed the opportunity to talk to her beloved Steve.

She sighed deeply, the weight of her memories pressing down on her heart. Jenny couldn't shake the feeling that despite her efforts, time's unyielding grip had proven too strong. The faces of those she had touched and lost played through her mind as a reminder of moments shared and dreams unfulfilled. It was the laughter of Joy Chen's son, the aspirations of Maddie, and the quiet heroism of Will Hayes that underscored the fleeting nature of happiness. As she contemplated the fragility of life and the inevitability of time's passage, Jenny came to a sombre realisation. She had fought against time, yet it was her own inability to reach Steve that haunted her most. Time was so cruel and should not be manipulated, she thought.

She looked up at Mel, 'So are you going to tell me about the future or not?'

Mel looked with love at the reluctant time traveller. 'I believe that for us the future holds more tea and another slice of cake, after that who knows?'

9 781918 156096